"From
to the n
are very few books I want to read twice. *Unleashed* made me want to go back and reread books one and two. And before I was even done with *Unleashed*, I wanted to read it all over again."
—BookSpot Central.com

"Magic, mayhem, and mystery make up *Unleashed*, a poignant yet often amusing urban fantasy that is filled with intrigue . . . a wonderful original urban fantasy whodunit."
—*Genre Go Round Reviews*

"Another solid, thoroughly enjoyable urban fantasy . . . Levitt's newest novel is a fast-paced, entertaining game of hide-and-seek played in San Francisco . . . Readers who enjoy a thrilling tale with plenty of heart are sure to love this book." —*SFRevu*

"As always, Lou, the dog/Ifrit, is both the perfect sidekick and conscience as this magical pair faces a bloodthirsty monster. Levitt has plenty of twists up his sleeve in this supernatural thriller."
—*Romantic Times*

Praise for

NEW TRICKS

"A lively new take on working magic. Along with his original take on familiars (in the form of Ifrits), Levitt is doing very nicely at creating his own niche in the urban fantasy landscape."
—*SFRevu*

"A suspenseful tale that's supported by strong characters and a delightful infusion of magic and mystery."
—*Darque Reviews*

continued . . .

"The second book in Levitt's Man & His Dog series is just as clever and twisty as the first. Mason's offbeat sense of humor and knack for finding trouble make him a likable, if somewhat cursed, hero. Lou, on the other hand, is a pure delight. This crime-fighting duo has plenty of bark and bite!" —*Romantic Times*

"If you like urban fantasy, this one is a cut above the rest."
—*CA Reviews*

"*New Tricks* came through in a huge way . . . This is urban fantasy at its best." —BookSpot Central.com

Praise for
DOG DAYS

"The supernatural lives, breathes, and slithers in a San Francisco where the dog days don't just get you down; they eat you alive." —Rob Thurman, national bestselling author of *The Grimrose Path*

"A compelling magical mystery, filled with twists and some uncomfortable turns as it follows a likable new character through a mostly familiar San Francisco . . . I thoroughly enjoyed *Dog Days*. It's proof that there's still a heck of a lot of potential for variation in the urban fantasy genre, and it's a highly satisfying read . . . an excellent start to a promising new series." —*The Green Man Review*

"Appealing, fully founded characters . . . Levitt promises to be a novelist worth watching . . . Readers will enjoy the roller-coaster ride through dangers both magical and mundane. Anyone who likes solid storytelling will enjoy *Dog Days*. Here's looking forward to the next adventure." —*SFRevu*

"Levitt has envisioned a lively world . . . [a] delightful take on good versus evil. Mason's character, with his self-deprecating humor, beat-up van, and list of odd associates, is entertaining and engaging, and will certainly leave readers looking for more from this unlikely hero and his dog." —*Monsters and Critics*

Ace Books by John Levitt

DOG DAYS
NEW TRICKS
UNLEASHED
PLAY DEAD

PLAY DEAD

JOHN LEVITT

THE BERKLEY PUBLISHING GROUP
Published by the Penguin Group
Penguin Group (USA) Inc.
375 Hudson Street, New York, New York 10014, USA
Penguin Group (Canada), 90 Eglinton Avenue East, Suite 700, Toronto, Ontario M4P 2Y3, Canada
(a division of Pearson Penguin Canada Inc.)
Penguin Books Ltd., 80 Strand, London WC2R 0RL, England
Penguin Group Ireland, 25 St. Stephen's Green, Dublin 2, Ireland (a division of Penguin Books Ltd.)
Penguin Group (Australia), 250 Camberwell Road, Camberwell, Victoria 3124, Australia
(a division of Pearson Australia Group Pty. Ltd.)
Penguin Books India Pvt. Ltd., 11 Community Centre, Panchsheel Park, New Delhi—110 017, India
Penguin Group (NZ), 67 Apollo Drive, Rosedale, North Shore 0632, New Zealand
(a division of Pearson New Zealand Ltd.)
Penguin Books (South Africa) (Pty.) Ltd., 24 Sturdee Avenue, Rosebank, Johannesburg 2196,
South Africa

Penguin Books Ltd., Registered Offices: 80 Strand, London WC2R 0RL, England

PLAY DEAD

An Ace Book / published by arrangement with the author

PRINTING HISTORY
Ace mass-market edition / February 2011

Cover art by Don Sipley.
Cover design by Annette Fiore DeFex.
Interior text design by Kristin del Rosario.

For information, address: The Berkley Publishing Group,
a division of Penguin Group (USA) Inc.,
375 Hudson Street, New York, New York 10014.

ISBN: 978-0-441-01964-9

ACE
Ace Books are published by The Berkley Publishing Group,
a division of Penguin Group (USA) Inc.,
375 Hudson Street, New York, New York 10014.
ACE and the "A" design are trademarks of Penguin Group (USA) Inc.

PRINTED IN THE UNITED STATES OF AMERICA

10 9 8 7 6 5 4 3 2 1

For my dad, Bill Levitt,
who would have liked this one

ACKNOWLEDGMENTS

Thanks go out to all the readers who've supported Lou and the series. And Mason, of course, but we all know who the real star is.

ONE

THE RAIN WAS VICIOUS, DRENCHING THE STREETS, bouncing off the pavement and running down the gutters. The wind had picked up, driving the rain sideways at times, and the bobbing red and yellow and black umbrellas danced erratically as the wind swept through.

A nasty gust caught one woman's black umbrella and flipped it inside out, instantly transforming it from a useful tool into a formless mass of wire and fabric. The woman clutched at it hopelessly and in faint surprise, as if she'd suddenly and unaccountably found herself holding a drowned bat.

Lou was one thoroughly wet dog, and he didn't like it a bit. He crowded next to my feet, trying to keep under the umbrella as well, but he's barely a foot tall, and by the time the rain reached him, the umbrella was essentially useless. He stopped every minute or so to give a vigorous shake, coupled with a sour glare in my direction. It was not fit outside for man nor beast, as they say. But the weather was entirely appropriate for my mission. I was on my way to see a black practitioner.

Black practitioners have a bad rep among the rest of us who aren't and it's not entirely undeserved, but not all of them are terrible people. I'd dealt with a few of them in the last few years, with mixed results. But I'd dealt with a couple of "normal" practitioners as well, with outcomes that were no better, and sometimes worse.

Still, normally I wouldn't waltz off to the home of a black practitioner I didn't know. They're unpredictable, and a practitioner's home is where he or she is most effective. There's enough danger in the magical world as it is, without inviting more.

So when I got a call out of the blue inviting me for a talk, my first instinct was to politely decline. But the person on the other end of the line was courteous and persuasive, and by "persuasive," I mean he mentioned a rather large sum of money. He wasn't the actual practitioner, though. When you reach a certain level of fame, or maybe notoriety would be a better word, you never just call up someone yourself. You have people for that sort of thing. And the name he threw out was impressive—I try not to get involved with practitioner politics, but even I had heard of her.

The representative understood I wouldn't be comfortable coming to a black practitioner's home, so he suggested a meeting at the downtown offices.

"Offices?" I'd said. That was a new one for me.

"Five hundred Sutter Street, suite 1092. Blue Bay Promotions."

So there I was, walking through the rain, headed for 500 Sutter Street. Which turned out to be a handsome older building, erected sometime in the 1920s, or maybe even earlier. It sports an elegant granite facade with scrollwork peeking out below the windows on every floor. The lobby is faced in marble and the elevator doors are constructed of engraved metal, so that when they're closed they seem like elegant bas-reliefs, hardly looking like elevators at all. It was the kind of building Sam Spade might have visited, back when San Francisco was a far different city, and probably a better one.

The elevator doors were ancient, but the elevator itself was modern and high speed. I shared the ride with a young woman. There's a particular type of awkwardness associated with elevator rides—you're stuck in close proximity with a stranger, and often people avoid even making eye contact. Small talk is rare. An unspoken agreement to stay encased in one's own bubble seems to be the norm.

Lou changes all that, though. He won't put up with staring blankly at the opposite wall, and he usually gazes up winningly at random passengers until they finally break down and comment on his cuteness factor. I'd just replaced his usual collar with a sleek black harness because he kept getting the collar hung up on random branches. It was quite stylish and increased the cuteness factor, which helped him in cadging treats from strangers. Some people don't care for dogs, of course. I guess it takes all kinds. This woman, however, had a corgi with her, so we shared a few dog pleasantries.

At the tenth floor, I walked down the corridor checking numbers until I came to Blue Bay Promotions. The outer office reminded me of a dentist's office, with bland prints on the walls and beige everywhere. The man behind the front desk looked up as I came in, noting my general scruffy condition and my wet dog, and raised his eyebrows ever so slightly in polite inquiry.

"I'm here to see Jessica," I said. He looked at me in some surprise.

"You're Mason?"

"The same." He picked up the phone on the desk, pressed a button, and spoke into it.

"Jessie? There's a Mason here to see you?" He listened a moment, then nodded and waved a hand toward the door at the far end of the room. "Go right in."

I knocked politely at the door before pushing it open. The inside office was as opulent as the outside was austere. Thick carpet, the obligatory expanse of mahogany desk, and, on each wall, hanging rugs that even my untrained eye could see were old and expensive.

"Come in," said the woman on the other side of the desk. "I'm Jessica, Jessica Alexander. Jessie to my friends, and everyone else, for that matter." She smiled disarmingly. "Yes, I use my full name, just like an ordinary businesswoman. Gauche of me, I know." She came out from behind the desk and offered her hand, glancing down at Lou. "And this is Louie, of course."

"You've done your homework, I see," I said, taking her hand. It was cool and her grip was strong.

"Wouldn't you? I assume you at least asked Victor about me."

Actually, I hadn't, so I just shrugged noncommittally. Victor was my sometimes boss, the unofficial head of magical enforcement in San Francisco. Jessica wasn't at all what I'd expected. First, she was way too young, and way too pleasant-looking. I'd expected more of an iron maiden, suitable for a black practitioner with an impressive reputation. Steely eyes, short hair or perhaps a tight bun, impeccably dressed in the latest of fashion. But this woman was none of those things.

At first I thought she couldn't be more than twenty-five, but the wrinkles in the corners of her eyes and the slight beginnings of a double chin when she held her head at a certain angle made me revise that upward. Long hair, loose and light brown. A long straight nose. Nondescript slacks and a soft, plain cashmere-type top, expensive but not obviously so. She looked more like the daughter of the CEO than the CEO herself.

Which made her doubly dangerous. One of the things I've learned from hanging around with Victor is the danger of unexamined assumptions. This woman looked harmless and friendly, and cultural conditioning would inevitably lead people to not consider her much of a threat. On an intellectual level they might realize her potential for danger, but emotionally it would be hard not to let their guard down, at least a little. Which, given her position, would be a mistake. Luckily, I wasn't there as a rival.

She sat back down behind the desk, pushing aside a large brown leather purse that was dangling over the back of the desk chair.

"Okay," I said. "So you checked me out. And there was the mention of some money. Quite a bit, actually, but I have no idea why. Blue Bay Promotions? What exactly is it you do here?"

She examined me thoughtfully, as if she hadn't yet decided whether she liked what she saw.

"You've worked for Victor for quite some time now, haven't you? And handled some difficult problems, some complicated situations?"

"I have my moments."

"I believe you. Victor has his moments, too, but he's old-school, to say the least. He likes the old ways, and tradition, and isn't fond of change. Am I right?" She was, but I wasn't about to be discussing Victor's psyche with her.

"He gets results," I said.

"I know he does. I'm not dissing him; he's an impressive man, and quite the character as well. But times are changing—he'd prefer to live in the nineteenth century if he could, where I'm ready to move into the twenty-first, redefining what it means to be a practitioner. So I've set up a corporation and opened an office—part public relations, part R and D. The old days of random knowledge and private fiefdoms are coming to an end."

I wasn't sure I liked the sound of that, and it also didn't answer what she wanted from me. She immediately saw that in my body language, and turned on her smile again.

"But that's neither here nor there. I gather you're not that interested in practitioner politics." That was putting it mildly. "That's not necessarily a bad thing," she continued. "For example, I've also heard that unlike many of your fellows, you don't hold any particular prejudice toward black practitioners."

"Maybe not, but I haven't had the best of experiences in dealing with them, either," I said.

"And have you had nothing but good experiences with those who aren't?"

"Not always," I admitted. She smiled.

"So if I were to offer you a job, you wouldn't automatically turn it down, then? You'd at least listen?" I thought about the dollar figure that had been mentioned.

"Well, I'm here," I said. "And it never hurts just to listen." Which of course is the age-old lie, but it's something we all tell ourselves.

Lou meanwhile had been quietly checking out the office, wandering around unobtrusively. He kept glancing over behind the desk where Jessie sat and then glancing back at me. I looked in that direction and thought I saw a slight movement. Jessie saw my attention straying.

"How rude of me," she said. "I haven't introduced my Ifrit. Naja, say hello to our guests."

I wasn't prepared for what came out from behind the desk. There are many types of Ifrits, which is what we call our magical companions. They almost always take the form of small animals, no more than fifteen pounds tops, and most are much smaller. Mostly they're cats, ferrets, sometimes small dogs like Lou, and occasionally even large birds. No one really knows what they are or where they come from, although my mentor, Eli, and I have come up with some pretty good guesses in the last couple of years. They can't do magic or talk, but they're smart, way smarter than a dog or a cat, and most of them can understand a great deal of what you say. And they do have some special abilities.

Not all practitioners acquire them, either—more don't have them than do. Lou of course is special, clever even for an Ifrit, and he's saved my hide on more than one occasion. But there was one form I'd never seen an Ifrit manifested in, and that was what came out from behind the desk. Slithered out, actually. I was looking at a large snake.

And not just any snake. It was five, maybe six feet long, heavy and speckled, and there was a thickening around its neck that would turn into a hooded cowl if it reared up and spread it out. A cobra.

Lou stood immobile, imitating a statue. Ifrits generally get along well with one another, even if their practitioners are in conflict. They'll fight to the death to protect their practitioners, and that's a two-way street. But there seems to be no personal animosity between them, no matter how deadly an argument between practitioners may become. They're almost like mercenaries on different sides of a battle—they may have to kill one another, but there's no hatred and even a certain respect and camaraderie that comes from being part of the same club, a club outsiders can't comprehend.

But like me, Lou had never run across an Ifrit that was a reptile, much less a snake, and a deadly poisonous one at that. I hadn't known there were such things. He didn't seem inclined to test the limits of the normal Ifrit bonds.

"I know, it's too perfect," Jessie said, laughing at Lou's reaction. "Black practitioner with a poisonous snake for an Ifrit. But she's harmless—quite friendly, actually." Sure she was.

Lou eased slowly behind me, putting a couple of strong, thick legs between Naja's fangs and his own precious skin. He may be willing to fight to the death for me, but he's also got a very strong sense of self-preservation.

"Interesting," I said.

"Yes, isn't it? I sometimes wonder why I'm the only practitioner with a snake for an Ifrit. It must say something about me."

It probably did, though I couldn't imagine what. I'm not one of those people who think that snakes are evil or creepy; I rather like them, in fact. They're no more evil than is a cat or a dog, just different. But it couldn't hurt to have an Ifrit that could scare the hell out of people, not to mention that whole poisonous fang thing.

Naja slid back around the desk and disappeared again.

Now I did feel a little nervous. It's one thing to have a large snake staring at you from across the room; it's quite another to have it lurking somewhere, unseen. Maybe Jessie had learned that trick in a management seminar. Gentlemen, ladies—if you want to gain the upper hand in a negotiation, there are many techniques designed to throw your opponent off his game. But may I suggest a six-foot cobra coiled up somewhere underneath your desk?

"So, what is it you want with me?" I said, trying desperately to regain some measure of equanimity. Jessie didn't answer right away, making me wait. Another technique designed to make one unsure. But I'd seen Victor pull the same sort of thing for years, and all it did was amuse me. She saw that, and changed tactics abruptly.

"Okay," she said. "Bottom line, I need your help, and I'm willing to pay for it. I want you to find someone for me."

"Money's always welcome," I said. "But you seem to have quite a little organization going here. You should easily be able to locate someone. Why would you need me?"

"Most of my 'organization,' as you put it, aren't practitioners. They're accountants and PR people and the like. And we were still in Seattle when this person left, but recently I've had word that she's been seen here in Frisco."

"San Francisco," I corrected automatically.

"Whatever. But she's here, and from what I've heard, you have a particular talent for finding people."

"You need better sources of information." I gestured down toward my feet. "It's not me who's good at finding people; it's Lou."

"Same difference."

"Not really. And he can't just trot out and find someone, anyway—he has to know the person, or at least have met them, and they have to be relatively near—if someone's in San Jose, they might as well be on the moon as far as his ability to find them goes."

"Oh." Jessie looked momentarily disappointed. "Well, that's too bad, but you still could be a great help. I'm relatively new here; you're a fixture in the community, dialed in to the scene here. Plus, you're a musician."

"I'm not sure what that has to do with anything."

"The woman I'm looking for is a musician as well—a jazz musician. She may change her name, and even her appearance, but she won't be able to give up the music. That much I know about her—it was an important part of her life, and she was good. So chances are you might run across her."

"What's her name?" I asked.

"Jacquiline. Jackie for short."

"And why are you looking for her?" A more incisive question might have been why this woman was hiding from Jessie, but as a prospective employee, I was trying to be tactful.

"That's not important. I just need to locate her."

"Well," I said, "it is kind of important, at least to me. If you're planning on draining the blood from her body for a ritual, for example, I doubt I'd want to track her down for you." Jessie laughed, not offended in the least.

"If I tell you why I want to find her, will you help then?"

"It depends. Obviously."

"It's simple, really. She stole something from me, something important, and I want it back."

"And what was that?"

"That's not important, either." I let that one pass.

"What happens to her if you find her?"

Jessie's face hardened for a moment, and I got a glimpse of how she could be running a large operation.

"She's a thief," she said. "Worse, I trusted her. If she weren't a practitioner, she'd go to prison. I won't try to con you; she'll be punished, and severely. Victor would do the same, would he not?"

"Probably."

"But no, I won't be draining her of blood or stringing her up from the ceiling fan."

"Maybe a little play toy for Naja, though?" This time, Jessie wasn't amused.

"Naja's not like that," she said, clearly angry. "She would never hurt another practitioner unless I was being attacked. She's an Ifrit, for God's sake, just like your Louie. She's not some mindless instrument of revenge."

"Sorry," I said, and I was. That had been uncalled for. Jessie nodded, a bit wearily.

"I get a lot of that, just because she's a snake. It gets old." We sat for a moment in an uncomfortable silence.

"If I did look for this woman, there's no guarantee I could find her," I said, pretending the exchange had never happened.

"Of course," she said. "I could put you on retainer, though. I know your reputation, and I know you'd give it your best shot." She named a figure three times what I usually make working a job for Victor. "And of course a bonus if you do locate her." She named another figure, significantly larger. She reached into the purse hanging from the chair, pulled out a photo, and pushed it across the desk toward me.

When she reached into her purse, I saw a small soft case inside, partly open. I just got a flash of it, but it seemed to contain a hypodermic syringe and some vials of liquid. What was that about? A diabetic, perhaps, but the syringe looked wrong, too long, and so did the vials. It's also not a disease that practitioners normally develop. Drugs? Was she a secret Demerol junkie? I pushed it aside to consider later.

"This the woman?" I asked, picking up the picture. She nodded.

The photo was an eight-by-ten black-and-white, almost like an old studio glamour head shot. It showed a young woman, a light-skinned African American. Large gold hoops dangled from her ears. Her hair was thick and hanging free, massed like a puff of smoke.

"Quite an attractive woman," I said.

"Yes," Jessie said, with no inflection. "Isn't she?"

I was tempted. Money's not usually the overriding thing with me, but my rent had been raised, my van needed a major overhaul, and although gigs had been coming my way, clubs weren't paying a whole lot these days.

But Jessie was a black practitioner. As I said, some of them aren't so bad, but some of them are, and I didn't know enough about her or the situation to judge which type she might be. I'd been joking about the draining-blood thing, but not entirely. I pushed the picture back across the desk, regretfully.

"Sorry," I said. "It's really not my sort of thing."

Jessie looked at me from her seat on the other side of the desk and didn't say anything. A slight flickering in her eyes told me she was running through a set of responses in her mind, trying to decide which one would work best.

"Think about it at least," she finally said. "You don't have to give me an answer right now."

It didn't add up. I got the feeling there was more to all this than she was letting on, and when you get that feeling it's best to pay attention.

Why had she called on me, of all people, in the first place? She'd given a bunch of reasons, but they didn't hold up when you looked at them closely. Finding people is not a particularly noted skill of mine, even with Lou to help, and since she'd done research on me, she must know that. I'm a musician, and the woman she was looking for was, too, but that was a tenuous connection at best. And although I don't have a huge prejudice against dark practitioners, they're not my favorite people, either. I should have just thanked her for her interest and walked away, but maybe it would be smart to keep my options open until I found out why she'd focused on me. Maybe I was just being paranoid, but it never hurts to be careful. And there was that money, after all.

"Well, okay, I'll think about it," I heard myself say. "I'll let you know."

She nodded, satisfied for the moment. When I got to my feet Lou immediately headed for the door, twisting his head back over his shoulder to keep an eye on the desk. Naja had made him very nervous. He didn't relax until we were out of the building and back out on the street, and then he had the rain to deal with again. All in all, not a great day for him.

Or me, either. I had a splitting headache, and that's rare for me. I hoped I wasn't coming down with something. Maybe I was allergic to black practitioners.

TWO

PRACTITIONER SOCIETY DOESN'T HAVE ANY FORmal structure; no one is officially in charge of anything. But there is a loose code of conduct based on tradition and peer pressure, which is usually enough to keep most practitioners in line and ensure that things run smoothly. That and a near-universal desire to keep a low profile and avoid the public eye. No one knew what the consequences might be if the existence of people and things magical were to become common knowledge, and not many were eager to find out. Change is not always for the better.

But occasionally practitioners do get out of hand, mostly in minor ways, but sometimes with deadly consequences. Some type of structure needs to be in place to deal with such people, and over the years a thoroughly unofficial group of enforcers has developed. Victor is one of those, and so am I, technically, since I work for him from time to time—mostly when I'm broke. I'm really not suited to the job, though.

So, much as I hated to involve Victor, it was probably a good idea to do so. A new black practitioner was in town, one with a serious rep, one who even I'd heard of. And contacting me with an offer of employment, for rather flimsy reasons, was worth a closer look. It might mean nothing, but it also might mean quite a lot. Victor would probably be keeping tabs on her already; he has a lot of sources and isn't often taken by surprise. But he wouldn't know yet that she had contacted me. He might have a much better handle on why she had called me than I did.

When I rang him up and told him about my meeting, I expected him to rant on angrily about my not telling him before I went. One of the basic areas of disagreement between us is that he feels I should inform him ahead of time about anything I do that might possibly affect him, and I don't. But he hadn't ranted at all; only a slight pause before he said, "Interesting." Another pause, and then he said, quite politely, "Why don't you come over for breakfast tomorrow—say nine or so? We should talk about this."

Something was not right. Victor seldom bothers to be polite to me; he feels it's a waste of effort. So either he'd undergone a radical personality transformation in the last few days or he wanted me to do something for him. And as I'd learned over the years, when he wanted something, my own health and well-being was often not his primary concern.

Eli was already futzing around in the ground-floor kitchen when I arrived at Victor's Ocean Beach Victorian next morning. Eli is often at the house, since he and Victor are usually working on some project or other. His day gig is at San Francisco State, where he's a full history professor, which gives him some flexibility. But his convenient presence here just reinforced my suspicion that something was up. He gave me a broad smile and shook his head when he saw I was about to pump him for information. More confirmation.

Victor was brewing coffee, and Timothy, Victor's current boyfriend, was busy cooking breakfast. The smell of bacon wafting through the kitchen almost threw Lou into a frenzy. He has a rather unhealthy preoccupation with food anyway, but bacon is his true weakness. It's like crack for him; I almost think he'd abandon me for a stranger with a rasher of bacon, although he might feel guilty later.

Maggie, the gray Persian cat, was curled up lazily on a chair seat. She looked up as Lou came in and yawned sleepily. Yawning sleepily is what she does best; sometimes it's hard to believe she's an Ifrit like Lou. She rarely leaves the house, although she had helped Lou out once when we were all in danger. She does suit Victor, though—like her, he's neat and self-possessed, and unlike myself, he doesn't often need help. I'd be lost without Lou; he's helped me out of more than a few tight spots.

Lou walked up and they touched noses briefly. In the past, they hadn't got along at all, which is unusual for Ifrits, but of late they seemed to have arrived at an understanding. They weren't exactly great friends, but they were civil to each other. Sort of like Victor and me, only the two of us aren't always civil.

"Cheese omelette?" asked Victor as I came in, civil as all get-out.

He'd lately reverted to his beard of sharp, thin lines, giving up his recent full-coverage look. He seemed to have put on some weight as well—muscle, not fat. A potbelly on Victor would have been as unthinkable as—well, I can't think of anything that impossible. Maybe he thought he needed more strength, since he's a short man, but I've seen him fight, and more strength would be an embarrassment of riches. Timothy interrupted his cooking long enough to hand me a cup of coffee.

"The condemned man ate a hearty breakfast," I muttered, too low for Victor to hear.

Timothy was looking a bit scruffy these days, but not in a bad way. He'd quit his tech job at a startup a couple of months ago, relying on the reputation he'd built up in the tech world to make it as a freelance consultant. Ironically, as the economy worsened and layoffs became the norm, he was doing better than ever. A lot of places could no longer afford a full-time IT staff, but they still ran into problems they couldn't solve from time to time—so they called Timothy. And the worse the problem, the more in demand he was. He's a regular savant when it comes to removing malware, tracking who's done which changes to what strings of code, and basically all things computer-related. I'll bet he'd been a serious hacker as a teen, before growing a conscience.

Timothy is a good-looking guy, dark hair, a ready smile, and rows of tiny gold hoops in one ear. But he's always had something of the geek about him. Now that he was on his own and more relaxed, he'd loosened up. Low-slung tight pants with rolled-up cuffs, tan canvas shoes—he was beginning to look more like the stereotype of a musician or a Mission hipster than a computer nerd.

He expertly flipped the omelette he'd been making onto a plate and shoved it in front of me. Eli looked at it longingly, before settling for a small cup of nonfat yogurt. He was still on a strict diet, and had already trimmed his normal two sixty down to two twenty-five or so, close to his college-football-playing weight. That was the pre-steroid era, of course. He looked good, but I could see he was suffering. He likes his food.

But this wasn't about food, anyway—it had more the feeling of a strategy session than a friendly breakfast. Or maybe Victor had decided on an intervention over unknown transgressions. One never knows.

Timothy tossed a couple of bacon strips to Lou and started in on another omelette. The rest of us sat around the old scarred kitchen table. Victor's kitchen, unlike the rest of his house, is a warm and plain and comfortable refuge, a far cry from the expensive antiques and ornate furnishings that he otherwise favors.

It would have been polite for me to wait until everyone had got their food, but cold eggs are no treat at all. I'd polished off my omelette before Victor even started on his. When I poured myself a second cup of coffee and leaned back in my chair, Victor gave me a friendly smile, indistinguishable from the smile he gives to a hearty breakfast plate. I looked back at him more in resignation than suspicion. Timothy was a good cook, and the cheese omelette had put me in a comfortable mood, which of course was exactly the point.

Timothy didn't know that; he was just having a good time cooking up breakfast for his friends. He's the only one in our circle who isn't a practitioner, and that sometimes provides a welcome balance and some common sense as well. He's very fond of Victor, naturally, but has no illusions about what Victor's like. Still, he doesn't really get just how manipulative Victor can be. Which is fine; if you can't turn something of a blind eye to the faults of your significant other, what's the point of a relationship?

"So," Victor finally said as I sipped my coffee, "you met Jessie. And how is she these days?"

"How do you know her? I thought she was new in town."

"She is. But we've crossed paths from time to time in other places."

"She's . . . impressive," I said.

"She is that. Always has been. Did you meet Naja?"

"Oh, yes." Victor's mouth quirked into a bare smile.

"Gave you a bit of a turn, I imagine. And what exactly was it she wanted from you?"

"Well, it seems that a woman in her employ stole something from her and then went missing. She wouldn't say what. She wanted to know if I'd consider trying to find her. She offered me a ridiculous amount of money to take it on."

"And what did you tell her?"

I looked over at Eli for some clue as to what was going on, but he just gazed back blandly at me.

"I told her that dealing with employee theft wasn't really my thing."

"I see. And she just let it go at that?"

"Sort of. She did ask me to think it over, and I said I would. I got the feeling there was more to it than she was letting on."

Out of the corner of my eye I saw Eli nod approvingly. Victor pushed around the remnants of his omelette with his fork.

"With Jessie there usually is." More omelette pushing. "Well, after you've given it some thought, it might be a good idea to call her and say you've changed your mind."

"Oh? And why's that?"

"How else are you going to find out what she really wants from you?"

"Do I care?"

"Maybe not, but I do."

Eli weighed in before we started sniping at each other again.

"You see, Mason, this Jessie woman has a long history with Victor. Very long. They differ on some very crucial matters concerning practitioner society."

"She mentioned something about that," I said. "Organizing practitioners. Moving into the twenty-first century. Apparently she thinks Victor is somewhat of a fuddy-duddy. But how long a history could she have had with him, anyway? She can't be more than what—twenty-nine, thirty, if that."

Victor gave me that half smile of his, the one where one corner of his mouth twitches up, just enough to let me know he knows something I don't.

"She's been uncommonly active," he said.

"Yes, and she's quite the organizer as well," Eli said. "She likes being in charge, and she's very good at it. And therein lies the problem."

"Because she's a black practitioner?"

"No, not precisely, although that doesn't help. But she's always been an advocate for a more formal society of practitioners—something that we've never had—an official set of rules and laws, not just guidelines based on tradition."

"And with herself in charge, naturally," Victor added.

"I see."

So it was basically a turf war. Victor's enforcer role was entirely unofficial, but he'd never been challenged about it. Sure, we'd had trouble with practitioners trying to kill us, or do other unpleasant things, but they were criminals, not political rivals. They had no problem with the system; they just thought it shouldn't apply to them.

"She's been building her base for quite a few years," Eli continued. "The fact that she's appeared in San Francisco now could mean she's ready to move. She considers Victor her greatest obstacle, and I think she's ready to take him on."

"You mean like an all-out war? Sounds bizarre."

"No, of course not; that would be ridiculous. That's not what she has in mind at all. She's a businesswoman, not an assassin. And although I think she wouldn't hesitate to kill someone if it were necessary, that's not what we're dealing with. She wants to rule by acclamation, not force."

"It'll never happen," I said, shaking my head. "Practitioners are a notoriously independent breed. They may put up with our little group because we're a necessity, but they'd never go for anyone actually being in charge of them."

"Maybe, maybe not. What if she proposed that practitioners be allowed to use their talents to win money at gambling? Or what if she proposed we finally come out of the closet, make ourselves known to society at large? Run for political office, using a bit of glamour to sway votes? Run the country, for that matter? A lot of younger practitioners aren't wedded to the old ways."

"Hmm. I never looked at it that way. But what does that have to do with her wanting to hire me?"

"Maybe she wants to make a convert out of you," Victor said.

"Why me? Why not Eli? He'd be a hell of a lot more useful."

"She knows Eli would be a hard one to convince, to put

it mildly. You, however, have somewhat of a reputation. One you encourage, I might add. Mason the loner. Mason the rebel, the man who goes his own way. Dirty Harry with a wand."

I opened my mouth to tell Victor where to put it, but Eli held up a warning finger. I acknowledged it and decided to keep the conversation light.

"I like to think of myself more as a cross between Sherlock Holmes and Indiana Jones."

"Yes, don't we all," Eli said. "More likely, I think, she's simply aware that you and Victor don't exactly see eye to eye on a lot of things. I can see why she might think you could be persuaded eventually to jump ship, and a secret ally smack in the middle of Victor's camp would be of tremendous use to her—if for nothing else, just for the information that could provide."

Timothy had been following the conversation with great interest.

"Sounds like you want Mason to act as a double agent," he said. "Couldn't that be dangerous?" Good old Timothy, right to the heart of the matter.

"Yeah," I said. "Couldn't Mason end up hanging from a meat hook somewhere, or providing target practice for a playful cobra?"

"That's not Jessica," Victor said. "If she found out you were running a con on her, she'd most likely just fire you."

"Most likely" is one of those phrases that does not inspire confidence. But I wasn't worried about my health, not really. I was more worried about taking on a difficult and possibly unpleasant assignment, for no good reason that I could see.

"Still, it seems like an awful lot of trouble for something based on supposition, and not anything I want to get in the middle of anyway. I think I'll pass on this one, thanks. The whole double-agent thing doesn't hold much appeal for me—too much like simply being a rat."

"It's not an admirable situation, I admit," said Eli. "But you might want to reconsider. This could well be more than just practitioner politics—it could affect our future in a significant fashion. And who knows, maybe she really does want you to find this woman for her. Maybe the woman really did steal something and it would be nice to know why. You don't steal things from a black practitioner without some very strong motivation."

"And don't forget the money," Timothy said. "I believe you owe me a few dollars, come to think of it."

I owed him more than a few, borrowed back when he was working and I wasn't, and I felt guilty about it.

"Well, the money certainly would come in useful," I said.

"Oh, you couldn't keep the money," Victor said. "I'll pay your standard salary for the duration, of course, just like any job, and you can turn over the money she gives you to me."

"Fat chance," I said. Victor leaned forward in his chair like a prosecuting attorney.

"Really? So are you intending to actually look for this woman who's hiding from Jessie?"

"Why not?"

Somehow I'd become turned around on my position about not doing this job without realizing it.

"And what will you do if you find her? Turn her over to a black practitioner you know almost nothing about, based on her claim that the woman stole something? You'd be comfortable with that, would you?"

"Well, no, I couldn't do that, not without knowing a lot more about the situation."

"And let's say this woman really is a thief. Then you'd be fine with being the instrument of her punishment, letting Jessie make the decision of what that punishment might be? Really?"

I didn't say anything. I hadn't thought the thing through. Victor continued, relentless.

"So let me see if I have this straight. You'd go to work for Jessie under false pretenses, with no intention of actually doing the job you're being paid for, and take a large sum of money for it? And at the same time, then betray her and report back to us about what you found out? And keep the money for yourself? That seems morally weak, even for you, Mason."

Victor was right, of course. I looked over at Eli for help, but he just looked at me with an interested and inquiring expression. Timothy started washing up, whistling nonchalantly.

"And what do you do with the money?" I asked. "Distribute it to widows and orphans?"

"Operating expenses. Upkeep for enforcement activities isn't cheap, after all. I know you think I'm made of money, but I'm not."

I didn't think; I knew. Still, he had a point.

"Let me think about it. I haven't decided yet," I said again, but of course I already had.

If nothing else, I was getting curious about the situation. Victor continued to look at me with polite expectation. I gave up. "Goddamn it. You win." Victor leaned back in his chair, satisfied.

"That's settled, then. But give it another day, just to make it look like you've really given it some thought before you call her. We don't want to have her wondering what might have prompted your change of heart."

"We can do better than that," Eli said. "How about if we stage a public disagreement between you and Mason, nothing serious, just some angry words. She's had her eye on Mason; it's bound to get back to her. That way, a change of heart on his part won't seem so unlikely; Mason will obviously be needing a new source of income. But be cautious. Her reputation for astute calculation is not unwarranted, and I don't think she'd take it well if she found out you weren't being on the up-and-up with her. You'll need to make your fight believable."

Victor and I looked at each other and both smiled at the

same time, which was a rarity. Eli saw that and sighed.

"Okay, I see that won't be a problem. Just don't get carried away, all right?"

WE NEEDED TO FIND A PLACE WHERE OUR LITtle tiff would be noted, and there aren't that many places where practitioners hang out. Mostly we're a solitary bunch when you come right down to it. But there is one bar over in Polk Gulch where you can usually find a practitioner or two. Most of the clientele are just normal citizens looking for a pleasant neighborhood bar, but the owner, Bill Gavagan, knew a lot of practitioners and always made them particularly welcome. And the occasional Ifrit, like Lou, was always treated as an honored guest, as well they should be.

Both of Bill's parents had been practitioners, which was why he knew so many of them. He had only the faintest trace of talent himself, if any, which was unusual. Talent sometimes appears in a family where there never has been any before, but the reverse is seldom the case. Just like two short people occasionally have a tall child, but two tall people seldom have a short child.

But Bill didn't really care about his lack of talent, or if he did, he'd come to terms with it long ago. He was a friendly and gregarious soul, born to run a drinking establishment. Which, naturally, he called Gavagan's Bar—a joke of sorts, but appropriate in more ways than one.

So that was where we all found ourselves later that night. Sherwood and Timothy came along—we hadn't all had a night out together in a while, and besides, they both wanted to see the show. Sherwood's an ex—a quite-a-while-ago ex. We also both had worked for Victor in the past, and we were still occasional work partners now.

A few years ago, on a case, my lack of ability had gotten her killed. Except it wasn't really my fault, and she hadn't actually been killed, but that's another story for another day.

Bill was behind the bar when we came in and greeted Eli with a huge smile.

"Eli! How long has it been? Mason, Victor. And . . . Sheridan, is it?"

"Sherwood. And this is Timothy."

Lou hopped up onto one of the high-backed barstools that ran the length of the bar, and looked at Bill expectantly.

"Ah, yes. Lou."

He reached behind him, took a cocktail wiener out of a large jar, and offered it. Lou took all of half a second to dispose of it and looked up hopefully for another.

"Enough," I said. "Don't be a pig."

"How about the rest of you? What can I do you for?"

Gavagan's has a nice selection of microbrews. I tried a Black Rock Porter, Sherwood picked out an amber Barleywine, and Victor of course went for a single-malt scotch with a name I couldn't pronounce.

We talked shop for a while, speculating on Jessie's motives, but of course we didn't have any more information than we'd had this afternoon, so we didn't get anywhere.

After a while the place filled up, and I noted a couple of practitioners in the crowd, a man and a woman I knew vaguely, though I couldn't remember their names. San Francisco is a small town for a big city. There aren't that many practitioners living here, and if you live here long enough, you get to know almost everyone, if only by sight. It's not so different in that way from the community of jazz musicians.

It seemed like as good a time as any. I looked over at Victor, and he nodded.

"Because I say so, and that's good enough," he said, voice a bit louder than usual. A couple of people nearby glanced over at us.

"Yeah?" I shot back, a little louder. "You're not the boss of me."

Timothy shook his head, Sherwood put her hands over her eyes, and even Eli came close to a smirk.

"Weak," he whispered.

"Actually, I *am* the boss," said Victor, gamely carrying on. "You'd do well to remember that, Mason, and I'll thank you to show me some respect."

"Respect is earned, not ordered up like Chinese take-out. At least I have some respect for good food."

Okay, maybe we should have scripted this. You'd think that as a jazzman my improv chops would be strong, but they weren't, not with this. And I hadn't given Victor much to work with for a comeback.

"Why don't you go back to playing your guitar for a living, then," he said. "Oh, that's right, you tried that and failed. That's why you came crawling back for a paycheck."

Now, that was over the line, even for a fake argument. Even when it was all for show, Victor had to win. I got pissed.

"Go fuck yourself," I said, standing up, and I meant it.

I reached over and knocked his scotch out of his hand. It spilled over his expensive slacks, and his eyes tightened. I might have gone too far myself; he was pissed as well now. By now most of the bar was watching. Victor also stood up and for a moment I thought he was going to deck me. He's smaller than I am, but he's a martial artist among other things and you wouldn't want to tangle with him for real.

"Victor," Timothy said warningly, and Victor relaxed just a bit. Timothy was the only one who could calm him down when he started losing it.

"Just leave," Victor said. "I'm sick of you, and I don't need to put up with any more of your crap."

"Couldn't have put it better myself." I motioned to Lou. "Let's go," I said, and strode out of the bar without a backward look.

When I got outside I realized I'd ridden over with Victor and Eli, so I had no way to get home. I ended up taking a bus, with the usual hassle about Lou, and then BART to the Mission. I was in a rather sour mood; even though the spat with Victor had been phony, there had been an undercurrent to it that left a bad taste in my mouth. And I could already see trouble coming from this. I'd managed to get myself talked into a dicey situation, and not even for money, either. I'd played a lot of cheap gigs in my time, but this was the first time I'd been suckered in by nothing more than a cheese omelette.

THREE

I CALLED JESSIE THE NEXT DAY AND TOLD HER I'd reconsidered. I didn't give her a reason.

"Might I ask what brought about this change of heart?" she said.

"Rent. Food. Victor hasn't had much work for me lately, not that I'd take it, anyway."

"Oh? No trouble between you, I hope."

She'd surely heard about the fight at Gavagan's, so this was my opening, my chance to rail against Victor, but I remembered Eli's advice. It would be just a little too pat, and Jessie was no fool. I let that sit just a moment longer than usual before I answered.

"No, not really. Just the usual. We have some differences of opinion."

"I can understand that," she said. "Anything in particular?"

Again I was tempted but I didn't push it. If I was going to worm my way into her confidence, it had to be done slowly. If you jump right in, sooner or later the person you're trying to con starts wondering why you're being so forthcoming.

"No," I said. "Victor's okay, I guess." I changed the subject. "If I'm going to be looking for this woman, I'd like to have that photo of her. Using words to describe people works only up to a point."

"Of course. I'll be up in your neck of the woods later today if you want to meet up."

I wasn't happy that she apparently knew where I lived, but then, she'd obviously had me checked out thoroughly before she ever called me. I do like my privacy but I'm not hiding, either, so I'm not hard to track down.

"Café Java," I said. "Sixteenth and Guerrero."

That wasn't one of my usual haunts, but I wanted to avoid my favorite spots. I'm not sure why; it just seemed like a good idea.

I was at an outside table later that afternoon, drinking a latte, when Jessie showed up wearing a floppy straw hat and carrying a large straw bag. It was big enough to hold all sorts of things—like a good-sized snake, for instance. She plopped herself down on the chair across from me, very much at ease.

The first thing she did, before even saying a word, was to reach into the bag and pull out the photo I'd seen at her office. When she did, I got a glimpse of something moving inside it. Lou's head had already snapped around the moment she sat down, and he was staring fixedly at the bag. Not very polite, but I didn't blame him.

"What are you going to do with it?" she asked. "Show it around like in a Raymond Chandler novel?"

"Something like that," I said. "You said she's a jazz player—what instrument?"

"Piano. Is that important?"

"Possibly. It gives me a few ideas about leads."

"Such as?"

I put on a faux tough face. "I'll ask the questions here, ma'am."

She laughed. "I'm sure you will. From what I've heard

you ask a lot of questions. I also heard something about some odd creatures roaming the city a while back, and you going around asking questions. Did you get any answers?"

"I did. Not always the ones I wanted."

She waited expectantly for further explanation, but I just smiled blandly at her. Mason, man of mystery, that's me. But it was interesting that she'd brought that up. We'd had to deal with some strange things indeed, some vicious, some not, that had been spawned by an energy pool. A gateway of sorts that I'd unwittingly helped to establish a while back.

We'd never been able to close it, though Victor and Eli had finally come up with a way to keep anything else from coming through, at least for now. But it was still a worry. I wondered if Jessie was aware of it, and if so, why she was asking questions about its consequences.

"Well, I'm late for a meeting," she said, when it became clear I wasn't going to say anything else. She knew enough about people not to push things, either. She scraped her chair back and got to her feet. "Mason. Lou." She nodded to each of us and set off down the street without looking back.

I looked at the photo again, this time more carefully. It's impossible to tell character from a photo, but that doesn't stop anyone from trying. I was hoping to see something in it, a sly look or a narrowing of the eyes. But all I saw was a good-natured humor in the face, and the relaxed confidence of someone who knows who she is. She didn't look like a thief. Then again, the good ones never do. Or maybe she just took a good photo.

I sat idly, sipping my latte and considering. I did have a good idea about how to go about finding her. If it didn't pan out, I'd be at sea, though; I didn't have any backup plan. But I'd deal with that when I had to.

According to Jessie, Jackie was a musician. Now, when you're in hiding, it's a good idea to change your routine and avoid those things that define you. If you're an avid skier, stay off the slopes. If you're a surfer, stay away from the beach. And if you're a musician, don't start up a band or hang around at jam sessions.

But that's easier said than done. At first, you're looking over your shoulder and jumping at every noise. But after a while, when nothing happens, you start to relax. You can't live in fear forever, watching every step—it's like being on a diet; for a while it's not that difficult, but sooner or later old habits creep back and before you know it you're scarfing down cheesecake.

And Jackie had last been with Jessie in Seattle. She might not even be aware that Jessie was now in San Francisco as well, much less that she'd been fingered as living in the city herself. So, the urge to play some music would seem harmless enough.

But where? You can't just waltz in and start playing with people at random. Sure, there are jam sessions for jazz players, quite a few of them, actually. But most of them are geared toward the intermediate player, with a house band sometimes providing the rhythm section. There aren't that many that cater to accomplished musicians, which, according to Jessie, Jackie was.

The prime jam session for jazz players is at the Dogpatch Saloon, four to eight every Sunday. Everybody's welcome, and the players are surprisingly kind, but some heavy cats drop in on a regular basis. It's intimidating unless you know your way around your ax, and mediocre players don't usually brave the bandstand more than once.

Dogpatch, over on Third Street, is named for the area of the city it's located in, namely Dogpatch. Whether that has anything to do with the old Li'l Abner cartoons, I don't know. I do know Dogpatch used to be an industrial area with a few clubs and lots of machine shops and vinyl repair stores. As a result, nighttime parking was once plentiful, perfect for a club location. But now, like everywhere else in San Francisco, the area developed a rep as a hip place to live and parking has become difficult.

The Dogpatch Saloon is another bar where Lou is welcome. I used to spend a lot of time hanging out there, back when gigs were scarcer and the magical world was quieter. Eventually, Lou wormed his way in. He was on his best behavior at first, as he always is until people get used to his being around. Then he starts in with shameless begging, but by that time no one would even think of banning him.

Another thing I like about Dogpatch is that it never seems to change. No matter how long you're away, you still see the same long straight bar with captain's chairs, the same scuffed pool table, and, mostly, the same familiar faces. The bar was packed whenever I walked in carrying my ax, and since I knew at least half of the regulars I always got a bunch of friendly waves.

When I headed over there the next day Shirley was tending bar, which she always did for the Sunday jam sessions. She's heavyset, short-haired, and knows more about fixing motorcycles than the average mechanic. The perfect stereotype of a particular type of gay woman, except that she's entirely straight with a doting husband.

A young kid was up on the stage, nervously fingering his alto while the house band thumbed through their real books looking for the tune he called. I guessed it was his first time up there. It might be his last. I walked up to the bar and ordered a Sierra Pale Ale. Shirley whacked it down on the bar.

"Mason," she said. "Haven't seen you in here for a while. I hear you're playing a lot around town, though. Too good for this place these days?"

"I've always been too good for this place. It's just taken a while for others to realize that." She snorted, looking down at my guitar case. In it, a blond fifties Gibson Birdland, my pride and joy.

"You going to honor us with a few tunes tonight?"

"I thought I might give it a whirl. Maybe I can even fool a few people."

Lou made it up onto one of the bar chairs and stepped

daintily on top of the bar itself, tail wagging hopefully, in search of a treat. Shirley reached behind her for some beef jerky.

"You need to teach that dog some manners," she said, but she didn't mean it.

"Yeah, sure. Good luck with that."

I kicked back, drank some beer, and listened to the band, with the new kid sitting in on sax. They kicked off with "Pent-Up House," an old Sonny Rollins tune. It was a good choice on the kid's part, because although the timing on the head is a bit tricky, the changes are straightforward and easy to solo over, with lots of room and a steady swing rhythm. At first the kid was tentative, trying hard not to make the slightest mistake, and so his playing, naturally enough, was rather stilted. But he definitely had potential, and I added some loud clapping to the crowd response when he finished his solo. It was more enthusiastic than he strictly deserved, but the regulars at Dogpatch are nice people and all musicians remember what it's like to be new and start playing out with the big boys—although not all of them care. But it worked; on the next tune he relaxed and just started to blow without thinking about it, and really caught fire. He was grinning when he stepped off the stage, just another jazzman.

Joe Antonelli, the guy on the piano, caught sight of me and motioned for me to come on up.

"Long time, no see," he said. "What do you want to play?"

"Something easy. You call it."

I could see him considering, trying to come up with the hardest tune he could think of, but finally he relented and decided to take it easy on me.

"'Stella'?"

"Sounds good."

"Stella by Starlight" is a standard I could play in my sleep. But it's a nice tune, with great changes, and the challenge is to find something new about it each time. I plugged into the little house amp and gave it a credible ride, though it didn't have my full attention. I was thinking about how to approach getting a line on the missing Jackie.

Since these were friends and acquaintances, it was a lot easier than it could have been. If you walk into a bar as a stranger and start flashing a photo around and asking questions, all you'll get is blank looks. And unless it's someone everybody hates, you can be sure that person will hear about it before the night is over.

But even though these were friends, I still had to tread lightly. She might well have friends here, too, and being an attractive young woman, maybe even more than that. The last thing I wanted was to let her know that someone was sniffing around after her.

We wound up "Stella" and then played "Song For My Father" as a Latin groove. After that, I unplugged and put my guitar away. There were more than a few players waiting their turn to sit in, and it's not polite to hog at a jam session.

"Say, Joe," I said, "you know any good keyboard players?"

"Not a one," he said, doing a quick arpeggio over the piano keys.

"Yeah, me either. But seriously, a friend of mine just moved to the city, and she's thinking of putting together an all-woman jazz quartet and needs a piano player."

"How about Wanda?"

"I thought of her, but my friend wants to put together something with all new faces, as a promotional thing, and Wanda's been around for years. You run into any new players lately, preferably talented?" Joe thought for maybe half a second before snapping his fingers.

"Shit, yeah. A new woman started coming around a couple of months ago. She's good, too, and I don't think she's playing with anyone yet. Her name's Melissa. I'm surprised she's not here today."

Jackie probably wouldn't be using her own name, so it could be her.

"Melissa?" I said. "I think I might know her. Redhead, kind of goofy-looking?"

Joe laughed. "No, not at all. A black chick, and goofy-looking's the last thing you would call her."

Bingo.

"Huh. You wouldn't have her number, by any chance?"

Joe shook his head. "I don't, but I'll give her yours if I see her."

I thought a moment, dug out a scrap of paper, and wrote down Sherwood's cell.

"Give her this," I said. "It's the woman who's putting together the group—her name's Sherwood. Maybe it'll work out."

"Maybe," he said. "She's a good player, but there is one thing your friend should be aware of." My ears perked up.

"Really? What?"

"She's kind of an eco freak—except for music, every conversation I've had with her comes back to how we're all destroying the planet."

"Well, we are."

"Don't I know it. But you can't go around yelling about it all the time. It gets old. Still, she can play; I'll give her that." Joe reached in his pocket and pulled out a wallet. "Hold on a sec." He fished around until he came up with a worn business card and handed it to me. "Melissa gave me this, said to come by if I was interested. Maybe you can find her there."

The card had a stylized graphic of a raccoon holding a small globe of the earth. On the top were the words *Earth Abides* and an address and phone number.

"I'm surprised you kept this," I said.

"What can I say? She is hot, you know."

I tucked the card away and returned to my seat at the bar where Lou was working the crowd. I stared him off the bar until he jumped back down onto the floor. I examined the card, but there was nothing else on it. Maybe I wouldn't need my scheme after all; maybe this address would lead me right to her.

It would be good to keep a backup plan, though, and I thought this was a pretty good one. Jackie would surely be skittish if she thought someone was looking for her, and any new acquaintance might be viewed at first with some suspicion. But if a jazz musician she knew told her that a friend of his, another jazz musician, was looking not exactly for her, but for a keyboard player, she'd have to be extraordinarily paranoid for it to set off any warning bells.

Still, given that a black practitioner was looking for her, she might well be that paranoid. As soon as I got home, I called Sherwood.

"I need a favor," I said.

"I'm shocked."

"It's work-related." I told her about my conversation at Dogpatch. "I gave Joe your cell number to give to Jackie if he runs into her. She's calling herself Melissa. If she does call, you're a bass player looking to put together an all-female band, like I said."

Sherwood wasn't a player, but she knew a lot about jazz and jazz musicians. She'd be able to fake it convincingly.

"What's my name?"

"Sherwood. I thought you knew that."

"Very amusing. And what if she's done some poking around the practitioner community since she got here and my name has come up in conversation?"

"I would guess she's been staying as far away from practitioners as possible. And if she's come across your name, she's surely heard the name Mason as well, in which case I don't imagine we'll be hearing from her anytime soon."

"I'm not sure I'm comfortable with this. Eli told me about your new job, helping a black practitioner hunt someone down. It's creepy."

"I get that. But it's not like I'm going to be turning her over to anyone. I'm just trying to find out what the larger picture might be, and get in good with Jessie. You can suggest she come over to my place for an audition."

That setup would have two advantages. First, we'd be two against one if things got out of hand. Second, we'd be at my place, and a practitioner is always strongest on home turf. That's why you never go to another practitioner's house if the situation is problematic—public places like coffee shops are the preferred neutral territory. I didn't expect any trouble, though. She'd be expecting to meet some musicians and play some music, and practitioners would be the furthest thing from her mind.

"Sounds perfect. And I'm sure it will all work out. Your plans always do, after all."

I didn't mind the gibe. Sherwood's occasional sarcasm is always friendly, more jokes than digs. Whenever I try that kind of thing, it just sounds petty and mean-spirited.

"Well, this plan will work," I said. "Why shouldn't it?"

"No reason. Except . . ."

"Except what?"

"Aren't you forgetting something?"

"Probably. Remind me."

"Well, she's a practitioner, right? And she doesn't know we're practitioners, right? She thinks we're musicians."

"So?"

"So we're inviting her over to your house."

"And?"

"Your *house*, Mason."

I still didn't see what she was driving at. I live in an in-law flat in the Mission, a converted garage in the bottom of a house. It's got greenery all around, a driveway that used to run up to the garage that I can park my van in, and is surprisingly cheap—for San Francisco. The landlord lives upstairs and travels a lot, which is a blessing for both of us. Sooner or later he'll be home when something odd happens, though, and that will certainly create a problem. I might even have to find another place. But it's pleasant and cozy, and not the sort of place you'd associate with a practitioner.

"What's wrong with my place?" I said. "It's perfect for— Oh."

Now I got it. Practitioners' homes are just like anyone else's—with one big difference. We ward our houses to protect them from magical attack, or even magical intrusion, for the less paranoid. It's as common and normal as having a lock on your front door, and few if any practitioners live unguarded.

Victor's house is as secure as Fort Knox—the wards are direct and powerful, set up by an entire team, and nothing gets through uninvited. He needs that level of protection; acting as the chief enforcer of magical mores has earned him some powerful enemies over the years.

Most practitioners don't have that level of protection, nor do they need it. My own wards, though effective, are comparatively modest. But although wards are not perceptible to ordinary civilians, they are instantly apparent to any practitioner. In fact, you can tell quite a bit about a practitioner by the type of warding they employ.

The moment Jackie showed up at my front door, she'd sense the wards and make me as a practitioner. And that would be the last we'd see of her.

"Hmm," I said. "I see your point. A café, then—that's neutral ground for practitioners, and it will make her feel more comfortable, even though she won't be expecting anyone but a musician. And it's natural to want to check out someone thinking about joining a group, to see if you're compatible."

"Any preferences?"

"Not really. Maybe you could have her suggest a place—she's likely to choose somewhere near to where she lives, so if things go south, we'll at least have an approximate location for her."

"Good enough," she said. "Tomorrow, then."

After I hung up, I thought for a while. The plan was good, but complicated. Maybe I should go a more direct route and save all that trouble. If that didn't work, the plan with Sherwood was still a good fallback option. So I made another call, to the number on the card Joe had given me. A woman's bright and sunny voice answered, friendly, but noncommittal.

"Hi," I said. "My name is Sam. A friend of mine gave me this number. I'm new in town, and looking for some environmentally conscious groups. I used to be an animal rights activist, but there doesn't seem to be much need for that here."

"Oh no," she said. "There's plenty of need everywhere, believe me. But we're always happy to have new people. Where are you from?"

"Chicago," I said.

"Really. What part? I used to live there myself."

I had actually spent some time in Chicago, which was why I picked that city. Anytime you're fabricating a cover story, it's best to stay as close as possible to the truth. Otherwise, you'll get tripped up in no time.

"Hyde Park," I said. "My girlfriend used to go to the University of Chicago." Another morsel of truth.

"Wow," she said. "I had a friend there as well. Lived close to campus, on Barrister Avenue. You know where that is?"

This was interesting. She was testing me, seeing if my story held up. Which meant this group was probably engaged in more than just talk when it came to environmental issues.

If I'd just picked Chicago at random, I would have had to guess at what to answer. If it was the main campus drag, you wouldn't want to say you'd never heard of it. But if she'd made up the name off the top of her head, then saying sure, you knew where it was, would be even worse.

"Barrister?" I said, letting a tone of doubt creep in. "I don't think I know where that is."

"Oh. Well, maybe I got the name wrong. It's been a while." Her tone changed, becoming a tad more relaxed. "Actually, we're having a get-together tonight at my house, if you'd like to drop by and meet some of the folks."

"That would be great."

"About nine, then. I'm Haley." She gave me the address, the same one that was on the card.

"I'm looking forward to it," I said.

THE ADDRESS WAS A HOUSE IN THE UPPER FILLmore, right off Fillmore Street itself. Upper Fillmore's not as snooty as the nearby Pacific Heights, but you still need some money to live there. Nice restaurants, elegant bars, patisseries instead of bakeries.

In the Mission you get a diverse crew of hipsters, down-and-outers, yuppies, and assorted other types. The upper Fillmore is more stylish; the men wear expensive casual clothes and the women wear outfits, ensembles that could have come right from the pages of *Glamour*.

I put a psychic shield around myself before I went up to the house; if Jackie was at the house, I didn't want her to make me as a fellow practitioner. And I left Lou in my van, with one window open as usual so he could come and go as he pleased. There wasn't anything to steal in it, anyway.

It wasn't that I thought Jackie might recognize him as an Ifrit if she was there. It was more about keeping a low profile, just in case. If I was going to be poking around for the next few days, he'd be too obvious an identifier. Describing me as six feet tall with dark hair is accurate. But so are a thousand other guys. Add a small black-and-tan dog tagging along into the mix, and you become instantly identifiable.

The woman who answered the door was blond, late thirties, pleasant-looking, and stylish.

"You must be Sam," she said. "I'm Haley. Come on in and meet the folks."

She led the way to a large front room with a hardwood floor and rugs scattered throughout with the random appearance that speaks of careful thought. "Everyone, this is Sam, new to the city. Sam, this is everyone."

I got a pleasant chorus of hellos and nods from the assembled group. I'd been expecting a more radical-looking bunch, some compilation of guys with dreadlocks and women in combat boots. But like most stereotypes, it was way off. They were a very ordinary-looking collection of people who would have looked equally at home discussing PTA issues, neighborhood dog-leash regulations, or at a cancer awareness fund-raiser.

I counted ten of them besides myself, four men and six women, all white, none of them Jackie. I sat down off to the side as unobtrusively as possible. They ignored me, not rude, just focused on the conversation at hand.

Most of the talk centered around a supposed developer's land grab involving the Point Reyes National Seashore. I don't know where they got their information, but that was just not a realistic concern. Apart from the legal protections involved, the public would never stand for it. I asked a few questions, which were answered politely enough, but mostly just listened. Finally that paid off.

"Is Melissa coming tonight?" asked one of the men. The way he asked made me think that saving the planet wasn't his only interest in the group. Apparently others thought the same, since I caught a few knowing glances thrown between the others.

"No, I don't think so," Haley said. "But Cassandra should be here soon. She's talked to Melissa and she'll know what the . . . status is."

She glanced over at me, not too subtly, making it clear she didn't want it gone into with me there, at least not right now. But I wasn't interested, anyway. I was interested in Cassandra, though, if she was tight with "Melissa."

About five minutes later the doorbell rang and Cassandra was ushered in. Again, not what I had expected. She was small, not quite five feet, with a neat afro and light brown skin. A dusting of freckles ran across the bridge of her nose, and when she smiled a greeting at the group, it stretched all the way across her face.

If she knew Jackie, she might well be a practitioner herself. But I got no sense of that; if she was shielding, she was doing it well. I could probe her a little, but if she was a practitioner, she'd feel it and know I was one, too, and that wasn't what I wanted at all.

"Nothing new," she said, in answer to the unspoken question from the group. "I'll find out more by next week." Her voice had a light and lilting Jamaican accent, just enough of one to fall pleasantly on the ears.

Her announcement didn't seem to be a big deal, though. Pretty soon they were all working out the logistics of a planned rally at City Hall next month. After that was finished, Haley brought out a little tray of cookies and pastry. Good thing Lou wasn't here or there wouldn't have been enough for everyone.

I edged over toward Cassandra, trying to get a line on her, what she was about, anything that would make it seem natural for me to see her again. Apart from the obvious—she didn't strike me as someone looking to hook up, even assuming I was irresistible. One of the women came up to her and gave her a hug.

"Cass, I've just got to thank you again. You were absolutely right—it was a wrong choice, and the wrong person." I gave an inquiring look, hoping to draw myself into the conversation, and the woman obliged. "Cassandra is a genius at arriving at the truth of a matter," she said.

"Really? Are you a therapist, Cassandra?"

The woman laughed. "Not likely. Cassandra does readings, and they're amazing."

"Oh? What kind of readings?"

Cassandra shrugged. "Life. Love. Relationship problems. Psychic readings. Not the sort of thing you'd be interested in, I'd guess."

I put on my most charming smile. "You never know." She looked at me skeptically. "Okay, you're right," I said, laughing. "It's not my sort of thing, But my sister, now, she's very much a believer, and she's having some doubts about her boyfriend."

"I tell you, Cassandra is simply the best," said the woman. Bless her.

"How much do you charge?" I asked. Cassandra perked up with interest.

"Two hundred dollars, usually. One hundred fifty for members of the group here."

"And worth every penny," the woman put in.

"Have you got a card?" I asked. Cassandra shook her head.

"No, but I have some time tomorrow if you're really interested."

"Absolutely."

"Do you know where the houseboats on Mission Creek are?"

"I do. You live there? That's fantastic."

"It is nice," she said. "You can't miss mine—it's bright red, the only one like that there." She took a scrap of paper, wrote something on it, and handed it to me. "There's a gate into where the houseboats are moored. Here's the combination. About noon, then?"

"We'll be there," I said.

I left soon after, promising Haley I'd be back next week. Driving home, I was well satisfied. Already I was one step closer to Jackie. This detective stuff wasn't turning out to be that difficult after all.

FOUR

I WOKE UP EARLY THE NEXT MORNING WITH another headache, but by the time I'd finished my coffee it was gone. I waited until a decent hour before calling Sherwood to ask for her help a second time.

"Again?" she said. "Why am I supposed to do all the work?"

"This will be easy, and you'll get a free psychic reading out of it."

"Just what I've always wanted. How did you know? Oh, wait, are you psychic, by chance?"

I explained about Cassandra and how I was supposed to bring someone over for a reading. Sherwood, of course, would play that role.

I drove over to pick her up. Sherwood had finally moved into her new place, a pleasant garden apartment on Potrero Hill. Mission Creek is nearby to Potrero Hill, but closer to the downtown area. It's a unique place to live, mostly industrial. The new UCSF Mission Creek campus is located there and a large medical complex as well, though they weren't totally up and running yet.

An odd collection of houseboats sits moored on the channel leading to the bay, inhabited by both bankers and eccentrics. Not far from where the homeless guy once known as Bridge Guy, now known as Rolf, hung out. And where the energy pool was located. The one we'd been unable to so far close off.

"This woman lives on a houseboat?" Sherwood asked as we drove over.

"So she says."

"I had no idea there was such a thing in the city."

Fifteen minutes later I pulled up and parked next to the small park that lay alongside the narrow channel. A mud flat ran down to the water's edge, ending in a jumble of rocks of various sizes. Two well-fed cats prowled cautiously by the water, jumping from rock to rock. Lou's ears perked up when he saw them, but there was no way he was going into that muck just to see them run.

Ramps led across the channel to where the houseboats were moored, each ramp blocked by a wire cage door with a combination lock. A gated community, though not the usual sort.

The houseboats were more house than boats. Some were small, but most were two stories and a couple of them were three. Right across from where we had parked, a pink three-tiered boat did a credible imitation of a wedding cake, each level slightly higher and smaller than the one below. Another, dark blue with white trim, reminded me of a top hat. All the houses exhibited the same curious mixture of ornate and ramshackle, with junk strewn over the long mooring dock and expensive-looking sailing boats tied up alongside. These houseboats weren't going anywhere, any more than the double-wide trailers in an RV park.

We strolled up to one of the entrance ramps, which was blocked by the tall wire mesh gate.

"They do like their privacy," I said, "but I was given the code."

I punched in the numbers and swung the door open. We passed along the row of houseboats, finally stopping at one of the smaller ones. The number thirty-two was visible over the front door, but it wasn't needed. There was no mistaking it; no two houseboats looked even vaguely similar, and this was the only one painted bright red.

"What's our story again?" Sherwood asked.

"You're having relationship trouble. You want to know if your current boyfriend is really the one."

"And you're the boyfriend?" She looked at me critically.

"No, that might be a hard sell. How could you possibly be having doubts about someone like me? I'm the skeptical brother, watching out for poor, credulous you."

"And Lou?"

"Lou's a dog." He threw me a dirty look. "He doesn't need a cover story."

I put a psychic shield over both of us. Cassandra might not be a practitioner at all, but on the other hand she might well be a wild talent—people we run into occasionally, those with talent who have little or no contact with other practitioners, sometimes unaware that others like them even exist. Mostly they're adolescents, when talent first manifests, but sometimes it's an older person. Generally they're harmless, but once in a while they have real power, and, being totally untrained, often wreak minor havoc.

Checking them out is part of Victor's responsibilities. If Cassandra was one of those, she might well sense our power. She might not recognize what she was seeing, but she'd sense there was something different about us, and that might make her uneasy and suspicious. Thus, the shield. Lou didn't need any shield, of course.

As soon as I knocked, the front door immediately popped open as if Cassandra had been waiting for us right behind it. Maybe she had seen us coming through the front windows.

"Cassandra," I greeted her. "This is my sister, Rebecca."

"Welcome, my dear. Welcome to both of you." She looked down at Lou and a puzzled expression flitted across her face.

"He's very well behaved," said Sherwood, following her gaze. Lou sat quietly at Sherwood's feet, doing a convincing imitation of a well-behaved dog. "I hope it's okay that I brought him along."

"Of course," she said. "All are welcome at Cassandra's house. Come in, come in."

When we stepped across the threshold I expected to feel the houseboat move under my feet, or at least have some sense of motion, but it was solid as a rock. The front room was light and airy, with windows that looked out on the bay channel. The widows opened out and a pleasant breeze with the tang of salt air came through.

I didn't get much time to look around. As soon as we entered, Cassandra led us through another door, heavy, with an iron dead bolt on the outside. A short flight of stairs led down to a basement, but unlike normal houses where the basement is underground, this room was below the waterline instead.

Cement walls, painted white, were another surprise. You'd think they would be damp and clammy with condensation covering the surface, but they were dry as a bone, tight and snug.

One corner of the room was set aside as a sleeping area, a low bed frame and mattress partially concealed behind a wooden screen. It wasn't somewhere I'd be comfortable sleeping; no matter how warm and dry it was, I'd always be aware I was under the waterline with the chilly waters of the channel only inches from my head.

The room wasn't cool, though; it was hot and close. Possibly the water acted as an insulator. On a low table at the back of the room a small fan was stirring the air, trying to provide some relief. In the middle of the room a larger table had been set up, with a shallow rectangular pan of water in the exact center of it.

Next to the pan, a small lamp was placed close enough to cast light over it. Several small square glass bottles, each a different color and stoppered with corks, sat next to the lamp. Two wooden chairs on either side of the table provided seating—one for Cassandra, the other for her client.

I looked around for another place to sit and settled on a more comfortable chair in one of the corners. Lou appeared to wander around aimlessly, sniffing at things, but he wasn't really being aimless. This was a job, and he was checking out the room as thoroughly as he could.

"Sit down," Cassandra said to Sherwood, motioning toward one of the chairs. She turned on the lamp, which cast a miniature spotlight on the pan of water, and turned off the other lights. Then she stooped down and flicked on another switch. Immediately, the ceiling of the room was transformed into a replica of a starry sky, complete with swirling blue clouds and moving points of light.

It was a laser projector, one of those high-tech toys that places like the Sharper Image used to sell. When I was five, my grandfather gave me his old planetarium projector. Actually, it was nothing more than a plastic globe covered with pinpoint holes, so that dots of light were thrown on the ceiling and walls, but I loved it. This was similar, in the way an Indy car is similar to a Model T. Technology has come a ways.

It was quite impressive, and had I been five again, I'd have been awestruck. But it also reeked of a carny scam—setting up the mark with a pretty display to distract them so they wouldn't notice the wires behind the scenes. Pay no attention to the man behind the curtain. Cassandra sat down at the table and took Sherwood's hands in hers.

"So," she said. "Your boyfriend. You want to know if you two really belong together, yes?"

Sherwood nodded.

"Concentrate on him. What he looks like. How he holds you. What you love about him. Then, what you don't like so much—the things that make you wonder."

Sherwood concentrated; then she relaxed and a faraway look appeared on her face. She closed her eyes and sat motionless. At one point a small sigh escaped. She was really playing it up, living in the moment.

But if it was method acting, it was also real. Sherwood believed in being fair, and was giving Cassandra every chance to show her stuff. Maybe there wasn't any boyfriend at the moment, but whoever Sherwood was envisioning had meant something to her at one time. It might have even been me—though that had been ages ago.

I took the opportunity to cast around, looking for evidence of true talent. It was there, faint but unmistakable, lurking in the corners. I focused in on Cassandra, and again I felt something. So she had talent, no doubt about it, but it was so faint as to be essentially useless to her. But maybe that was what had drawn Jackie to her, apart from the eco agenda they seemed to share. Maybe it flared up at random moments, giving her some real insight and a flash of power. That might explain why she was attracted to her psychic profession, and would also explain why her clients sometimes got real results.

Cassandra had closed her eyes as well, and she sat quietly, as motionless as Sherwood. Then she gave a start, as if waking up suddenly, and disengaged her hands.

"I have enough," she said. "Now we shall see what we shall see."

She picked up one of the bottles, uncorked it, and carefully tipped it sideways. I moved in closer to see what she was doing. A thin stream of black ink splashed into the pan of water and curled around like smoke from a fire. She replaced the stopper, picked up another bottle, and repeated the process. This time the ink was red. Next, she stirred the water ever so gently with a narrow wooden paddle. The two ink streams intersected, forming swirling patterns in the liquid.

"Ahh," I said. "Inkromancy."

Cassandra turned her head and fixed me with a glare. Not a trace of that previous good humor I'd seen remained on her face. This was clearly not a joking matter to her.

"Sorry," I said, retreating away from the table. "My bad." She turned back and bowed her head over the pan, examining the patterns in the water.

"I see a face," she said. "A man, strong, handsome." Sherwood nodded slightly. "But he seems troubled."

No indication of power or talent was in evidence. She was doing a cold reading, speaking in generalities, using logic, and taking cues from Sherwood's body language.

A "handsome man" was a fairly safe bet. Sherwood is a very attractive woman; slim, strong-featured but not harsh, with dark shoulder-length hair shot through with purple highlights. Sure, she might have hooked up with some poor schlub, but the odds were against it. Attractive people usually end up with other attractive people. Maybe that's not fair, but it's a fact of life.

And "troubled" was another good bet. If relationship problems had arisen, he surely would be troubled about that.

Still, no power was apparent as Cassandra gazed into the water. I don't think she was pulling a con; she probably thought she really saw things in those swirling patterns. Maybe she did, but they were all in her mind.

I edged back toward the table to get a better look. All I could see were swirls of ink, but Cassandra seemed to have no problem in discerning a pattern. I wondered what she would do if something truly recognizable were to appear in those twisting strands of ink. No sooner thought than done.

I don't have the artistic skill to create a portrait from scratch, so I just let out a little talent, ran the energy through my body, and let it flow into the pan of water. The curls of ink immediately started to form a picture of my own face, like a fine-lined pen-and-ink drawing. Sharp angular features formed, a shock of dark hair, and a dark, brooding expression on the face that was a caricature of my real self. The red ink pooled around my eyes, giving the face a demonic air. Sherwood saw what I was doing and glared at me.

Cassandra drew her breath in sharply as the face in the water became more detailed and lifelike. She looked up at me, then back at the water, then at me again. Then she spoke, but the words were not anything I expected.

"Who sent you?" she said. "Jessie?"

I was caught off guard and stammered incoherently for a moment. Cassandra pushed her chair back and stood up slowly. She fixed her gaze on me and advanced, all four foot eleven of her. It should have been funny, but there was nothing funny about her. I could feel the energy crackling around her. I'd made a bad mistake; she was a practitioner, all right. The second I'd let down my shielding and used some talent, she'd pegged me. That residue of talent I'd sensed floating around earlier wasn't the random emanation of a meager talent at all; they were wisps that had escaped her own shielding. I backed up instinctively as she approached me.

"Take it easy," I said. "We don't mean you any harm."

She laughed, barking it out like a curse. "Don't you, now? Well, that's good of you, a very fine thing."

Her lilting Jamaican accent grew more pronounced, at odds with the angry intent of her words. She broke off her advance and walked over to the door, fast but not panicky. When she reached it, she turned and faced the room, clasping her hands above her head. "Go free," she said, and unlocked her fingers, clearly implementing a spell. She stared at us, opened the door a fraction, and squeezed through. "Good luck."

The moment Cassandra passed through the doorway, Sherwood sprang up from her chair.

"Shouldn't we go after her?"

That question was answered by the unmistakable sound of the dead bolt being slotted into place. As if the sound had triggered it, a set of wards sprang up around the door, glowing with jagged lines of force. Not literally—wards are perceived on the psychic plane, and you don't exactly see them—that's just a metaphor. But the important thing was that Cassandra wasn't running from us at all. She didn't have to—she had neatly trapped us in her basement room.

Usually wards cover an entire house, or at least a room.

And sometimes you can locate weak points. But this room was cement, and underwater. There was no need to ward the entire area—just the door, the only way out. So they could be concentrated there, making them all the more difficult to defeat.

I was sure that between Sherwood and myself we could dismantle them, given enough time. But there was still the dead bolt. Getting out was going to pose quite a problem. Meanwhile, a more pressing issue presented itself.

The whirling stars on the ceiling had grown brighter and were moving faster, now with urgency. I didn't like the looks of them, and neither did Sherwood. She walked over to the laser projector, searched for the on/off switch for a moment, and finally just unplugged it. The light went out, but the moving points of light didn't. If anything, they blazed brighter, and now they occasionally detached themselves from the surface of the ceiling and whizzed around a few inches below it.

As we watched, the points of light dropped down even farther, now just brushing the tops of our heads. Lou liked this new development even less than we did. He quickly headed toward the table, intending to take cover underneath. Right before he reached it, one of the bright sparks flew out of its orbit and struck him squarely on his back leg. He yelped and dove under the table, finding relative safety for the moment.

A second later one of the light points swooped down and nicked my forearm. I almost yelped myself; it felt like the sting of an angry wasp. The room was now thick with the swirling points of light; they didn't appear conscious or malevolent, just random. But there were enough of them so that soon intent wouldn't be an issue. We were in serious trouble.

Sherwood grabbed my arm and pulled me toward the far corner of the room.

"We need to set up a barrier shield," she said.

I nodded and yelled over at Lou to join us. His hiding

place under the table wasn't going to be effective for long. Sherwood and I had worked together long enough to be an efficient team. Usually two practitioners using talent end up at cross purposes, but we'd found ways to divide up tasks without getting in each other's way. We used the two sides of the corner walls as a natural barrier and quickly set up an energy shield to cover the rest.

But this was only a temporary fix. Protective physical shields are an active use of talent, and take a lot of energy to maintain. A static shield, like a warding, is different. It's like putting up a barbed-wire fence; it takes some time and effort, but once it's up, it's done. You don't need to expend energy to keep it in place. You need to keep up maintenance, like if you had to replace a rusted wire or loose post, but otherwise it's just there.

Same goes for aversion spells, and passive spellwork like personal shielding of talent or creating illusions is even easier. You have to keep your concentration, but a trickle of energy will suffice to keep them going.

But an energy shield is like an electrified fence, and the power has to come from somewhere—usually from your personal store. The stronger you are, the longer you can hold it steady, but sooner or later you tire and run out of energy. Then the shield collapses. But we had a moment's respite, and Sherwood took out her cell phone.

"I think we could use a little help," she said, and started to punch in a number. Then she stopped and stared at the phone.

"Let me guess," I said. "No service." I waved at the flecks of light. "The energy animating those things is going to disrupt any electromagnetic signal."

"Of course. Otherwise it would have been easy. So what now?"

"Just the question I was asking myself."

"How much time do we have?" she asked. "How's your energy holding up?"

"Not bad. I'd guess we've got an hour, give or take."

My forearm was still smarting from where the speck of

light had grazed it. I examined it, expecting to find a welt like from a bee sting, but it was more like a burn. An angry red line, turning black around the edges, ran down the arm. I showed it to Sherwood, who whistled.

"Nasty," she said. "Those little points of light must be super hot, like little flecks of molten metal. What do you think—can we douse them?"

"I don't see how. Too many of them, and they move too fast, anyway."

The air was now thick with them. Another problem was the nature of the energy shield. It protected us, but it also protected the lights. In order to deal with them, we'd have to drop the shield, and we might not last long enough after that to do anything much.

"Fuck!" Sherwood yelled, and slapped at her neck. An angry welt appeared there as if by magic. Which of course was precisely what it was. "One got through."

Still another problem. The lights were too minuscule to be blocked completely. The shield was like those Kevlar vests police wear—they'll stop a large-caliber bullet with no problem, but narrow the point of focus and now it's trouble. A stiletto, wielded with sufficient force, will punch right through it because the point of the knife is small enough to squeeze through the fibers. And these little fiery points of light were small enough to squeeze through the shield.

And each time one broke through, it weakened the shield and made it just a bit easier for the next one. We didn't have an hour to figure things out; we had minutes.

A disturbance toward the back of the room caught my eye. The random pattern of swirling flecks coalesced into something less random there. All the points of light that entered that specific area suddenly glowed brighter and swooped off in the same direction for a short distance before dissolving into chaos again.

What was causing this? Of course. The fan, sitting on its table, blowing air. When the air moved, so did the flecks, and the extra breeze energized them like a bellows stoking up a fire, making them light up like fireflies on steroids.

I could use this. My strength lies in improvisation, taking cues from the environment around me, weaving in various aspects and using my talent to effect spells. But that sort of thing isn't instantaneous. It always takes a little time, and we'd have to drop the energy shield for me to put things in motion. And the second the energy shield came down, we'd be riddled with white hot holes.

"Sherwood," I said. "If we drop the shield, how long could you protect us?"

"Completely?"

"No, just enough so that I can do something about these things without getting fried."

She looked out at the swirling points of light. The room now looked like a miniature snowstorm.

"Maybe a minute if I can keep total concentration. Maybe less if I blink."

"Plenty of time. If it works."

"And if it doesn't?"

"People will remember us fondly, I'm sure."

"Hmm. Me, perhaps. And Lou, of course." She looked out into the room again. "You hold the shield in place for a minute. I'm going to need all of my energy for this."

I could feel talent moving as she gathered energy, even taking some from the shield itself, forcing me to pour even more of my own into it to keep it up and running. She flexed her arms, and energy was coursing down them into her hands. She took a deep breath and nodded.

"Ready," she said.

I dropped the shield, redirected my energy out into the room, and the flecks of white-hot light swarmed in. I was focusing on the task at hand, but from the corner of my eye I saw Sherwood whip out both hands and let loose concentrated pulses of energy. Every time a group of spots intersected with Sherwood's energy pulse, they flared brightly and winked out of existence. It was like a 3-D video game or a miniature fireworks display, inches from my head.

I heard Sherwood curse and Lou yelp, and a moment later I felt burning on the back of my neck. She wasn't intercepting them all. I ignored the pain and reached out with my talent. I gathered the essence of the electric fan in the corner and enhanced it, both the movement of air and its circular motion. Then I sucked energy out of one side of the room and poured it into the other, creating an imbalance. When I cast out the essence I'd gathered, it created a perfect little whirlwind. The floating points were swept up in the airflow, burning even brighter as the miniature tornado whirled them around.

I brought the whirlwind close to us, where it sucked up the random bits that Sherwood had been fending off. Then I pushed it toward the door, compressed it down, and focused it on a spot just above the doorknob. The heat from the now-concentrated light flecks was palpable even from ten feet away.

The spot on the door started to smolder, then char; then under the onslaught of concentrated heat, a section just dissolved away, leaving a gaping hole with flickers of flame licking around the edges. At the same time, I poured the rest of my energy into the sparks so that it now spilled over, the sparks being unable to contain the extra power. The wards around the door sensed this as a severe magical threat and attached their own energy to combat the threat.

"Push it through," I said to Sherwood. "I've got to concentrate on holding it all together."

She directed a rush of air toward the hole in the door and the energized points of light streamed through, taking the wards with them. Five seconds after, there wasn't a single speck of light left in the room, and the wards around the door were gone as well.

I reached through the hole in the door, felt around, and slid back the dead bolt. We moved cautiously out of the room and back up the stairs, watching for Cassandra, but she was nowhere to be seen. I wanted to look around the place, but Sherwood pulled me along.

"Let's get out of here," she said. "She might be back at any time, and we're both drained."

"Hold on a sec. I need to do something first."

I signaled Lou to keep watch at the front door, scanned the front room, and grabbed a couple of dog-eared paperback books and a half-eaten chocolate bar from a table. As soon as we got outside I picked up a smooth twig and put all the items together on the plank leading to the front door. I put out some more energy and diffused it through the objects there, then another, weaker pulse into the plank itself. I ran back in and put the books and the candy bar back where I'd found them. No point in alerting her.

The twig went into my pocket. I now had an efficient alarm system; the twig was keyed to both Cassandra and the wooden plank, and if she returned, it would glow the minute she set foot on it.

"Okay," I said. "Let's go." Lou took the lead, still keeping watch.

Before we even reached the car, the cell clipped to Sherwood's belt went off. She made a face as she put it up to her ear. Then she made another face, this one directed at me, with sudden interest and raised eyebrows.

"What?" I mouthed. She waved her hand at me for quiet.

"Yes," she said. "This is Sherwood." A pause. "Melissa? Yes, I'm looking for a keyboard player." Another pause. "Bass." A longer pause. "Mostly originals, a few standards. I'm pretty open to different styles, though."

"Set up a meet," I mouthed frantically. Sherwood waved me off impatiently and turned her back, but I waved my hands in her face until she said, "Hold on a moment, will you?" and put her hand over the phone.

"What?" she said.

"Try and set up a meet right away. The next time she talks to Cassandra, we'll be toast." She nodded, and went back to her conversation.

"Sure," I heard her say. "I'm out and about right now, but I could meet you somewhere and we could talk it over.

Where? How about Potrero Hill; that's up where I live. Do you know the Thinker's Café on Connecticut? . . . Good. About an hour, then." I tapped her on the shoulder and pointed to Lou, and she nodded. "You'll know me because I'll have my dog along—he goes everywhere with me. A little black-and-tan guy, like a mini Pinscher . . . Okay, see you then."

"So we're on?" I asked as she snapped her cell shut.

"Apparently. She sounds nice. I'm still feeling a little creepy about this. I don't like lying to people much, even if it's for a good cause."

"Yeah, I know."

"Why all this elaborate make-believe, anyway? Why don't you just grab her if that's what you're going to do?"

"I don't want to grab her. I want to find out where she lives and what she's been up to and maybe who she's hanging with. And if she stole something, and if not, why Jessica's really looking for her. Grabbing her, as you put it, isn't going to do a thing for me."

We walked the last little bit back to the van, Lou keeping an eye out for Cassandra, but she was making herself scarce. Just as well—right now I didn't want any trouble. The important thing was to get over to the café before Jackie did.

Only one of the outside tables was open when we got there, but that was fine. I parked the van a block away where I could see but not be too close. I didn't want to take any chance of spooking her. I grabbed Lou by his harness to get his attention. Once he got a good look at Jackie, he'd be able to use his talent to track her down like a bloodhound. Locating her again and finding out where she lived would be simple for him.

"Lou. Go with Sherwood. She's meeting someone, and pay attention to who it is. And you're a dog, remember? No tricks; you've got to be a dog or she'll know something's wrong. Got it?"

He yawned in my face, his way of saying, *Of course I've got it.* He can't completely understand sentences, though he's pretty good with words, but I've managed to get some complicated ideas across to him in the past. This time it was pretty straightforward.

I wasn't worried about Jackie tumbling to what he really was, even though she'd obviously know all about Ifrits. But magically speaking they're amazingly neutral, and most spells slide right off them. Even a practitioner sometimes can't tell an Ifrit for sure, especially if the Ifrit wants to stay unrecognized.

Sherwood's persona was more of a worry, but she was good at shielding. If Jackie suspected her and really probed, she'd be able to tell Sherwood was a practitioner, but why would she? There was no reason to do that. It takes some energy, and it's not practical to examine everyone you meet on the off chance they might be the odd practitioner, even if you're hiding out and super paranoid.

Sherwood walked down to the café, Lou dutifully trotting beside her like a faithful dog, and went inside. She reappeared a minute later with a cup of coffee and sat down at the open outdoor table. Lou hopped up onto the chair beside her and scanned the area carefully, looking for any leftover scraps of sandwich that might have fallen on the ground around the tables.

Twenty minutes later Jackie showed up, wearing a bright red sweatshirt. I recognized her instantly from her picture, though she was shorter than I had expected, no more than five-two or so. She paused in front of Sherwood before sitting down across from her. She reached over a hand for Lou to sniff. He did so, playing his part, and then sat up in his all-purpose begging position, the one guaranteed to melt the heart of dog lovers and even coax a smile out of dog cynics. She was clearly the former, and she made a big fuss over him, ruffling his ears and thumping him gently on his side.

I was too far away to hear what they were saying but it seemed to be going well. Sherwood laughed a couple of times, and so did Jackie. After a while Jackie looked at her wrist and stood up. Sherwood stood up as well, they hugged briefly, and Jackie walked away with a little goodbye wave. Sherwood stayed on her feet, looking after her. I could see she was now even less comfortable with her Mata Hari role.

I waited a couple of minutes before joining her, just in case Jackie made an unexpected return. When I finally walked over and sat down at the table, Sherwood gave me a sour look.

"Okay, I did my part. Now what?"

"What did you think of her?" I asked.

Ever since Sherwood had "returned" to us after a year's absence, her natural empathetic abilities have increased considerably. She could get a pretty good reading on people almost instantly. Practitioners were harder to read for her, and some people were naturally closed off to that particular ability, so she wasn't always right. But her take on people was not to be dismissed lightly.

"I like her," she said. "We talked about music, naturally, and she's serious about it. Sort of like you, actually. Made me wish I really could play instead of just faking it."

"Anything else?"

"She's passionate.

"Really?"

"Not like that, you idiot." She shook her head in resignation. "Men. No, passionate about life. Passionate about music. Passionate about things she believes in, the all-or-nothing type. You can see it burning in her. Maybe she could be a bit obsessive, but there's nothing at all nasty about her."

Interesting. Not that it meant that much, though. Thieves aren't necessarily bad people in other ways. And even a person who is honest, loyal, and trustworthy can be dangerous, if their values and worldviews are opposed to your own.

"Did she tell you where she lived?"

"No, but she gave me her cell number. And she did say she was temporarily living downtown somewhere. We're going to set up a session later, supposedly."

"Good enough. Lou will be able to find her. And we'll see where she lives, and maybe who she's hanging out with. After that . . . well, we'll see."

"Count me out," she said. "I don't want any more to do with this. I'm not sure helping to track her down for Jessie is such a good idea, anyway."

"You could well be right. But I won't know until I find out a little more about her."

AFTER I DROPPED SHERWOOD OFF BACK AT HER house, I continued on downtown. San Francisco is a small city, geographically speaking, but the downtown area covers quite a bit of space. However, when someone says they live downtown, that's more specific than it sounds. Usually they'll use a more exact description for wherever they live—I live in SOMA, I live in North Beach, or the Financial District. Only places that don't fit neatly into those specific areas become the amorphous "downtown," which doesn't cover that much territory. Maybe she lived in one of those elegant high-rises that dot the downtown area like the one Jo and Rolando had been staying in last year.

I parked on Mission Street and Tenth, right outside where "downtown" starts. Lou could direct me from the car, using body language and the occasional bark; he's done it before. But driving around at random and interpreting his barks at every intersection is not the most efficient method. Traveling on foot usually works better.

Lou hopped out and looked up at me expectantly.

"Time to do your stuff," I told him. "That woman? The one with Sherwood? I need to find her. Find, okay?"

He started off down Mission without a pause, which meant Jackie was fairly close. If she'd been farther away, he'd have cast around for a while until he got a whiff of her, or however he does it.

There weren't a lot of places to live close by, though. Maybe she was shopping at a store, or on her way somewhere. When we got to Sixth and Mission, Lou took a right, sliding through the street denizens clustered on the sidewalk.

Sixth and Mission is street person central, not as rough as the Tenderloin, but filled with citizens on the fringe: men pushing shopping carts that hold their life's possessions, drug addicts, alcoholics, desperate women who are thirty and look sixty. Scattered throughout are the rundown resident hotels where you can get a cheap room for a day or week or month.

Halfway down the block Lou stopped in front of one of those hotels. A surprisingly elegant sign proclaimed it to be the Hotel Carlyle but the dingy lobby with an iron grate across the door showed its true colors. Lou stopped in front of the door and looked over at me, ducking out of the way of a friendly drunk who had stopped and was clumsily trying to paw at him. I stood on the sidewalk, hesitant. This was odd. The Carlyle was one step up from a crack house, not the sort of place Jackie would choose. Even if she was trying to keep a low profile and hide out, it made little sense. With her fashion model looks, she'd stand out in a place like this like a delicate warbler amid a flock of city sparrows. People would notice, people would talk, and talk like that has a way of making its way up to unintended ears.

But she was in there. Lou's never wrong, not about stuff like this. Maybe she was visiting someone. I stood in front of the entrance for a few moments; then, as a resident came out of the hotel and opened the iron grate, I squeezed past him into the lobby.

The guy manning the lobby desk was reading a paperback book and didn't even look up. I followed Lou up a flight of stairs that angled off to the left and then down the hallway that ran the length of the building. The walls were covered with patterned wallpaper so old it was almost one dull color, plaster showing through in places where it was ripped. Sounds of rap music leaked through closed doors, harsh and tinny over the booming bass. I walked past one door that was propped open, and the two guys sitting inside the cramped room looked at me with a mixture of wary suspicion and passive indifference.

Lou ignored them and continued on until he reached the next-to-last door on the right. He sat down in front of it, then got up and sniffed at the door. He seemed oddly unsure of himself, but finally gave a little shake and sat back down. I came up close to the door and listened for the sound of voices. Silence.

After standing there for a while I knocked. No sounds from inside, and after a short pause I knocked again. Still nothing. I tried the doorknob, just in case, and it turned easily. A slight pressure and the door swung inward. This was all too easy, so I stood in the doorway a moment, scanning the room from outside. But only for a moment. In the middle of the floor, surrounded by clutter, lay a figure, dressed in a bright red sweatshirt. Even from the doorway I could see dark red blood pooled around the figure's head, lots of it.

I'd found Jackie, all right.

FIVE

MY FIRST INSTINCT WAS TO RUSH IN AND CHECK the body, to see if she was still alive, and that was what I would have done a few years ago. But I'd learned a lot from Victor since then, now that I'd finally stopped ignoring anything he had to say. Secure the room was now my first priority. When finding a body on the floor it's a good idea to make sure whoever put it there isn't hiding behind the kitchen counter waiting for you to bend over the body, back conveniently turned.

I took one step through the doorway and closed the door behind me. There wasn't much space to hide in the small room, but there was a closet. I glanced around the room and saw a walking stick leaning against the wall next to the door. I picked it up, then realized I might have just placed my fingerprints on a murder weapon. Oh, well.

I moved quietly across the room, jerked the closet door open, and jumped back, holding the stick at the ready. A few jackets and a dead TV were all that was in there. The bed was a twin with no room underneath for anyone to hide, but I pointed to it just the same.

"Lou," I said. "Check under the bed."

He wormed his way under and reappeared a moment later. All clear, at least for now. I put the stick down and bent over the body, reaching for the throat to find a pulse. Lou circled around me, looking at the body from different angles as if trying to figure something out. Finally he sidled over and sniffed at her. That was totally out of character for him; he doesn't like death at all—he's rather squeamish about such things. Usually he wanders over to the farthest corner and waits for me to be done. This time he simply walked over to the door and stood there impatiently.

No pulse at the throat, which was what I expected to find. Or rather, not find. The side of her head showed a depressed area matted with blood where someone had struck a blow, but other than that she could have been sleeping. Her face was untouched and she looked almost peaceful, as if she'd be waking up soon from a refreshing nap. There was a slight odor of perfume coming from her hair, mixed in disturbingly with the odor of fresh blood. Her skin was cool but not cold, so whatever had happened had been recent. Which made sense. I'd seen her laughing and talking with Sherwood a scant hour ago.

One thing was for sure: this was no random murder. Sure, the cops might think so when they showed up, but I could feel the magical residue of a powerful talent hanging in the air. This murder had been done by a practitioner—maybe even by a killing spell, with the knock on the head an afterthought to make it look mundane and believable to the cops. It wouldn't be the first time someone had been bludgeoned to death in this hotel, no doubt. There was something strange about the traces of talent, though; it was muddy and unfocused.

I stood up and took a quick look around the room, looking for anything that might provide a clue. A small bureau sat in the corner, but when I pulled out the drawers there was nothing in them that could have belonged to her. Only men's clothes, and if the shirts were any indication, a large man at that. So this wasn't her hidey hole at all—she had been visiting someone.

It was time to get out of there before someone came by and found me in a situation that would be difficult to explain. But first I needed to search the body, unpleasant as that would be. Again, a few years ago I would have been filled with dread and loathing, but I'd seen too much death since then. They say you can get used to almost anything, and although I wasn't exactly blasé about it, my emotional reactions had definitely been dampened.

As I grabbed the body to roll it over, Lou came over and gave one sharp bark. At first I thought he was warning me about someone coming, but when I paused he just stood there looking at me with a definite air of frustration.

"What?" I said, but of course he can't answer.

I bent back to my task and he slipped by me, standing right next to the body. Calmly he lifted one leg and peed on her, as if marking his territory. That got my attention. I stared at him, baffled, and he blandly stared back at me. Either he'd gone completely nuts or I was missing something and he was trying to tell me what it was.

Lou wouldn't randomly piss on a dead body, not for any reason. Unless he had gone insane. That wasn't an option, so the logical conclusion was that it wasn't a body at all. I'd been so focused on the dead Jackie lying crumpled on the floor that I hadn't paid proper attention to the reek of talent permeating the room. Somebody had performed a powerful spell. I'd assumed it was connected to her death, but maybe it wasn't. Maybe it had to do with making something seem to be what it wasn't.

I took a step back and viewed the scene critically. If this was an illusion, it was a top-rate job—visual, tactile; even the sense of smell was involved. It was possible to create such an illusion, though it was beyond my own abilities. But not beyond my ability to see through it, hopefully.

I concentrated my vision and drew power from the mundane room, very much in the here and now. I narrowed my attention, let out some talent, and focused on the figure lying there. The body flickered briefly like a strobe light before returning to solidity. I walked around in a circle and examined it carefully from every side. It wasn't quite perfect after all. The hair that lay across the red sweatshirt was sharp and detailed, but only on the side you were looking at. On the side of the head farthest away it blurred slightly, bleeding into the fabric. When I walked around to the other side the same thing happened. So it was definitely an illusion, but damn impressive nonetheless.

Usually I can cut through illusions easily, but this one was special. It would take a hell of a practitioner to pull it off. I reached out to examine the odd magical residue again and realized why it was confused. It wasn't just traces from one practitioner; it was the remnants of two practitioners working together. That was why it had seemed so muddy.

Two practitioners working together would explain the illusion's quality, but two practitioners can't work well together unless they're personally close and have had a lot of practice time. So it had to be someone powerful, and also someone Jackie knew well.

It wasn't Cassandra, though. The remains of talent are recognizable; if you know the person's talent signature, you can always recognize it, and Cassandra's spell at her houseboat had given me a taste of hers.

And like voices, some signatures are more recognizable than others. If you've ever heard Jack Nicholson or James Earl Jones, you instantly recognize their voices when you hear them again. And the talent signature of both practitioners involved, though similar, were distinctive.

There was another issue. What was going to happen when the owner of the room came back? And then called the cops? Could the illusion stand up to an autopsy, when the pathologist sliced it open with a scalpel? Highly unlikely. Eventually it would fade anyway; no illusion is permanent, no matter how strong. And then there would be hell to pay.

The one thing every practitioner is aware of is the need to keep our abilities quiet, to not expose the practitioner community to widespread scrutiny, and something like this would surely cause some ripples. Then again, Jessie had hinted that she thought it was time for a change; maybe she was involved in some way I didn't understand. I didn't have enough information to come up with a plausible explanation, so I filed it away for the time being.

One strong possibility was that the illusion was specific to me, and only me. Jackie might have set it up to throw me off her trail. But if she had set it up that way, how had she done it? To implement that sort of a personally specific spell, you need to use something physical as a trigger, something from the person you've targeted. Or some object you've planted on them. But she'd never met me, never even been in close proximity to me. I ran over everything she'd done at the café with Sherwood. Had Jackie even glanced my way? Had she handed something to Sherwood? Had I inadvertently taken anything from Sherwood?

Then it clicked. There was one connection between her and me—Lou. She'd fussed over him, running her hands all over him. A spell wouldn't stick to his Ifrit persona, but . . .

I called him over, loosened the Velcro on the harness, and ran my hands along its length. I found it right between his shoulder blades, a small slip of folded paper, sticky on one side like a Post-it.

I unfolded it, and there was a neat drawing of the famous optical illusion where you can't decide if it's a vase or the profiles of two faces. The note felt magically inert, but when I tore it in two a huge burst of energy rushed out, amazing for such a small piece of paper.

Immediately the body on the floor shimmered, and then, like the vase picture that looks like the one thing and suddenly flips into the other, I was looking at a pile of jumbled clothes. A can of Pepsi had been overturned by one end and the liquid had poured out across the floor, dark and sticky. Right by the can, nestled ludicrously in the clothes, was a dented cantaloupe—the supposed head. It was ludicrous and creepy at the same time.

So the only ones affected would have been me and Lou. The average Ifrit might have been fooled, even though they're resistant to such magical tricks, but Lou's not your average guy. He'd seemed confused before entering the room, as if Jackie were there but not there. And he'd circled the supposed body, trying to figure out exactly what was wrong with the scene, like a bloodhound who temporarily loses the scent when the hunted backtracks and grabs an overhanging limb. But it hadn't taken him long to see through it, even with the spell paper tucked securely under his harness. That was when he sat by the door, ready to pick up the scent again, or whatever it is he does when he tracks someone.

He must have wondered what I thought I was doing investigating the room and its contents, blithely unaware of the true state of affairs. Finally he figured out that I wasn't as smart as he was and helped me see the light.

"Let's book," I said, but it was too late.

The door swung open and a man stood in the doorway. I couldn't be sure of his race, but he looked like a Pacific Islander, Samoan or maybe Tongan. I'd guessed he'd be large from the size of the shirts in the bureau, but I'd had no idea. He wasn't much taller than I was, but his shoulders brushed both sides of the doorway. He had to weigh three hundred pounds if he weighed an ounce, and he wasn't fat, just thick and solid. He looked momentarily surprised to find me there, and then asked the logical question.

"Who the fuck are you?" he said, squeezing through the doorway and taking a large step forward. "And what are you doing in my room?"

These were both rhetorical questions, mostly a ritual of speech to be uttered before pounding me into unconsciousness. Lou threw himself onto the floor in front of him and rolled over, paws waving in the air in the typical submissive dog pose, and looked up pleadingly with liquid eyes. It worked, at least temporarily. The man hesitated, momentarily taken aback. Before he regained his momentum, I jumped in.

"I'm looking for Willie," I said, letting a whine creep into my voice. "I thought this was his room. He owes me some . . . stuff. I even fronted him the cash."

I sniffed a couple of times and lay down a quick illusion. Maybe I couldn't create a totally realistic dead body, but I could at least make it look as if my nose was running uncontrollably.

"Fuckin' junkie," the man muttered. "There ain't no 'Willie' here, Jack."

"Maybe you could help me out?" I said, not giving him time to think. "It's not for me, man; it's my girlfriend. She's really hurting."

He stood away from the door and gestured with a large hand. "Get the fuck out of my room."

I ducked my head as if I thought he was going to hit me and edged toward the door. Lou had already scrambled to his feet and was waiting outside in the hallway. Just as I passed the guy he reached out and grabbed me by the shoulder, almost crushing it. For a second I thought he'd changed his mind about the pounding idea, but he just said, "Hold on. Turn out your pockets."

I meekly followed his instructions. As soon as he was satisfied I hadn't snagged anything of his, he let go.

"Now get out," he said, pushing me into the hallway hard enough so I bounced off the opposite wall. I'd got off easy; apparently he was the mellow sort. I hurried out of there before he noticed the mess on the floor and came after me to clean it up.

Once back out on the street, Lou hesitated, then started down the sidewalk again past the hotel. I called him back.

"I don't think so," I said. "Let's just go home."

Despite the deflection, Lou could still track Jackie down. But I wasn't sure I wanted to find her right now, not just yet. I needed to know more about what was going on first.

She wasn't just randomly hiding out in San Francisco—she had to be dialed in to the practitioner community to some degree. She'd known all about me, all about Lou, and had known that we were looking for her. Or maybe Cassandra had gotten to her first and warned her. Either way, she'd seen through my ploy about forming a jazz group with no trouble at all. Sherwood needn't have worried about conning a poor innocent—we were the ones who'd been conned.

It was a clever ruse. She couldn't hide from me forever, so she'd taken preemptive action. If I thought she was dead, I wouldn't be looking for her any longer, would I? No one would. She'd be free to go about her business. But thanks to Lou I knew she wasn't dead—but she didn't know that I knew. I now had the upper hand, except I still didn't understand what the game was.

SIX

"WHAT THE HELL IS GOING ON HERE?" I ASKED. "Is this eco stuff for real, or just a smoke screen? If a smoke screen, for what? It's not making sense."

I'd hightailed it back to Victor's house and laid out the whole scene for him and Eli. Victor leaned forward and put his elbows on the polished wood of his giant desk. The desk would have been overwhelming in most rooms, but in Victor's faux Victorian study it seemed natural.

"On the contrary," said Eli. "I'm sure it makes perfect sense, only we're not in possession of enough information. But I'd guess now that there's more going on here than just a simple theft."

He was ensconced in one of the big padded armchairs with Maggie on his lap. Lou was curled up on a nearby throw rug. Maggie didn't like me much, and she despised Lou, who returned the sentiment wholeheartedly. They were the only Ifrits I knew who genuinely didn't like each other, despite the recent détente. Maybe that animus had something to do with the difficult relationship between Victor and me. But she liked Eli. He stroked her abstractedly with huge hands.

"Maybe it's time to press Jessie about what was supposedly stolen, and why it's so important," I said.

Eli considered it briefly, then shook his head. "No, I don't think so, not yet. Without more information, you'll have no way of knowing if what she tells you is true or not. And remember, your main focus is to find out what Jessie's up to, not what Jackie is doing."

"Disagree," Victor said. "They're related; they have to be." So it was one to one. Big help.

The sound of the front door opening told me Timothy was home. The fact that he and Victor were still together still amazed me. Not only that, they were living together. And ever since Timothy had quit his IT job and was freelancing, he was at the house most of the time, as was Victor. I thought that would surely spell the end of the relationship—it would with me—but so far it seemed to be working out. Relationships for Victor rarely reached the live-together stage, and the only other time I could remember anyone else living there it hadn't ended well. Which was partly my fault; I'd arrived at Victor's with a horrible creature hot on my trail and, after seeing that, the guy moved out the next day.

He hadn't been a practitioner, of course, and neither was Timothy. But unlike most nonpractitioners, Timothy managed to take everything in stride. I think he rather enjoyed it, to be honest—except for the dangerous parts. When he came up the stairs to the study Lou got up to greet him, looking for his usual treat.

"Sorry, Lou," he said, showing empty hands. "I didn't know you'd be here."

Lou returned to his rug good-naturedly. He wasn't that hungry anyway.

"What's up?" Timothy asked, sprawling out on the couch by the front windows.

I laughed. "That's the question of the day."

"Tell you later," Victor said. "It's a long story."

"And speaking of long stories," I said, "did Sherwood tell you about Cassandra?"

"She did."

"Any thoughts?"

"Not yet. I did some research, and found out who owns the place, but that was no help. He's out of the country, and apparently rented it out to a friend, who sublet it to the woman. Who she is, I haven't a clue, and I doubt she'll be returning to the houseboat anytime soon for us to find out."

"She might come back to pick up personal stuff, though," Eli said.

"I set up an alert system," I said. "I'll know if she does." Victor nodded approvingly.

Eli hauled himself up out of his chair, carefully lifting Maggie off his lap, and stretched. "But we still have no idea who she thought you were or why she attacked you, or why she thought Jessie might have sent you. Until we know that . . ."

"Well, just as long as we're making progress," I said. I hunched my shoulders in resignation and headed toward the door. "I'll call if anything new comes up."

"What are you going to do?" asked Eli.

"I'm not sure. See Jessie, for one. Maybe it's not a good idea to tell her anything, but if I stir her up a bit, maybe something will shake loose. If it does, Lou can track down Jackie again—only this time I'll be better prepared. After today she's bound to think we've been thrown off the trail, so her guard will be down."

"And then what?"

"Play it by ear, I guess."

Eli looked unconvinced, but he didn't say anything. After all, he didn't have any ideas, either. I left Victor's rather disappointed. I hadn't expected any brilliant deductions but I'd hoped for at least something.

When I got home, there was a message on the machine. When I hit play I heard Jessie's voice.

"Mason. Any luck so far? Call me."

So she wanted to know how the search was going. Or wanted to keep an eye on me. I had nothing to tell her but I couldn't just ignore her call, not if I wanted to keep working for her.

If I could get hold of Cassandra, it would help. I put the twig from her walkway, the one that was now an alarm system, on the kitchen table and stared at it hopefully. It remained stubbornly twiglike without a sign of magical activity. My mind remained as obstinately blank without a wisp of an idea.

When you're stuck it's always better to do something than nothing, though. Jessie wanted to know what was up. But instead of calling her back, I'd show up at her offices downtown and see if stirring would produce anything.

I headed over toward the Twenty-fourth Mission BART station, Lou trotting a few steps ahead of me. It was another beautiful day, and Valencia Street was as crowded as if it were the weekend. We hadn't gone more than a couple of blocks when Lou stopped, almost tripping me. He stared fixedly down the street, then back at me.

"What's up?" I asked.

He took several steps forward, stopped again, and looked back over his shoulder. So he was either telling me there was someone he wanted to follow or asking me if I wanted him to follow someone. There was only one logical person.

"Jackie?"

A short bark. Jackie it was. I scanned the street on both sides, but didn't see her. That didn't mean she wasn't around, though. She could be shielding, making herself look like just about anyone, and if she was a block away, there wasn't any way I'd be able to tell. After the illusion of the dead body, I wasn't sure I could tell even if she bumped into me. But Lou could.

A bit of a coincidence, though. San Francisco's not that big a city, but it's big enough so that you don't usually run into someone you've been looking for by accident. So either she was keeping an eye on me, wondering if the ploy had worked, or she knew Lou would notice her and was leading me on for her own unfriendly purposes. Either way, I was game.

I nodded at Lou and he started up again, moving purposefully, but slowly enough so I didn't have to hurry to keep up. We passed Clarion Alley, well remembered from a couple of years ago, but Lou trotted past without a look.

We wove through the usual Valencia crowd without incident: twentysomethings with odd hairstyles headed for their favorite cafés, homeless people sleeping on the sidewalk, Hispanic families shopping at discount stores. Then, right before we reached Sixteenth Street, something odd.

A large branch lay across the sidewalk, blown down from God knows where. There weren't any nearby trees large enough to account for its presence. Lou paused, then hurdled it gracefully at the same time I stepped across. I immediately felt a sticky sensation, as if I'd pushed through some gelatinous barrier. It wasn't exactly magical, but it wasn't normal, either. I stopped and looked around, understandably wary. Lou went into a sneezing fit, which he does whenever there's an overload of magical energy. If Jackie had been setting a trap, I was pretty sure we'd just sprung it.

But there didn't seem to be anything wrong. People were still walking down the street, chatting. A homeless man was sleeping on the sidewalk, half blocking it. The breeze was warm in my face, laced with the odor of diesel fumes and gasoline.

I stopped at a café and picked up a latte to go. It was terrible, weak yet bitter, like something that might be labeled "coffee-style beverage." I drank only a few sips before tossing it in a trash can. You assume that anyone can make a decent cup of coffee, especially in San Francisco, but I guess not. That's one reason we all have our favorite places.

I continued on and fell behind two young men, one tall and blond, the other shorter and Hispanic-looking. We were all walking at the same pace, and I couldn't help but overhear their conversation. I was close enough to catch the words, and it was standard Mission District conversational fare.

"He said he'd call, but he hasn't yet," said the tall one.

"Typical. What did you expect?"

"I don't know. I thought we made a connection. But now he's playing it all cool and disinterested."

"Or maybe he's just not that into you."

Lou meanwhile was cutting back and forth across the sidewalk, casting around as if for a scent. At first I thought he was confused, but I've learned to read his body language pretty well, almost as well as he reads mine. He wasn't confused. He was annoyed, but I didn't understand why.

I refocused on the two guys ahead of us just in time to catch the second one saying, "Or maybe he's just not that into you." Either his vocabulary or his thought processes were rather limited. That was what I thought until after some idle chatter, the blond guy said, "He said he'd call, but he hasn't yet." And the response came back, "Typical. What did you expect?"

This was bad. It wasn't a real conversation at all. They were on a conversational loop, providing mere background noise like extras in a film.

I stopped and sat down to think on the stoop of a deserted store with dust-caked boards nailed over the window. The parade of Mission types trooped on by, and the more I watched, the more I realized that was exactly what they were. Types, not individuals. Stereotypes, like a bad Hollywood film.

In fact, now that I paid attention, the street had the air of a movie set. The entire scene had the feel of a staged reenactment, complete with actors. Not bad actors, but actors nonetheless. Nothing rang quite true. When I looked up at the street sign on the corner and saw the word "Valençia" was now spelled with a cedilla, I was only mildly surprised. Not only was the sign different, but modern Spanish doesn't even use that mark anymore.

I wasn't in the Mission anymore. I was in a singularity—one of those odd constructs that mirror the real world, but aren't entirely real themselves. I was no stranger to such things—the last time I'd been in one, there were no people around, but no two are quite alike. I'd managed to escape with the assistance of Lou—and some helpful wolves, my totem animal. The wolves had since abandoned me; why, I don't know. And the magical talisman that helped call them had also become inert. A shame—I could have used their help from time to time.

I'd also been to several places that weren't constructs at all—more like alternate dimensions. I'd found some on my own, and some I'd been thrust into. Some of them were as real and complex as our own world; others were a weird amalgam of real and not real. The entire cosmology of such things was far beyond me.

Jackie had set me up for this. She must have seen that her death illusion hadn't thrown me off the trail after all. She had some real talent, and a surprising facility with constructs—not a common skill. I don't understand them very well myself, though Eli does. He knows a lot about many things. At least she was just trying to get me out of the way, not do away with me altogether, although stranding me somewhere like this might add up to the same thing.

The only thing I knew for sure about constructs was that Lou is a master at slipping in and out of such places. Left to my own devices, I might never find my way home, but he could, and I could follow.

"Home?" I said. "Can you get us home?"

Lou darted over into a nearby mini park, did a circle around the perimeter, and came back up to me, tail wagging. He looked at me and yawned, his saying, *Of course*, again. He never lacks for confidence, although I could have reminded him about several previous incidents where that confidence turned out to be misplaced.

He jumped to his feet and started down the street, with me a few steps behind. The physical aspects of the singularity were almost perfect—the buildings, the uneven paving of Valencia Street, the trash swirling in little eddies at the corners. Where it broke down was in the depiction of people. Which made sense—after all, people are more complex than streets and buildings.

As we walked along the sidewalk, passersby moved quickly around us, eyes flicking incuriously over us. It made me wonder; just as they weren't exactly real to me, perhaps we weren't entirely real to them.

I stopped and motioned Lou over to the middle of the sidewalk.

"Do your sit pretty," I told him, that cute begging position that always melts hearts and elicits aws. He looked at me with something close to contempt. What—I thought he was a dog, eager to do stupid tricks on demand?

"No, I'm serious. It's an experiment."

He sighed and sat up, holding his front paws in the air. If it's possible to beg grudgingly, that was what he was doing. I got out of the way and leaned up against the side of a nearby building so that he would seem to be on his own.

Two men passed by without a second glance. Then, two young women, walking side by side, split when they reached him and passed him on either side. Not a flicker of interest. That settled it. On a normal day, they'd have been cooing over him, ready to adopt him off the street.

It wasn't like they couldn't see him; they'd walked around Lou to avoid stepping right on him. But he didn't quite register with them, as if he were something totally outside their experience. But could they even interact? What would happen if I actively confronted one of these individuals?

A young man about my own size and build, six feet or so, approached. I stepped out from where I'd been lounging and stood directly in his path. Without pausing, he veered off to one side, but I stepped over and blocked his path again. He stopped, confused, as if it were something completely outside his realm of experience. He tried to pass on the other side of me, but I blocked him again, and just for good measure grabbed him by the arm.

He stopped, looking confused. Or maybe not confused, exactly, but disturbed, like a bird trying to process an unfamiliar situation. He tried to continue on, but I wouldn't let go of his arm.

Finally he stopped trying to move and looked at me, really looked for the first time. The expression on his face didn't change, but he unexpectedly opened his mouth wide, letting out with a harsh, quavering ululation, like a mullah at daybreak calling the faithful to prayer.

I let go of his arm and stepped back. The moment he gave the call, every person on Valencia, for as far as I could see, stopped moving. A second later, in perfect unison, a hundred heads swiveled toward me, and the same harsh noise erupted from a hundred throats. Grabbing this guy might have been a slight mistake.

Lou didn't wait around to see what I would do next. He flattened his ears and took off down the street at a good clip. Ever the faithful companion. He's always there in a pinch, but sometimes when I do something particularly stupid, he pretends to leave me on my own just to teach me a lesson. I had the feeling that one of these days he wasn't going to be pretending.

I followed him, walking at a good clip myself, resisting the impulse to break into a trot. I glanced back over my shoulder to see what was happening with the people behind me and promptly ran into a woman in front of me. This time there was no hesitation; she made the same noise, only an octave higher. As soon as she did, people began converging on us. Even those from across the street had no problem getting there, since all traffic had also come to a halt.

Now was the time to utilize my store of magical talent, improvising to fit the situation. Only, we were in a singularity. In some of them, talent didn't operate at all. In others it was intensified, and in still others it manifested in unexpected ways. That's why if you ever find yourself in an unfamiliar situation, the first thing you need to do is test a basic spell, like igniting a piece of paper or casting a simple illusion. Otherwise you can end up making problems worse, not better. But I'd been so interested in what was going on around me I'd neglected to do that.

I picked up the pace and dodged by a couple of grasping hands. Lou saw I was in trouble and doubled back, throwing me a glance that said I would pay for my idiocy later on if he had his way. As two more of the crowd closed in on me, he darted in and sank his teeth into the calf of the closest one. That certainly earned Lou some attention. The bitee jumped and spun around, kicking out and reaching down to grab at him at the same time. Lou skittered out of the way and headed for temporary safety under a parked car.

I faded back and leaned against another storefront wall, trying to make myself invisible. Not literally; that would be too difficult even if my talent here turned out to be at full strength and under control.

True invisibility involves a tremendous expenditure of energy, even for the most powerful of practitioners. Plus, intense concentration. It's like playing a complicated guitar solo as fast as you can—it can be done, but you can't do anything else at the same time and you can't keep it up for long. And of course one wrong note and you wink right back into visibility.

The usual way is a variation of an aversion spell. You make it so people are disinclined to look at you; their eyes just flick right by without their brain noticing. Considering the odd makeup of these particular denizens, that might work well. But it works best in a passive situation, like blending into a crowd. If you're standing alone in the middle of a football field and someone is looking for you, sooner or later they're going to notice you, no matter how good the spell.

The third way is the easiest, and that's nothing more than laying an illusion over yourself. People can still see you, but they don't realize it's you they're looking at.

I let out some talent and let it wash over me, concentrating on several of the people milling around the car Lou had ducked under. I took a little of one, a little of another, until I resembled a generic person, not myself and not any of them. I couldn't see myself, of course, so I didn't know how good the illusion was, but I did feel the surge of magical energy that told me my talent was still working. I also felt a twinge of fatigue, which meant that my power was severely limited here. I was going to have to do less with more.

Meanwhile, Lou was still hunkered down under the car. Two women had positioned themselves at the back end of the car while a man crouched down at the other end. Three more guarded the street side. The sidewalk effectively blocked the other direction so that Lou had no way out except through the gauntlet.

The guy at the front had crouched down and was cautiously extending his arm under the car, trying to snag Lou by his harness. He whipped it back just in time to avoid losing a finger. So far Lou was holding his own, but he couldn't get out and sooner or later someone was going to come up with the idea of long sticks or something similar.

Just in front of the car, right past the engine compartment, an old oil stain discolored the street. I sucked out its essence and cast it onto Lou—an old trick I'd used before, but still reliable. Lou is supple and adroit, not easy to catch at the best of times, and now he had the added advantage of being slippery as a seal. That should do it.

"Lou!" I yelled. "Over here."

Heads turned in unison again, but they couldn't tell where the voice had come from. The second they turned their heads, he shot out of there like a greased pig at a fair. The guy in front made a quick grab, but Lou slipped through his fingers.

As he ran by where I was standing, I muttered, "Two cars down. Cover, and don't move."

One great thing about Lou is that in a crisis, he assumes I know what I'm doing even if he doesn't understand it. Of course, a lot of the time I really don't, but at least we don't end up working at cross purposes. He continued on with the crowd in pursuit, ducked under the proper car, and crouched down without moving. I used the trash in the gutter and sent out another wave of illusion. In seconds, he took on the aspect of a pile of old and dirty rags, with a torn milk carton in the middle for good measure. The first of the crowd to reach the car threw himself down, looked under the car, then scrambled to his feet. A second later, he dropped again, making sure. As far as he could tell, Lou had vanished, sneaking out of the opposite side, perhaps. The rest of the crowd fanned out, checking under nearby cars and in doorways along the street. I joined in, poking aimlessly around, never getting too close to anyone.

After a while, the crowd lost focus; some of them kept searching randomly, but others picked up their looped dialogue and went on their way. In five minutes, the street was the same as it had been before I'd foolishly grabbed that arm. I circled around and continued strolling down Valencia past the car, signaling for Lou to follow. He wormed his way from car to car, hugging the street like a feral cat. At the intersection of Fifteenth, he emerged, no longer looking like a pile of rags, and we continued on our way.

No one gave us a second look. Either they'd forgotten already, or it no longer mattered to them. After we left the Valencia corridor, fewer people walked the streets, and most of them were far off, blurred by distance. That seemed typical; Valencia was a carefully constructed imitation, but the farther away we got, the less realistic it was. Constructs by their nature are limited; there was no way an entire major city, complete with masses of people, could be maintained.

We passed under the 101 freeway overpass and down Harrison. Usually Lou doubles back and twists and turns whenever he's trying to find his way out of an unknown dimension or construct, but this time he kept up a steady trot, hardly looking right or left. Farther down on Harrison was the construction site where the energy pool sat—in the real world, at least. Eli and Victor had managed to tamp it down, which was a good thing, since more than one unpleasant creature had come through it in the past. One of its functions seemed to be to provide a path transport between dimensions, so it was a good bet that was where Lou was headed.

The construction site is also home base for Rolf, where he spends much of his time at night, he and a few others like him, doing a credible imitation of a group of homeless minding their own business. Rolf used to be a practitioner, but over the years he'd changed. He was something else now, mostly still human, but not entirely. I wondered if he, or someone like him, would be here. There was a lot I didn't know about Rolf, and not much would surprise me.

A half hour later we were standing in front of the wire fence and gate that blocked access to the site. I hadn't seen a soul on the streets for the last couple of blocks. The site was deserted and the fence around it had its usual strands of barbed wire on top. The gate was secured with a heavy padlock, but when I looked more closely at it I saw it wasn't a lock at all, just a solid chunk of lock-shaped metal. Out here on the edge of the singularity, things were degrading.

There was no way of getting the gate open, but the strands of barbed wire weren't any truer to life. The barbs weren't true barbs at all—no jagged edges, no snagging points, and the wire itself was thin and easily broken. I climbed over with far less trouble than I had in the past, when I'd had to negotiate the real thing. Lou ran along the fence until he found a sloppy place where the fence bottom didn't fully meet the ground, and squeezed under.

I kept an eye out for Rolf, but the place was deserted. The energy pool, however, was there and going strong. It's usually almost undetectable in daylight, even to me, but this one was all too present. It swirled and leapt like a miniature whirlpool, flinging out tendrils of multicolored energy like spumes of spray off ocean rocks.

I edged up cautiously, keeping well back. We'd got the original pool contained, if not closed down, but this doppelgänger was fired up and pulsing with uncontrolled energy. I kept a close eye on Lou; he'd had a tendency before to become almost hypnotized by the pool, and wandering too close could have consequences.

He obviously thought this was the way out of here, and it made sense. But how to go about it wasn't clear. We'd both been through the pool before, and it wasn't anything I was eager to try again. Where we'd end up was anyone's guess.

"Okay," I said. "We're here. Now what?"

Lou ignored me. He sat down and stared at the energy pool again, but now without that blank, hypnotized expression he'd had before. This time he wasn't so much staring at it as he was studying it. His eyes flicked from side to side, and occasionally he would turn his head and focus on one area or another. I had no idea what he was looking for.

A half hour later, just as I was about to pull him away and tell him to get on with it, he finally seemed satisfied. He stood up, stretched, and glanced over at me. He gave a short bark, ran a few steps at an angle to the pool. Then he doubled back behind me, nipped at my left heel, and sat down in his original spot again. I got it.

"The next time you jump up, you want me to take off after you, right?"

He looked at me, puzzled. I tried again.

"Follow? You want me to follow?"

A short bark. Okay, we were on the same page.

He focused on the pool again and I watched him closely. A couple of times I saw his muscles twitch, and once, he leaned forward as if he were about to lunge, but they were false alarms. I tried looking at the pool at the same time, to see if I could get a sense of what was going on, but it was just a swirl of colors with no discernable pattern, at least to me.

When he sprang to his feet he almost caught me by surprise, but a quick warning bark alerted me. Then he was off, and I tore after him, almost stepping on his rear paws. We ran about fifteen feet, toward a jumble of broken concrete chunks. He vaulted over the pile and I followed him, hoping I wouldn't twist an ankle when I landed. As soon as we were across, he doubled back and vaulted it again, then headed straight for the pool. I thought he was going to plunge right into it, but at the last moment he turned aside and vanished behind a pile of old rebar and metal duct pipes.

I stayed right behind him, and as I turned the corner I felt a familiar tearing sensation, the same as the last time I'd actually plunged through the pool. At the same moment, everything went dark. I thought for a moment something was wrong with my vision, but a half-moon in the sky made me realize it was now night. So we were back home—time dislocation was a common by-product of moving in and out of singularities.

My sense of relief lasted only a second. A noise behind me made me flinch, and before I could react someone bolted past me and out toward the gate. I started to go after him, but something else was close behind, moving past me like a breath of cold wind. Lou jumped two feet back, then moved up closer to me. I got a vague look at a shadowy something evaporating into the darkness.

The sight of yet another figure moving slowly toward us was not reassuring. It was more solid, large and menacing, scarcely human, gnarled and twisted and powerful. But I recognized it.

"Rolf?"

The figure seemed to diminish in size, subtly shifting and looking suddenly more human. Rolf came out of the shadows and looked at me in disgust.

I didn't know if I was glad to see Rolf or not. He'd been a lot of help to me in the past and although I certainly didn't consider him an enemy, I wouldn't exactly call him a friend, either. An interesting acquaintance, perhaps.

He looked the same as always—except for those times when he didn't. A rough face, wild hair, a stained army jacket, and a long beard plaited into dreadlocks. When people passed him on the street, they swung a little wider as they walked by without even realizing they'd done so. He wasn't a threatening figure, not exactly, but he made people wary, like antelopes passing by a well-fed lion. No real danger, but you just never know.

"Rolf," I greeted him.

"Mason." He looked down gravely. "Lou." Rolf took matters of formality very seriously, and to him, Lou was as worthy of recognition as I was. More so, probably. "You been playing with the pool?" he asked.

"Not by choice."

He looked carefully at me. "Been somewhere?"

"Just took a short vacation. What day is it?" Rolf looked baffled. Keeping track of time wasn't one of his strong points. "Never mind," I said. He peered at me in the darkness.

"What do you think you're doing?" he said. "Don't sneak up on me like that. There could be an accident. And what the hell was that?" He gestured out toward the darkness. "Friend of yours?"

"No," I said. "I don't think so."

Rolf came up closer and smiled, showing his disquieting collection of strong teeth. "Anyway, it's good you dropped by. I got some information for you if you're interested."

"Always interested."

"Got anything to trade?"

Another little quirk of his. Rolf was willing to provide information, but not from the goodness of his heart. Although sometimes it really was—but he refused to admit it. So he always demanded something in return.

"Not offhand," I said. "Anything you particularly want?"

"Can't think of anything. Shame, really."

He hesitated. I could see he wanted to tell me, which meant whatever it was probably impacted him as well as me, but he still couldn't get past his barter obsession. And I couldn't offer him money, even if I had any to spare. That would have been a deadly insult.

"Come on," he said. "You've got to have something."

"Tell you what. Anything that helps me, I'll return it in kind. You tell me what you know, and anything I find out that might affect you, I'll make sure you know about it, too." Rolf looked doubtful. "It wouldn't be the first time," I reminded him. "We've helped each other out before. A trade doesn't need to be all at once to be a valid bargain." That argument was weak and probably wouldn't have swayed him if he hadn't wanted to tell me anyway. But he did.

"True," he said, pulling at his dreadlocked beard. "Okay, it's not that big a thing anyway. A while back I was sleeping in my spot, right over there." He pointed back in the darkness. "Then something woke me up, a surge of energy like I haven't felt for a while."

"From a person?"

"No, not exactly. It was coming from the energy pool. You guys had tamped it down pretty effectively, but this felt like it was coming to life again. I could sense it from all the way across the area. So I got up and quietly drifted over to where I could see."

The thought of Rolf drifting quietly made me smile—he was large, bulky, and rock solid. But he could be hard to notice if he didn't want to be seen.

"And?"

Rolf stared at me, his aspect subtly changing with a hint of his other, troll-like persona. He didn't like to be interrupted, and my smile wasn't helping.

"You want to hear about this or not?"

"Sorry," I said. He waited a few moments until I'd been properly chastened.

"The pool was roiling around, almost like it had been

before. And walking around it was a young woman, attractive, but I could tell she was a black practitioner, and a strong one at that. None of your evil wannabes."

Jackie. If she'd been playing with singularities, it stood to reason she'd be interested in a gateway like the pool as well.

"Was she causing it?" I asked.

Rolf paused, considering whether this was a legitimate question or just another interruption.

"I'm not sure. She was walking around it, and every so often spoke a few words and made a few gestures. Each time she did, the pool jumped a little. But I don't know if she was trying to build it up or shut it down, or just experimenting."

Experimenting, I'd guess. But that wasn't the only question. Normal people can't perceive the pool at all, which wasn't surprising, but practitioners couldn't either, for the most part. Jackie must possess some real power, as if the illusion she'd set up hadn't already told me that.

"Did you follow her?" Rolf pulled on his beard.

"Saw no reason to. I could find her again if I needed to. Once I get a look at a practitioner, I can catch their vibes anytime I'm near. The stronger the practitioner, the easier they are to sense." He showed his teeth in what might have been a grin. "Kind of like Lou here, but nowhere near as accurate. But since you guys have been so interested in the pool, I thought you might be interested that a black practitioner was sniffing around it."

"Yeah," I said. "It's something to think about."

"Thought so. And that woman, the practitioner? Quite a looker."

"I know. And she never noticed you?"

"Nope. Or if she did, she thought I was just some homeless guy. Kind of like you did the first time we met, remember?"

"Yeah," I said.

"But I'd be careful if I was you. You might be able to

deal with her, but I'm not so sure about her Ifrit. Damnedest thing I ever saw."

"What Ifrit?"

"Didn't I mention it? A big-ass snake, and poisonous to boot, I'm guessing."

SEVEN

SO JESSIE, NOT JACKIE, HAD BEEN THE ONE MESSing around with the energy pool. I remembered Jessie asking me questions the first time I'd seen her. Having more information was supposed to make things clearer, not more confusing, but it wasn't working out that way.

Rolf didn't ask me any more about where I'd been. He doesn't like to reveal much about himself and as a result he doesn't ask many questions himself, either. If nothing else, he's consistent.

He walked me out to the front gate. Unlike in the singularity, the padlock on this one would be real, and Rolf's better at opening locks than I am. I certainly didn't want to climb over that fence again, especially now that it would be topped with actual barbed wire. But the lock was already open and the gate slightly ajar. More questions.

It would have been a long walk home, so I walked over to Mission Street and hopped a bus. I should have thrown an illusion spell over Lou; dogs are not welcome, even off-hours, unless leashed and muzzled. And they pay full fare. But it was late, the bus was almost empty, and I was tired and not in the best of moods. When I boarded, the driver shook his head.

"Sorry. You need a leash for your dog."

I put a couple of bills in the fare box as Lou ran down to the back and wedged himself under a seat.

"What dog?" I said.

He shrugged and closed the door. He had a long route to finish. He wasn't looking for a hassle over a dog.

I walked the last few blocks to my house, needing some time to mull things over. How had Jackie created that singularity? It wasn't the easiest thing to do, even for a strong practitioner. No one I knew could pull it off—not without special help.

And equally pressing was that *something* had followed Lou and me out of the singularity. I had no idea what it was, but past experience told me it was trouble.

I passed a newspaper box on a corner and checked the date. Tuesday. That meant I'd lost about a day and a half; not bad considering. It could have been a week or even a month.

I grabbed some turkey from the fridge as soon as I got home, gave some to Lou, made a lame-tasting sandwich, and checked my messages. There were two from Jessie, the first one annoyed that I hadn't got back to her yet, the second stronger, with just a hint of threat. Jessie wasn't one who took well to the notion that she was being blown off.

Should I call her, or wait until tomorrow? That question was answered when the twig on the table, the one from Cassandra's houseboat walkway, sprang into life. I'd almost forgotten about it. It flickered briefly, then settled in and glowed a steady fluorescent green. Cassandra had just stepped onto the plank that led to her front door.

"Come on," I said to Lou, who had just curled up on the bed and was looking forward to a pleasant nap. I was tired, too, but that didn't matter. The woman might have just slipped back to pick up some belongings and if I didn't catch her now, we might never see her again.

I stuck the glowing twig in my pocket and grabbed my old binoculars. When I held the door open for Lou, he took his own sweet time about getting up, stretching fore and aft like he'd been asleep for hours. He can be annoying when he's trying to make a point.

Fifteen minutes later I was across from the houseboat, a couple of blocks away. Masking spells take energy, and distance plus binoculars works just as well with a lot less effort.

Lights were on in the houseboat, but no sign of Cassandra. That wasn't a problem. When she exited through the gate that led out of the houseboat row, there was only one direction she could go. I took out the roll of duct tape I keep in the glove compartment and headed down there on foot. A block down from the gate, the sidewalk narrowed to accommodate a large fuchsia bush. Perfect.

First came the tape. I pulled off a long strip and folded it lengthwise in half, so that part of the sticky side was face-up, and laid it carefully down on one side. Then, another on the opposite side and two more, forming a large sloppy rectangle. The twig came next; I dropped it in the middle of the rectangle and threw some dirt over it to hide the glow. It still had Cassandra's essence attached to it.

I gathered energy, ran it through the rectangle I'd made, sucked up the stickiness of the tape and Cassandra's essence from the twig, and poured it all into a small rock I picked up from under the fuchsia. The trap was set—as soon as Cassandra walked into the area, I'd activate the rock, throw it in with her, and she'd be caught. More important, it would negate her talent and keep her from doing anything effective. It wouldn't hold her forever, but it wouldn't have to. I would be right there alongside to keep her in check.

Back to the van. I settled in, wishing I'd thought to pick up something to eat on the way over. I'd give it a while; I could always go down to her houseboat and confront her there, but engaging a hostile practitioner on her home turf is seldom a good idea. I could wait.

Nothing happened for a half hour or so and then the lights in the house went off. A few seconds later the front door opened. When I focused my binoculars on the door I couldn't see much, since it was dark, but I could see a short figure toting a duffel bag almost as large as she was. Cassandra had picked up whatever stuff she thought was vital, and was on her way out. She crossed the plank, went out the gate leading to the road, and walked down toward the parking lot. She acted nervous and kept glancing over her shoulder.

I slipped out of the van and signaled for Lou to circle around and come at her from the other side. He'd played this game before; I didn't need to tell him what to do. I moved up closer to her, but still stayed well back, out of sight. I was too far back to see Lou, but when she reached the area I'd prepared, she suddenly stopped short and let the duffel slip to the ground, so I knew she had spotted him. She stared off into the darkness. Then she whipped her head around as he showed himself again.

Lou was hiding in the fuchsia, taking advantage of urban cover, letting her get just a glimpse of him from time to time. She wasn't quite sure what she was seeing, but she knew something was up. Unfortunately for her, she was so focused that she forgot to look behind her. I got right up within ten feet before she became aware of my presence, and by then it was too late.

I tossed the rock at her feet just as she spun around. She raised her hand and flung it out at me, but of course nothing happened. She'd been neutralized. I raised my own hand and walked up closer to where she stood.

"Take it easy," I said. "I'm not looking for any trouble."

"Then you've come to the wrong place," she said, and flung her hand out again.

Still nothing. She stood there like a statue as the state of affairs dawned on her. She slowly lowered her hand as Lou came out from the bushes and stood on the other side. For a moment I thought she was going to try to bolt, but thought better of it. Her next words were a little calmer.

"So, who are you, then?" she asked.

"Mason." I waved a hand at Lou. "That's Lou."

She nodded. "Huh. I've heard of you, actually. Supposedly you're not so bad. What in God's name are you doing working for someone like Jessie?"

"A good question. But I'm not exactly working for her, and she at least never tried to kill me. That seems a bit of an overreaction from someone who doesn't even know who I am."

"Those fireflies?" Cassandra made a sound of disgust. "They wouldn't have killed a child, just taught you a lesson; that's all."

"Sure."

"And you're telling me you don't work for Jessie?" Her tone was as skeptical as it gets, and I hesitated. "Thought so," she said.

"She thinks something was stolen from her," I finally said.

"By Jackie, right? That's what she told you?"

"Something like that."

"Did she tell you what it was?"

"No. Just that it was something valuable. Some magical object, I'd imagine."

"And you agreed to track Jackie down, just on Jessie's word. Brilliant. Do you have even the slightest clue what Jessie's like? She's a black practitioner, you know."

"Oh, I have some idea," I said. "Anyway, Jackie's a dark practitioner, too, isn't she?"

"That's different."

"Yes, I'm sure. But I would like to hear her side of it."

"I'll bet."

"No, really. I would."

Cassandra seemed a bit more measured now that it looked like I wasn't going to do anything to her right away.

"Not going to happen," she said. "Jackie's not stupid. She won't let you get anywhere near her."

"Well, I'll just have to keep looking for her, I guess."

She gave me a long look, shrewd and calculating.

"What if I told you what Jackie took? What if it wasn't some magical object? Would that change your mind?"

"I doubt it. But you could give it a try."

She stared at me for what seemed like a very long time before she spoke again.

"It's not a magical object. It's not anything magical at all, and it's not worth anything."

"The perfect crime."

She ignored me. "Have you ever heard of Sun City Inc.?" I shook my head. "It's a real estate development group. Very upscale; they buy prime areas of pristine land and sell lots to people with money."

"For homes or for stuff like shopping malls?"

"Both. Integrated communities, they call them. They get hold of wilderness land and turn it into suburbia."

"And?"

"Their latest interest is part of the Point Reyes National Seashore. That's what the meeting you came to was all about."

"Good luck with that. Never gonna happen."

"You'd think. But Jessie is connected up with the deal and there's been a lot of under-the-table negotiation going on. Mostly about money, of course, but she has her talent as well—something no one else is aware of. No one but other practitioners.

"She's been talking up state representatives, federal government people, even senators, for all I know. A lot of money has exchanged hands, but even more important, there's been coercion—coercion on a magical level. Those poor saps don't even know what hit them. They're agreeing to stuff they would never have dreamed they'd accept. Plus, good old-fashioned blackmail. You can lean hard on people when you know secrets. And it's hard to keep secrets from a practitioner."

"What does any of this have to do with Jackie?"

"This all started up in Seattle. Jessie got wind of an opportunity here and started working on it. There are files—

e-mail messages, payoff ledgers, notes about what was done and to whom. Jackie copied them all onto a CD, wiped the computer hard drive, and took off. It screwed things up royally—that's why Jessie came down to San Francisco. She had to see a lot of the players in person after that.

"Not to mention if all that stuff were made public, it would sink the deal, and the deal is worth millions—no, hundreds of millions. Jessie's desperate to get them back—and shut up Jackie for good."

"Shut her up how? You mean, like permanently?"

Cassandra looked at me in amazement.

"No, of course not. Don't be absurd. I mean, we're talking about *Jackie*."

"Okay," I said, as if I knew what she was talking about. "And what exactly is your role in this?"

"I've known Jackie since forever. We tried starting an environmental movement among practitioners, to help heal the earth before the ordinaries destroy it. But it never got off the ground—it turns out that practitioners are as greedy and apathetic as anyone else."

She had that right.

"So then we tried working through normal channels, like the group you met. At first we tried talking to people, to convince them, to show them the damage we're all doing to the earth. But we've been met with indifference at best, or a patronizing tolerance like we were kids who needed to be indulged. So we decided on more aggressive methods."

"Like theft?"

"Among other things."

"So how did Jackie end up working for Jessie, anyway?" I asked. "Did she sell out and join magical corporate America?"

"You really don't know?"

"No, I don't. That's why I'm asking."

"Wow. Maybe you are just a dupe, after all."

"Thanks. I appreciate the vote of confidence."

"Well. Let me show you something," she said, leaning down toward the duffel bag.

As she bent down, she lunged sideways, catching me off guard. In less than a second she'd torn one of the duct tape strips off the ground and was out of her cage. Two seconds later she was swallowed up by the darkness, and probably by a concealing spell as well. Lou took off after her but I called him back.

"Let it go," I said.

I'd learned what I wanted from her, and I wasn't eager to go chasing after her through the dark in any case. She'd already shown she possessed some talent and ability, and although I had no desire to harm her, the reverse wasn't necessarily true.

I made my way back to the van, thinking hard. I'd assumed the problems between the two of them were of the magical variety; that only made sense. But money is the motivating factor in more disputes than anything else. That and sex, and the sex angle didn't apply here. Or perhaps it did; anything was possible. Or it could even be exactly as Cassandra had made it out to be. Sherwood had pegged Jackie as a woman of principle, passionate about her beliefs. Maybe she truly was a caped crusader for the environment. But somehow I didn't think it was that simple.

EIGHT

JESSIE WAS MAD AS HELL WHEN I STOPPED BY her office the next morning. Naja was nowhere in sight, which didn't make either me or Lou any more comfortable. I could have defused Jessie's anger in a second by explaining about Jackie, the singularity, and the time glitch, but until I knew more about what was going on I wasn't explaining anything to anyone. Especially since Jessie had been screwing around with the energy pool.

"Sorry," I said. "I was out of town."

"Really. Where?"

"Not relevant," I said, which was a lie. "I ran into some trouble." That much at least was true.

"I'm paying you a lot of money," she said. "I expect you to be looking for Jackie, not dealing with your own stuff on my time."

"Sometimes it can't be helped." I changed the subject. "I did run into a practitioner who seems to know you, though. Cassandra?"

I watched for some reaction, and I got one. It wasn't very helpful, though. Jessie just looked thoughtful.

"Cassandra. Surprising. I didn't know she was in San Francisco, too."

"She seems to hold you in high esteem," I said.

Jessie laughed. "Yes, I'll bet. She's a good friend of Jackie's, and she's trouble. She's one of those eco freaks—earthers."

"Earthers?" I said, like I had no clue what she was talking about.

"Earthers. It started out as a small movement, a save-the-earth movement among practitioners. Nothing wrong with that, mind you—I'm rather fond of the planet myself, and humans are certainly messing it up. That's one reason I think practitioners should have a voice in running things.

"But the earthers, and Cassandra in particular, are extremists. They're the magical equivalent of tree spikers, and nothing is beyond them. They're just getting started, and God knows what's next."

"And she's a friend of Jackie's."

"Yes, and she's filled her head with the earther crap. Jackie used to be levelheaded and reliable, but Cassandra's really had an influence on her, and not a positive one. I'd guess she knows exactly where Jackie is."

"Quite possibly. She left before I could ask her. But here's the thing: Jackie isn't just hiding from you; she knows you've moved to San Francisco and she could have left at any time if she simply wanted to avoid you. And she apparently knows who I am, knows very well. So if she stole something from you, and now you're in San Francisco, too, why hasn't she simply left town?"

"That's complicated," Jessie said, using one of my own favorite phrases.

"Okay. Does it have anything to do with Sun City?"

"No. And where did you hear about that?"

"According to Cassandra, Jackie stole a bunch of files that implicate your company with some crooked business practices—influence peddling, bribery, stuff like that."

Jessie smiled. "Perfect," she said. "And you believed her?"

"I haven't decided. Care to enlighten me?"

Jessie got up from behind her desk and walked toward the window overlooking the city streets. Naja materialized from out of somewhere and glided over to her, and Lou moved a little closer to me. Jessie looked out the window for a minute before she turned back to me.

"Cassandra's a clever woman," she said. "She told you part of the truth. That's the best way to sell a lie, you know. Yes, Jackie took some files, but that's just an annoyance. It was the other thing that's important."

"Which was?"

"Have you ever heard of Wilhelm Richter?"

"Of course."

Richter was a black practitioner from the nineteenth century. He's venerated by black practitioners, much like Alistair Crowley is among ordinary black practitioner wannabes. Except while Crowley was a philosopher who got almost everything wrong, Richter was a practitioner, and a practical man who got a lot of things right.

"Well, Richter kept a lot of secrets to himself, but he also left a great many notes and descriptions of what he called 'experiments.' In fact, he wrote a book. A lot of it we can't use anymore—that was a rough time, and modern practitioners, even black ones, frown on some of the methods used back then. It was thought to be lost, but it wasn't. I found it."

"Ah," I said. "A grimoire. Secret spells of the master."

"Don't mock, Mason. It's not an attractive quality, especially from an employee. No, it's not spells, not exactly. But it is an operating manual of sorts, with specific instructions on how to achieve desired results. And Jackie stole it from me."

"Why? To gain power for herself?"

"More to accomplish her aims, I suspect."

"Sorry to seem skeptical," I said. "But talent is dependent on personal ability and power, not a bunch of secret stuff written down in some arcane book."

"So you've never studied and refined your skills?"

"Well, of course. But I've had people who could guide and mentor me."

"Oh. Sort of like having an instruction manual, then?" I saw her point. "One needs talent, certainly," she said. "Without a certain level of intrinsic ability, no one becomes anything more than a journeyman practitioner, no matter how hard they work. But the reverse is also true—I'm sure you know some immensely talented practitioners who fritter away their gift and slide by on natural aptitude. But they never fulfill their potential, do they?"

I had an uncomfortable feeling she was talking about me, which meant she knew more about me than I did about her.

"What about Jackie?" I said. "Talent, I assume?"

"Oh yes. And that's the problem. That book describes how to implement many things, and with the talent she has, she'll manage quite well. But she's young, and reckless. There's stuff in there I wouldn't want to try, and I've been around awhile."

"So she could hurt herself."

"Yes, and others as well. The book is priceless; I spent a great deal of my life trying to find it. But it's not only priceless; it's dangerous."

"Dangerous for who?"

"Everyone, as I said." She sat back down at her desk and tented her hands, placing her fingertips together. Not to mention . . ."

"What?"

"Toward the end of his life, Richter became very interested in alternate dimensions, 'gateways between the worlds,' as he called them."

"A bit fanciful."

"The language, maybe. There was nothing fanciful at all about his results. According to his notes, he succeeded in creating what he called 'thin areas,' places where you could slip between dimensions."

Like what Lou could do. Or the energy pool.

"There's a lot in the book about those things," she continued. "And one other thing. One of the things the book covers is how to go about creating singularities—are you familiar with those?"

"Somewhat," I said cautiously.

"Well, it takes a lot of skill to create them. Or a lot of power. Like if you had power objects, talent enhancers, as it were. But those items are hard to come by, as I'm sure you know. And even if you have them, it's still tricky. There can be unintended consequences."

"Such as?"

"When singularities are created the edges become thin, and things can slip through. All kinds of things, and some of them are not nice." She smiled at me, knowingly. "I believe you've already found that out—something about an energy pool, a portal?"

The pool that Jessie had been sniffing around. I wasn't getting the whole story, not by a long shot. I wasn't sure if Jessie was lying to me about the book, but as she herself had noted, the best lies are composed partly of truth. One thing did make sense: if there was such a book, with notes by Richter about singularities, that would explain how Jackie had managed to whip up such a good one.

But Jessie being so worried about theoretical consequences that didn't affect her directly didn't mesh with what I knew about her. That wasn't the kind of person she was, as far as I could tell. And hiring me, specifically, to locate Jackie still made no real sense. Developing a line into Victor's camp seemed a more likely motive.

Or, she could be killing two birds with one stone. She might as well get some value for her money, even if putting a wedge into Victor's operation was her main objective.

"So in essence we've got a kid running around out there with a loaded gun," I said.

"Basically, yes. Which brings us to the point. Obviously you haven't located her, but have you at least found a trace? Anything?"

"Well, I did find Cassandra. And I tracked Jackie to a

cheap residential hotel over on Sixth and Mission, the Hotel Carlyle. Ever heard of it?"

"No," she said. "Is she living there?"

"I doubt it, and if she was, she's not living there now. She knew I was looking for her." I didn't mention details. "But I do have some other leads," I said, standing up. Lou was up instantly and at the door. He didn't like being in the same room with a poisonous snake, Ifrit or no.

"Like what?"

"Just some ideas. I'll let you know if there's anything to know."

Jessie wasn't happy about my vagueness, but there wasn't much she could do short of firing me, and that wouldn't help her at all.

"Just be sure you do," she said, and her tone changed subtly, becoming flat in affect. "And if you get any idea about finding that book and using it for your own purposes, don't. Naja's a sweetie, but she does what I ask of her."

That came out of nowhere, and I wasn't sure if she was making a bad joke or if she was deadly serious. Especially since she'd been so outraged at me when I'd suggested something similar at our first meeting. Why can't people be a little more consistent?

I didn't respond, just headed out of the office, but before I made it to the door she spoke again, and this time her tone was light and friendly.

"Oh, on another subject, are you free tonight?"

"That's flattering," I said, "but employer/employee dating never works out."

She flashed me a smile. "Not for the employee, maybe, but what does that matter?"

"I see."

"No, I'm having drinks tonight with a few colleagues, discussing some things. They're interesting people. I thought you might like to meet them."

"What sorts of things?"

"The usual. The Giants' chances next year. The proper

use of bat's blood." She held it a beat, like a trained public speaker. "The changing role of practitioners in today's society."

Ah, there it was. I feigned disinterest.

"Not really my thing," I said.

"Sooner or later it will be everyone's thing. You should come by."

"Where?"

"Gavagan's Bar. Eight o'clock or so."

So my public tiff with Victor had got back to her after all, and she was letting me know. I shrugged.

"Why not? I'll try to stop by."

THAT AFTERNOON AT VICTOR'S I FILLED IN ELI and Victor—the singularity, Cassandra, Jessica's invitation for drinks. When I told Eli about the singularity, his reaction surprised me. Usually he's like a little kid at Christmas where all things new and magical are concerned. But he didn't ask many questions; I guess singularities and such were old hat to him by now. He'd never had to find his way out of one, though.

He was more interested in what might have followed me out of there, especially the second thing. The last time something uncanny had slipped into our world, there had been a spot of trouble over it. Like people dying.

"You didn't get a look at it?" he asked. "Nothing? Not even a glimpse?"

I shook my head. "Barely an impression, like it was made of shadow. I couldn't even tell if it was human or not."

"Or human-looking. I doubt anything that came out of there was actually human." That thought didn't make me feel better.

"What about Jessie's idea of things slipping through?" I asked "The thin places."

"Absolutely," he said. "We all need to keep a sharp eye out."

"Moving forward, how are you planning to handle Jessica's social hour?" Victor asked.

"By ear, as usual. Any suggestions?"

"Just the same caution: don't overplay your hand; don't seem too eager. If she wants you on board, she'll keep at it. Let her drag you reluctantly into it. The essence of every good con game is to get the mark pleading to be taken."

"I know," I said. "But one more thing. Jessie made a veiled threat about sending Naja to visit me if I don't toe the line. She's a powerful practitioner, and Naja, being an Ifrit, isn't as discouraged by wards as most things are. I'd hate to be sitting quietly at home some evening and have her come slithering through the back window."

"Yes, I can see how that might be worrisome."

"Talent isn't reliable, either, when it comes to Ifrits," I said. "Can I borrow that sawed-off shotgun of yours? Just in case."

"I'm not sure that's the best weapon. It sprays pellets like a garden hose, even in a small area. You could easily hit Lou as well if you fired it inside. And if you were outside your house, anyone walking by would be at risk."

"Any other ideas?"

Victor gave me a calculating look. "Do you play tennis?" he asked.

"I used to. Why?"

"Any good?"

"Not bad. Not great."

"Follow me," he said, and headed down to the basement.

The basement of the house was where Victor has installed his gym. He works out almost every day, which is how he stays in such good shape. I should do the same, but keeping up with an everyday exercise routine would be too obsessive for me.

He opened a locker at the far end of the big room and took out what appeared to be a slightly curved sword resting in a scabbard.

"Wow," I said. "For me?"

"No."

He reached into the locker again and came out with an identical sword, only this one was constructed of hard black plastic.

"Ahh," I said. "I get the training wheels."

"If I just handed you the katana with no preparation, you'd probably cut your own ear off. Do you want to learn the basics, or not?"

"Sorry," I said. "I'm all ears. So far."

He started to put the sword back in the locker, but I quickly apologized. He takes all that martial arts stuff very seriously and was doing me a favor, so I needed to behave.

"Sorry," I said again. "Do you really think you can teach me to handle that sword properly?"

"Sure. If I had a couple of years. But I can also take an hour and show you how to use it well enough to be effective."

He handed me the plastic copy and went through some basics—footwork, balance, grip, how to turn the edge to the right angle for a strike.

"Don't strike at the target," he said. "It's not about power; it's about smoothness and speed. Strike *through* the target, like it's not even there, like it's simply in the way of where the sword wants to go. It's like hitting a two-handed forehand or backhand in tennis, except there's no topspin involved."

When Victor was satisfied I had the basics down, he attached a thick piece of rope to a hook in the ceiling, the kind you'd use to moor a small boat. He stepped back, did a figure-eight move with the sword, dropping into a crouch at the same time, and sliced it cleanly through three feet from the floor.

He stepped back, replaced his sword in the scabbard and took another one out of the locker, and offered it to me. I took it gingerly; a plastic practice tool is one thing, a razor-sharp blade quite another.

"Your turn," he said. "Don't try a fancy move; just remember what I told you and swing through it."

I stepped forward and gave it my best shot. The rope swung wildly when I struck it, just as if I'd struck it with the practice sword. When it swung back, it was frayed and half-cut through where I'd hit it.

"Not bad," said Victor. "Try again, and this time make sure the edge of the blade is perpendicular to the rope, and don't swing quite so hard. Speed, not power."

The second time wasn't much better, but after a few more tries I got the hang of it. The last two times the rope parted cleanly, barely moving at all. Victor nodded, satisfied.

"I pronounce you apprentice serpent killer," he said. "Just don't get carried away. And Mason?"

"Yeah?"

"You'll be tempted to feel the blade with the ball of your thumb to see exactly how sharp the katana is. Everyone feels that impulse. I'd advise against it."

AT EIGHT THAT NIGHT, WHEN I MADE MY WAY into Gavagan's, Bill greeted me from behind the bar. I picked up another Black Rock Porter and a glass, since I hadn't had time to enjoy the last one I'd got there.

Jessie was at a booth in the back, and as I made my way over toward the booth, Bill gave me a quizzical look. He wasn't much of a gossip; successful bar owners keep things pretty close to the vest when it comes to the peccadilloes of their customers. But first a public fight with Victor, then a meet-up with a black practitioner? This would surely test his powers of discretion.

Jessie was wearing black jeans and a black top and she made the outfit look slinky. Across from her sat a practitioner I knew slightly, at least by sight, a large balding man with a bushy red beard. He was a black practitioner, I knew, but I'd never had any dealings with him. Next to him sat a middle-aged woman I'd never seen. And next to Jessie was a surprise, a practitioner I knew fairly well. The booth was full, so I pulled up a chair.

"Warren," I said to the man sitting next to Jessie. "How's life?"

"Not as easy as it used to be," he said.

About a year ago Victor and I had busted him pulling a scam on ordinaries, and he was obviously still pissed about it. He'd advertised himself as a life coach, assuring clients that he could change their lives, give them self-confidence, and make them more attractive to the opposite sex.

For all I know, he might have given them some good advice, but that wasn't all he was doing. After each session, he'd laid a glamour over their appearance, nothing drastic, just enough to make them more attractive. They could have got the same benefit if they'd lost weight and worked out for a year, but that was never going to happen. He also included the opposite of an aversion spell, sort of an attraction spell, very subtle, a nice piece of work, actually.

At least he wasn't cheating them. They got results. But the spell lasted only a couple of days at most before fading away. So they needed to come back for additional "self-esteem" sessions, after which the bar scene became much easier for them. Warren charged an arm and a leg and people were happy to pay it.

He didn't see that he was doing anything wrong. "It's not like I'm hurting anyone," he'd said. "It's not a con—they do get what they pay for."

I didn't entirely disagree with him, but Victor was having none of it. He made Warren stop, but for some reason Warren decided I was the one pushing the issue. He didn't like me much.

"I see you two know each other," Jessie said.

She didn't introduce the others, which was a rather old-school form of etiquette among some practitioners, a throwback to the days when people believed that knowledge of names conferred power. If they wanted to introduce themselves, they would. They didn't.

I poured my porter into the glass and watched approvingly as it developed a creamy head.

"So," I said brightly. "The conspirators assemble."

Warren started to say something, but Jessie raised her hand. "Not so far off, actually, except that we're out in the open. And we're conspiring to change practitioner culture, by logic and reason."

"In what way?" I asked.

"I'm pretty sure you already know. Practitioners have been in the closet for years. We hide in plain sight, and we make sure that ordinaries don't know about us. It's been that way forever, and everyone accepts it's the way things have to be. But have you ever really thought about it? Haven't you ever wondered what the point of all this secrecy is?"

"Occasionally," I admitted.

"Well, at least there's that. A couple of things to consider: One, if anyone found out about us, chaos would result. Demonstrably false. Every one of us knows someone who is not a practitioner, yet who knows everything about us, yes?"

Timothy immediately sprang to mind. I knew a few others who didn't have the whole picture, but did know at least a little about us.

"That's true."

"And has society collapsed?"

"That's different," I said. "A few trusted friends aren't the same as the world at large. People would freak out."

"Are you sure?"

"We wouldn't just spring it on the world, all at once," said the middle-aged woman. "It would have to be gradual, of course, get people used to the idea over time."

"What would be the point?" I asked. "It's not like things are terrible—in fact, the whole setup has worked pretty well, for centuries."

"Well," said Jessie, "for one thing, we could do a lot of good. You may have noticed that society in general hasn't had a great history. We could help to change that."

The bald practitioner weighed in. "And to be honest," he said, "our talents would be in demand. Maybe you're satisfied to live hand to mouth, but I'm getting a little tired of it."

There it was. Money. At least he was honest about it.

Warren couldn't help but chime in. "Come on, Mason. You've got to be sick of Victor telling you what you can and can't do. Who is he to make decisions for everyone?"

Jessica was watching me closely. This was the crucial moment; I had to sell her on the idea that I could indeed be flipped, and she was no fool. A misstep would blow it.

I looked off into the distance, as if remembering ancient grudges. I let my head nod slightly, as if in agreement, then gave a little shake and returned to the present.

"Sorry," I said, reluctantly. "I just don't see it."

Jessie smiled enigmatically. I might not be buying into it, but she had bought into my act. She thought she almost had me.

"Well, think about it," she said.

I shook my head. "It's all academic anyway. Victor and those like him aren't tyrants. They just fulfill a need. If practitioner society didn't want him doing what he does, he'd be out of a job."

"Exactly. I'm not some evil black practitioner out to overthrow the order of things. I'm just going to convince people to see things my way. Democracy in action. What's wrong with that?"

I let an expression of uncertainty flash across my face. Then I dismissed it and stood up.

"Nice talking to you," I said. "But politics bores me. Besides, I've got work to do."

I hated to leave my beer unfinished again, but you can't utter an exit line and then linger. I was well satisfied with my performance. Jessie believed she had me on the hook, and the next time we talked I'd let her push me a little further. I still didn't know what she was up to, but it wasn't about building a grassroots consensus. That much I was sure of.

FOR THE NEXT FEW DAYS I PUT IN SOME TIME searching for Jackie, but it was a brick wall. I was just spinning my wheels. I prowled the streets with Lou, looking for her, but she'd either finally left town or was holed up where I couldn't find her. I also kept an eye out for whatever had followed me out of that singularity. I even went out a couple of times late at night, hoping to lure it into showing itself if it had bad intentions. But there wasn't a trace of it. I was beginning to think I'd imagined it until I remembered Lou and Rolf had seen it, too.

But now that I was looking for it, I did notice all kinds of small anomalies, signs that Jessie had been telling the truth. Squirrels that Lou didn't want to chase, squirrels that looked more ratlike than squirrel-like. The occasional brightly colored bird that seemed out of place. A procession of centipedes scuttling down a gutter, nose to tail, hundreds of them. Minor things, all, but out of place and disturbing.

I'd just about decided to pack it in and kick back for a while when the late-night knock at my door came. Lou bounded up from his spot on the bed, instantly alert. No growl; he wasn't disturbed, but it wasn't a random friend dropping by for a visit, either.

I'm pretty secure in my own house, so I opened the door. Two people stood there; I didn't recognize one of them but I sure did the other.

Jackie.

NINE

"MAY WE COME IN?" SHE ASKED.

I stepped back and motioned her inside. The person with her was unremarkable and rather unprepossessing—short, heavy, round-faced, thinning sandy hair, big ears that stuck out comically. He'd grown the type of little mustache people sometimes do when they're trying to add character to an otherwise undistinguished face. His eyes gleamed a pale watery blue, and his shoulders slumped as if he were afraid a stranger might lash out at him at any moment. A more inoffensive-looking man I'd never seen. I immediately marked him as someone to watch very carefully.

"Coffee?" I asked, as if they were casual friends just dropping by for a visit.

"No, thank you," Jackie said politely. Her companion held out his hand.

"I'm Malcolm."

From his looks I expected his palm would be damp and sweaty, but it was warm and dry. He might look like a nervous Nellie type, but his skin told a different story. And in more ways than one. A series of intricately designed tattoos peeked out of his sleeve, coming all the way down to his wrist. I recognized several runes there that I'd seen black practitioners use in the past. He looked like a good candidate for the one who'd helped Jackie with the dead-body illusion, and yet I felt not a trace of talent coming from him. Was he shielding? I couldn't imagine what the point would be if he was.

"You've been looking for me," Jackie said.

"True. But if I'd known you'd be dropping by, I wouldn't have wasted the effort."

"I suppose my mom told you I've done all kinds of dreadful things?"

"Your mom?" I had no idea what she was talking about.

"You didn't know?" She laughed, delighted, and then I got it.

"No," I admitted. "I didn't. But she's . . ."

"White? My dad was a black practitioner, if you'll pardon the pun."

"I was about to say too young. Just how old is she, anyway?"

Jackie laughed again. "I had no idea you were so naïve. Let's just say she's older than she looks."

I felt foolish. Now things started to fell into place. Jessie had naturally trusted Jackie; she was her daughter, after all. She must have experienced an incredible sense of betrayal. And she'd be worried not just that Jackie's inexperience and willfulness would cause trouble, but that it would be dangerous to her daughter as well. A typical family dynamic, now so obvious.

"Well, whatever," I said, struggling to regain control of the conversation. "But you did take something from her, didn't you? And she wants it back."

"Well, yes, but it wasn't really my fault. She wouldn't let me even see it. So I took it. And she doesn't just want back what I took; she wants *me* back as well. She's afraid I'll do something dangerous."

"Like creating a singularity?"

Jackie smiled, almost beaming. "Impressive, wasn't it?

I tried to throw you off the trail first at that hotel, and when that didn't work, I tried to get you out of the way for an extended time."

"Kind of drastic, don't you think? I might never have gotten out of there."

"Oh, it would have dissolved after a while. A couple of months at most." Jackie was still at an age where losing a couple of months wasn't that big a deal. "Besides," she said, "I knew he would get you out eventually." She pointed at the corner of the room.

"Lou?"

"Sure. He's kind of famous, you know."

Lou looked at her, then at me, then stretched, elaborately. This was just what I needed: Lou with a swelled head.

Malcolm had been quiet up to now, looking at us both with a sort of bemused interest. But now he nodded. "That's why we're here, actually."

Jackie took me by the arm and looked at me earnestly. "I knew you'd find me sooner or later. I've been hunkered down in a shielded house, afraid to go out, but I couldn't stay there forever. Then Malcolm found me." She jerked her head in his direction.

"If the house was shielded, how did he manage that?" I asked.

"He's clever. But that's beside the point. He'd noticed the singularity, and such things are kind of a passion of his, so he found me. He wanted to know how I'd done it."

"You had Richter's book to help you. That's how you managed it, right?"

"So my mom finally told you about that, did she?"

"She did. It's a big deal, apparently."

"Indeed it is," said Malcolm. "You saw what Jackie could do with its help. And with my expertise and assistance, there's no limit to what we might accomplish."

"That's great," I said. "But who are you, anyway? And why are you here? What does any of this have to do with me?"

Jackie interrupted. "Malcolm's a friend," she said, which

was no answer at all. "As to why we're here, first of all, I want to convince you to leave me alone. Second, I need your help, too."

Great. It looked like everybody wanted me on board these days. It would have been an ego boost if I had any idea why. Malcolm chimed in.

"And third, it's not so much you as it is about Lou here."

"Of course," I said. Lou had been quite in demand these last few years, and now his already swelled head was going to grow even larger. Malcolm pulled out a chair and gestured.

"May I?" He delicately seated himself at the kitchen table.

"I've made quite a study of singularities. With what I already know, Jackie's help, and Richter's manual, I'm now fairly certain we could create a singularity so complex it would be indistinguishable from an actual world. Plants, flowers, buildings, and three-dimensional people—even a real society, with its own history. All identical to the real thing. For all I know it might actually be the real thing—at a certain level of complexity, things take on an independent existence."

Not a chance, I thought. Malcolm was suffering from a god complex.

"That would be quite the feat," I said. "But what would be the point?"

"A test. If we can accomplish that, we'll be ready for the next step."

"Which is?"

"That will be made clear later on. But the thing is, the only way to test this would be for the two of us to enter the creation, to actually go there. That's no problem, but I'm not so comfortable about navigating a way out once we're there. Accessing it is one thing. Getting back might be a different matter."

I caught on. "I see. And you believe Lou could help you get back."

"Yes."

"Even if he could, he's not about to go off with you."

"Oh, I'm aware of that. That's why we want you to come along."

"Hmm. Assuming for the moment you could accomplish such a thing, why would I want to go there with you?"

Malcolm looked genuinely baffled.

"Why, it's the chance of a lifetime," he said. "A whole new world? Who wouldn't want to explore such a thing? Think of what you might learn, what wonders you might see there."

"I think you've got me confused with Eli."

"Who?"

"Never mind. But just to be clear, are you talking about making a construct of your own or about creating a gateway to an actual dimension?"

"An interesting philosophical question. But difficult to answer. It's not always a case of one or the other."

My God, he really was just like a pint-sized Eli. I knew better than to pursue that line of questioning; I'd get the same kind of semantic runaround that always drove me crazy. I brought Jackie back into the conversation.

"On a more practical level, what exactly am I supposed to do about you, Jackie? I was hired to find you and get back what you took from Jessie, remember? And she's paying me quite a bit for my services."

"I still can't believe you're working for my mom," Jackie said. "I've talked to a few people about you. I wouldn't have thought you were the type."

"You never can tell."

She shrugged and reached into the shoulder bag she carried and took out a couple of CDs.

"Here," she said. "The first one is the copy of Richter's book I took—I scanned the pages into my laptop and then destroyed the book."

She said this with the thoughtless arrogance of youth, unaware of the enormity of what she'd done. Eli would have called it a crime; he venerates books. It was like someone casually mentioning they'd burned a Shakespeare First Folio.

"And the other?" I said, reaching for the disks. There was no point in commenting on it.

"The other is the dirt on the Sun City deal. Cassandra told you about that, didn't she? I'm not even keeping a copy of that one. I don't care anymore."

"Why is that?"

"There's no point. If it's not Sun City destroying Point Reyes, it will be someone else. There's money to be made, billions, and as long as there's big money involved, it'll never end. Sooner or later the bad guys will win. They always do."

"That's a bit cynical, don't you think?"

"Not cynical. Just realistic. This planet is already dead; it just hasn't quite stopped breathing yet. But there's still hope—you just have to think out of the box. That's what this is all about, you know." I didn't know, but she wasn't paying any attention to me. She had the slightly glazed look of a true believer in her eyes. "We've screwed up one world, and it's too late to fix it now. But maybe if we could start over again, we'd do a better job."

Now it was starting to make sense. Not actual sense; both of them were verging on bat-shit crazy in my book, but I could see where she was coming from.

"Not much of a student of human history, are you?" I said.

"On the contrary. That's why it will work. But anyway, now you've done your job. You can give her the disks. Unless you're planning on tying me up and delivering me to my mom in person."

"No," I said.

"Then why don't you help us instead? It wouldn't hurt you any and you'd be doing a lot of good, more than you know."

"It's an interesting proposal; I'll give you that. But it's something I'd have to sleep on."

"Of course," Malcolm said. "Who wouldn't? But the experience will be more than worth it; that, I can promise. Trust me."

I don't think I'd ever heard anyone I'd just met say "trust me" before. It would have been another warning sign if it wasn't clear that Malcolm was basically clueless about nuances. He'd make a lousy conspirator. I guessed he hadn't spent a great deal of time around other people. Too much time exploring the phenomenon of singularities, perhaps.

"Hey," I said to him. "You're an expert on singularities, right? Supposedly."

"I do have some knowledge, yes."

"Well, the one I was in last week? The one Jackie set up? Something followed me out of it. Any idea what it could have been?"

The two of them exchanged a quick glance. So neither was very good at conspiracies. That was reassuring.

"Are you sure something came back with you? What did it look like?" Malcolm asked warily.

I thought for a moment of making something up, to test his reaction, but thought better of it. I was pretty sure he was lying anyway, so better I just play it straight and let him think I was unaware.

"I never got a look at it." They both relaxed slightly.

"I can't think of anything. Unless I'm very mistaken, nothing in that singularity had an independent existence—there's no way anything from there could exist in the real world."

"Huh. Well, maybe I was imagining things," I said.

Malcolm nodded. "Stress can play tricks on the mind."

"I guess." Tricks were perhaps being played, but it wasn't my mind that was doing it.

"So what do you think?" Jackie asked, still pressing.

"About your offer of a magical mystery tour? It's not impossible. But as I said, I'd have to sleep on it."

Jackie seemed to want to discuss it further, but Malcolm pulled her toward the door.

"Come on," he said, in what he thought was a hearty tone. "Give the man some time."

"Are you going to tell my mom I was here?" she asked.

"Probably. I have to hand over the disks, anyway. She's going to ask how I got them."

"You don't have to tell her." I didn't say anything. "Fine," she said. "Just don't tell her about what we're intending to do, okay? At least not until you make up your mind about if you're coming or not. She'd interfere, and then you wouldn't be able to make your own decision."

That was a sad and clumsy attempt at manipulation on her part, reminding me that Jackie was barely more than a kid, despite being powerful and clever in many ways. But since I had no intention of telling Jessie any more than I had to anyway, it didn't hurt to let Jackie think she'd succeeded in convincing me.

"All right," I said, with seeming reluctance. "I'll wait on that part of it, then. How am I going to let you know when I make my decision?"

"You've got my cell number, right? From Sherwood?"

She smiled mischievously, a subtle reminder of how easily she'd played Sherwood and me. I had to give her props on that one.

"Yeah," I said. "Come to think of it, I do."

As soon as she and Malcolm left I waited a few minutes and then went outside and walked around the entire building, checking the wards, just to make sure. Everything seemed tight.

I loaded one of the CDs into my computer, curious about what all the fuss was about. But I was in for a disappointment. It was a PDF file, obviously scanned in from the original book. Some of it was printed, and some handwritten in black ink. But the text was in German, with fancy lettering that I assumed was some sort of Gothic script. I couldn't even identify some of the letters, much less understand what it said. Runes, numbers, symbols, and other things that were gibberish to me were scattered throughout. This was something for Eli to deal with.

It was a bit late to head over to Victor's, so tomorrow morning would have to do. At least things were finally moving in some direction, although it wasn't clear what that direction was.

TEN

NEXT MORNING I CALLED ELI, MADE IT OVER to Victor's, and handed the disks over to Timothy. He loaded them up, made copies, and gave me back the originals. Then he scanned the monitor screen, briefly paging through the file. The first disk was nothing but office memos, contracts, and e-mails, all relating to Sun City. But the second, the one I'd looked at briefly, was what Eli had been waiting for.

He'd canceled a class he was supposed to be teaching and rushed over; he was that eager to take a look at the fabled Richter book. He almost pushed Timothy out of the seat in front of the monitor to get a look. In addition to the treasure trove of scribblings in black ink, diagrams, and text, there were also drawings of plants and creatures, none of which looked familiar. And although the text was incomprehensible to me, Eli, naturally, had no problem with it.

"Wow," Timothy said, looking over his shoulder. "This is amazing, whatever it is." Eli just grunted, already engrossed.

"Does it make any sense?" I asked.

"Hmm?"

"Can you read it? The disk. Is it full of secret knowledge, or just recipes for sauerbraten?"

"Recipes? Oh, a joke. No, it's quite interesting." He muttered something that sounded like "Fraktur," whatever that meant.

I asked him a few more questions, but after answering abstractedly for a while, he started responding with incomprehensible mumbling sounds. So while he sat mesmerized, staring at diagrams on the screen, I talked with Victor. Malcolm's proposal interested him. But he'd never heard of Malcolm, and my description of him didn't jog any memories.

"Odd," he said. "If he can do half of what he says he can, he'd be an amazing talent. You'd think we'd have at least heard of him."

"Well, I couldn't sense any talent," I said, "for whatever that's worth. Maybe he's a reclusive genius, hiding out from the world. He doesn't seem that good with people."

Something of our conversation must have filtered through to Eli's consciousness because he suddenly swiveled around in his chair.

"Oh, you have to take him up on it," he said.

"You think?"

"Absolutely. Who knows what you'll find there, what questions could be answered?"

"The last time I did something like this I was looking for Lou, and the only question was whether we'd get out alive."

"I think this is very different. This Malcolm is talking about a world, a society, and Lord knows what else. I seriously doubt that anyone could *create* such a thing, but he might be able to access some place that's already there. And who knows what it might lead to?"

Victor wasn't quite so enthusiastic, but he agreed. "They're up to something," he said." And I don't buy that they just want to test it out. They know what they're doing. There's a purpose behind it."

"Maybe they're hoping to find something there," I said. "Something not available in this world, like those rune stones that gave us so much trouble." Victor nodded.

"Not a bad thought. But again, what? The only way to find out is to take him up on his offer."

Truth be told, I was curious myself. The singularity Jackie had created was impressive enough, and if Malcolm could go her one better, it would be quite a feat. Accessing a complete other world would be even more so. But curiosity has been known to kill more than cats.

"Be careful, will you?" Eli said, already lost back in the computer screen. He assumed I would jump at the chance, because that's what he would have done.

"Always," I said, but I doubt he heard me.

WHEN I CALLED JACKIE AND SAID IT WAS A GO, she told me to meet her and Malcolm at the north entrance to Mount Davidson at six. Jackie was acting subdued when I got there but Malcolm was upbeat and bouncy. He wore a fanny pack around his waist, much like the one Victor carries for magical forensic investigations.

Mount Davidson is an odd place, a thousand-foot-high hill covered with tall eucalyptus trees and choked with thick undergrowth. It rises up unexpectedly from an area of residential streets, and a narrow path leads up to the summit where a massive hundred-foot-tall white concrete cross dominates the clearing at the top.

Malcolm and Jackie led the way with Lou and me trailing behind. Neither of us wanted to walk up that narrow path with the two of them at our backs. A lot of people enjoy Mount Davidson, but I've always found it just the slightest bit creepy. It has an amazing microclimate, like something plucked from the Pacific Northwest coastal rain forest and set neatly down in the middle of San Francisco. Even on sunny days the light doesn't quite penetrate all the way down to the forest floor, and the fog lingers there long after it's cleared away from the rest of the city. The tree trunks are perpetually damp, the dirt path always muddy in spots.

Rarely do you see a bird in the surrounding woods, although you can often hear crows squawking in the distance. Flowers are few and far between, and sound is muffled. The narrow path winds up to the top of the hill, and you can't see much of anything except the trees, even when you're within fifty feet of the summit. But when you finally crest the lip at the top and reach the clearing, it all changes. The sky overhead glows blue and the city stretches out in the distance like a panoramic postcard. And best of all, the huge white cross that dominates the clearing exudes a quiet peace, no matter your religion.

The sun was low when we arrived at the summit and its rays lit up the top of the cross, adding to the supernatural sheen. I saw why Malcolm had picked this place.

"Impressive, isn't it?" he said, following my gaze. "Richter lived in nineteenth-century Austria, so of course he was surrounded by Christian symbology. Many of his rituals and instructions depend on them—I probably could get much the same results using different symbols, but why mess with that when you have something that you know will work?"

"Don't fix what ain't broken."

"Exactly," he said, as if I'd uttered a profound truth.

He reached in the fanny pack and pulled out some crystals, which is standard for rituals. Then a glass bottle full of a grayish powder. He laid down a trail of parallel lines that led to the other side of the clearing, maybe ten feet or so, like a gunpowder trail leading to a powder keg. Arranging the crystals in a semicircle, he stepped back, considered them, and then, obviously dissatisfied, rearranged them. The next things out of the pack were a plain wooden cross, maybe six inches long, and a vial of liquid, dark red and viscous. I looked a question at him.

"Blood," he confirmed. "Can't do a black ritual without blood."

He unstoppered the vial and sprinkled it over the crystals. I didn't ask whose blood or where he'd obtained it. I was just happy it wasn't mine, for once. But no such luck.

"We need a bit more as well," he said, digging out what looked like a large pen from his pack. It was a spring-loaded lancet device, the kind diabetics use to test blood-sugar levels. He pricked his finger, drawing a bead of blood, then rubbed the blood into the wooden cross. He slipped a fresh lancet into the device and handed it to me.

"Sterile technique is all the rage these days," he said. "I just need a small drop."

I'm never thrilled about giving up any of my blood to a black practitioner, even a drop. I held it loosely, making no effort to use it.

"Why do you need more blood?" Jackie unexpectedly asked. She seemed a little ill at ease herself.

"We all need to contribute," Malcolm said. "That's one of the things that makes the singularity complex. All your life experiences are encoded in your blood, and all of mine in mine, and all of Mason's in his. The more input, the more complexity. If I could collect a drop of blood each from a million people, I could create a new world indistinguishable from this one."

Jackie took the device from my hand, pressed the end firmly against her little finger, and quickly produced a drop of blood. She rubbed it into the wood of the cross just as Malcolm had done and handed the device back to him. He inserted a new lancet and offered it to me again. There was no point in balking now. If Malcolm had bad intentions concerning me, there were easier ways to get at me than this elaborate ritual. I did the finger thing and rubbed it into the cross with the other drops.

Malcolm puttered around, adjusting the crystals, until finally he was satisfied. The last things he took out from the pack were an old work glove, a can of lighter fluid, and a sheet of paper covered with drawings and diagrams.

"Jackie, stand over here," he directed. "Mason, you on the other side here, so we form a triangle."

Lou had walked away and was now watching us from a safe distance. He hasn't had the best of experiences with rituals.

Malcolm picked up a long stick, and holding the paper for a guide, he drew a series of diagrams in the dirt. At the same time, he pronounced a series of words, some in Latin, some in German, pausing at different intervals between them. About halfway through, he threw the stick down in disgust, erased the diagrams, and began to redraw them.

"Damn it," he said.

"What?" asked Jackie.

"I made a mistake. I'll have to start over from the beginning."

This sort of thing always puzzles me. My belief is that magical operations are a result of simply using talent to access power, nothing more, nothing less. Rituals, objects, spells—all are mere focusing devices to channel talent. But events of the last few years had made me wonder if it was as simple as that. It may take a practitioner to activate them, but there surely is an intrinsic power and magic inherent in certain objects. I've seen that. And I've seen other things that I don't understand at all.

Still, I find it hard to believe that the exact sequence and proper pronunciation of words chanted in a spell can mean the difference between success and failure. Malcolm obviously believed it, though, and he was the one constructing the ritual.

I couldn't tell any difference the second time through, but Malcolm was satisfied. He finished, took a deep breath, pulled the work glove over one hand, and doused the wooden cross with lighter fluid. I thought he might set it ablaze with a simple fire ignition spell, but instead he produced a wooden kitchen match and struck it against a rock. It flared up, catching the lighter fluid alight at the same time.

Holding the burning cross in his gloved hand, he turned

to face west, mirroring the larger cross at the end of the clearing. Then, three clear syllables, almost Arabic in sound. Quickly, he crouched down and placed the cross over the lines of powder he'd laid down earlier. The fire shot down them with a sputtering sound, and then they burned quietly with a deep violet flame. He turned to Jackie.

"Quickly, now. You know I can't do this part. Throw your power into it."

This was odd. But maybe Malcolm was a weak practitioner despite his knowledge, somewhat like Eli. Eli had limited power, but his immense knowledge of magical operations more than made up for that lack.

Jackie lifted her arms and sang a high, keening double note, like a Tuvan throat singer. Energy flowed from her and the air above the lines of fire shimmied and wavered before solidifying into a faint passageway.

"That's done it," said Malcolm, breathless from exertion and adrenaline, but almost crowing. "I've done it; I've duplicated Richter. A few short steps, and we'll be exploring uncharted territory."

He gestured to Jackie, walked down the path between the lines of fire, and turned his head toward me.

"You coming?" he said.

ELEVEN

WE WERE STILL STANDING ON A PATH THAT wound down a hill, but now there was an actual forest around us. It was cold—not that San Francisco chill of a rainy day when the wind blows and the mist swirls around your head and down the collar of your shirt; more like the icy chill of the Sierras on a fall day that speaks of the coming winter. I turned up my jacket collar, wishing it was heavier.

"Notice how fresh the air is," Jackie said.

I took a deep lungful. "No hydrocarbons. Maybe."

"No sounds, either," said Malcolm, "except for natural ones. No traffic. No sirens. No engines. No leaf blowers or chain saws."

I listened. I could hear wind and the squeak and groan of tree limbs rubbing together. I could hear water running somewhere up ahead.

"Is this what you were aiming for?" I asked.

He looked thoughtful. "I wasn't really aiming for anything in particular. I just wanted to create the most complex place I could. The details weren't under my control, but that's something that eventually will change, I believe."

I looked around for something to try my talent on. This time I wasn't going to wait for an emergency before testing my limits. I listened to the sound of the running water, amplified it, and directed the sound farther up on the hillside. It worked; the reassuring sound of a fake waterfall echoed down among us, and Jackie looked up in confusion until she caught on to what I was doing.

"What's that for?" she asked.

"Just seeing how things work here," I said.

We set off down the path, Lou in the lead. He was perkier than usual, almost playful, which was a good sign. He wouldn't be prancing along if bizarre and dangerous creatures were lurking unseen in the woods. Probably.

The path was narrow, moist and muddy. Dead leaves choked parts of it and crooked trees leaned over one side. The other side was overgrown with lush broad-leafed plants and thick bushes. Occasional outcroppings of rock pushed their way through, dripping with a viscous green slime exactly like the gunk every kid buys for Halloween.

Gradually the woods opened up and the path wound through to where the trees were spread out every fifteen feet or so, sandy soil and leaf clutter providing a thick mat on the ground beneath them. Black squirrels scampered between the tree trunks. Lou whined in the back of his throat. He wanted to go after them, but restrained himself for once. If he ever caught one, I don't know what he'd do with it, anyway. Surely he wouldn't eat it. Or maybe he would.

He stayed on the path, though, all business despite his playful demeanor. Eventually we came to a broad stream, almost a river, the source of the water I'd been hearing. It curved in from the opposite direction until it ran parallel to the path. Moss-covered boulders squatted in the middle of the stream and tall, cattail-like rushes crowded together near the banks. Blackbirds with yellow wings fluttered among the reeds, uttering piercing whistles. Fifty yards from where the stream met the path, the water broadened out and gentled down. The path became a dirt road; the road became a long, solid stone bridge that crossed the stream, arches reflected in the water below.

We walked along the path until it became the road, crossed over the bridge, and followed the road down to where it bent around a shallow lake. The lake was broad and muddy, almost a swamp. Large trees with gnarled roots dotted the water, popping out like tiny green islands in a sea of brown. About twenty feet from the shore, I could see ripples in the muddy water. Probably catfish or something, but we stayed well back nonetheless.

The road continued past the lake and rolled into a narrow valley. A couple of miles farther down, a small village nestled into the slope of an encroaching hill. Buildings, mostly constructed of stone, overlapped on the slope like a giant jigsaw puzzle. Slanted roofs of red tile seemed to be the universal covering of choice. Smoke drifted out of several chimneys and the sound of hammering carried all the way up to where we stood. Picturesque didn't begin to describe it.

This didn't appear to be a construct to me. It was far too complex, and far too large. There was none of that telltale blurring around the edges that spoke of a singularity. And Lou seemed entirely at ease.

But on the other hand there was also something slightly unreal about the scene. It was like a Disney version of the mythical days of yore, like an illustration in a book rather than an actual flesh-and-blood village. I didn't see any people, either. Or maybe it was inhabited not by people, but by giant talking lizards. If this was Malcolm's magical creation, I supposed anything was possible.

Lou glanced back over his shoulder and danced impatiently. He was cold and wanted to keep moving. We continued on down the road toward the village. Ruts appeared in the dirt, indicating that wagons or the like sometimes passed this way. On the edge of the town a few buildings stood close to the road, not quite barns but larger than sheds, with gray, weathered wood patched so many times it looked as if they had been constructed of driftwood. Closer in, more substantial structures appeared, but still no people.

By the time we reached the base of the village I was feeling distinctly on edge. Lou was trotting happily along, however, ears perked as if he hadn't a care in the world.

Finally we arrived at one particularly large building that stood out from the others. It was two-storied, broad and solid, made of stone with thick and narrow glass windows, almost opaque, and a large front door of dark wood. The door sported an ornate brass handle, so there was at least some modicum of technology here. A wooden sign hung over it, suspended from metal chains, adorned by a crude painting of a large barrel with a tap.

Everything was amazingly detailed, from the ornate brass door handle to the wonderful smell of fresh, clean air. I'd been skeptical about Malcolm's ability to pull this off, but I was starting to believe. But not completely. I couldn't put my finger on it, but something still seemed off. At least Lou was having a good time.

"After you," I said, opening the door and holding it for Malcolm and Jackie. They hesitated and Lou bounded through in front of them. This was not the sort of place where anyone would be unduly worried about a dog in a bar.

Inside, a large room opened up with a modest fireplace at the far end and a small fire burning cheerily away inside. A medium-sized brown dog, sharp nosed and long haired, was lying by the hearth with its eyes closed. It looked up as we entered and Lou immediately walked confidently over to make dog friends.

Several wooden tables were pulled up close to the fire. Across the room, the long, rough-hewn bar would have been right at home in any Northern California logging town. Behind the bar, a middle-aged man in a brown wool shirt and apron was busy stoking up a small woodstove. He had longish hair and a dark beard, and again, would have fit right in to any logging town back home. No giant lizards were in evidence. So far, so good. He looked up as we came in and nodded a welcome.

"Sirs," he said, "and lady. Welcome, welcome. Chilly out, is it not? Can I get you something to warm your bones?"

So. He spoke English. That swung the weight of evidence over to it being a construct.

The delicious scent of hot cider, mulled with spices and what smelled like rum, wafted toward me. This place might not be the real thing, but Malcolm had got the important details down pat. My mouth was already watering in anticipation before I remembered an unfortunate complication.

"I'm afraid we don't have any money," I said regretfully.

The man's face narrowed in instant wariness, the wariness all bar owners develop from long experience in dealing with indigent lowlifes. Then he looked me over carefully, then glanced at Lou. His face relaxed and he brightened up.

"Well, you're a magician, aren't you?"

I assumed he meant a practitioner. Another twist.

"Why, yes," I admitted. "I suppose I am at that."

He looked satisfied. "Thought so. We don't get many passing through, but I mean, you have the look and all. And the dog."

When he said the word "dog," he lowered his voice and jerked his head over toward the fireplace as if perhaps I hadn't noticed Lou standing there sniffing noses with the house dog. He looked at me with an expression that was an odd combination of thoughtful and sly.

"I'm Carver," he said. He didn't ask for my name. "Maybe we can work a trade, then?"

He motioned for me to come behind the bar and lifted up a trapdoor at the far end. Wooden steps led down into the opening. There must have been a belowground level window dug out since it was dim but not pitch-dark. He started down the steps, again motioning me to follow. Whatever he was after, it didn't seem love potions were high on the list. I hesitated, then followed him down into the dark. Lou saw me at the last moment and bounded over the bar, doing his Olympic hurdler imitation. He might be distracted and having fun, but he wasn't going to let me go off into a dim hole in the ground by myself.

As soon as my eyes adjusted to the dim light I saw I was in an old-fashioned root cellar. Potatoes and carrots, turnips and onions and yams, plus vegetables I couldn't even identify, were stacked neatly or hanging in mesh baskets from the ceiling. Unfortunately, the cellar smelled like a fish tank long overdue for cleaning. I wrinkled my nose and Carver immediately took me by the arm.

"Yes! Exactly! This place is so moldy it's ruining my winter store. The smell is starting to creep up into the front room, and that's bad. Bad for business, bad for my reputation."

"You want me to get rid of the smell?" I asked.

"No, no. Not just the smell. The mold. I've tried everything, even spraying the wall with beryl root water, but nothing works. It just comes back."

"That's bad," I said. "If beryl root doesn't work, you've got a tough case here."

Pretending that I knew what the hell beryl root was made me feel a bit of a con artist, but at the same time it was kind of fun. It was like participating in an intense role-playing game.

I made a show of looking around the room, running my finger across several walls, and muttering to myself. One thing I've learned over the years is the importance of putting on a good show. If you simply do a workmanlike job without the trappings, people tend to be disappointed whether you get results or not. You can't make it look too easy, even if it is. That's why a lot of great musicians never get any recognition—they make it look so simple that no one except other musicians recognize their brilliance.

"Bones," I said solemnly. "I need bones, the older, the better."

Carver drew back. "You're not going to do any of that black magic stuff, are you? No offense."

"Why?" I said. "Does it matter?"

"I guess not. It makes me nervous; that's all. Doesn't seem natural, you know?"

"Don't worry," I said. "I never use the dark arts." He didn't seem entirely reassured, but started back up the steps.

"I think Georgie has an old bone he's about worn out," he said. I assumed Georgie was the dog I'd seen lying by the fire. At least I hoped so.

It took him only a couple of minutes to locate the bone and return to the cellar. I took it from his hand, ignoring that it was a truly disgusting object. I wrapped my mind around the deadness and let the energy flow through, meanwhile spinning around like an out-of-control lawn sprinkler, flinging lifeless pulses throughout the room. In five seconds I had coated the walls and floor so that nothing would grow there for five years. No mold. No fungus. No bacteria. I made it as sterile as a hospital operating room. Perhaps I had found my true calling. Transdimensional disinfectant specialist.

"Is it done?" asked Carver as soon as I stopped twirling. He ran his hand along the wall, where the mold was already starting to turn brown.

"Problem solved," I said.

We climbed back up the stairs to the main room. Jackie had taken a seat by the fire and Georgie, if that was who it was, was resting a shaggy head in her lap. Malcolm was on the other side of the room, deep in conversation with a man who looked like a Hollywood version of a sheep farmer.

I sat down next to Jackie, and Carver brought us two large ceramic mugs of the hot spiced cider. It was the best thing I'd tasted in a long time. He also insisted on two steaming bowls of stew, also delicious. Jackie ate hers with enthusiasm, which surprised me.

"I would have thought you'd be a vegetarian," I said, "given your other eco principles."

"I am. But sometimes I do eat meat." I let it go at that.

I looked around the room, which was almost empty, except for the sheep farmer and a lone figure at the bar. Malcolm joined the guy at the bar and struck up another conversation.

"Where is everyone?" I asked, as Carver came over to clear away the soup bowls and refill the cider mugs. "No customers? This is a bar, right? And an inn?"

"Oh, yes," he answered. "But this time of year I don't get much out-of-town business, and anyway, it's still early. People will start coming by in a couple of hours, and by nightfall there'll be a good crowd. Are you staying the night?"

I hesitated. I didn't know what Malcolm had planned, and there was that money thing as well.

"No charge," he said. "I owe you, after all." He smiled. "We have some musicians playing tonight." That settled it.

"Thanks," I said. "We'll take you up on that." Malcolm would just have to live with it.

Carver nodded and returned to the bar as Malcolm ended his conversation with the sheep farmer and joined us.

"Anything?" Jackie said.

Interesting. Malcolm was asking around, trying to get a line on . . . what? He made a little gesture at Jackie and shook his head.

"Did you help our barkeep with his problem?" he asked me, deflecting.

"I did. He offered us rooms for the night. I accepted."

"Good, good," he said, abstractedly. "Tomorrow is soon enough."

For what? I wondered.

I CAUGHT A SHORT NAP IN THE ROOM CARVER provided, then sat by the fire as the inn slowly filled up. Everyone who came in appeared to be working class—farmers, carpenters—men with rough hands and women with rough clothes. They were friendly enough, but reserved. They talked easily among themselves about work, weather, and that universal topic of humanity: who was doing what to whom. The people of this singularity, if that was what it was, were close to perfect. It wasn't long before I stopped thinking of them as pawns or window dressing and started to think of them as very real people.

Just after dark, a bunch came in carrying musical instruments and were greeted warmly. A young woman with long red hair took a beautifully polished and well-cared-for fiddle out of a battered case. She had a face that was delicate but roughened by weather, as were her hands. When she tuned up and tried a few practice runs, it was clear she could play.

A tall, balding fellow brought a set of hand drums, and a smaller guy with more than a few missing teeth came in later. He looked like he could have come straight out of *Deliverance*. He was carrying an odd-shaped case, and when he removed the instrument it appeared to be a cross between a mandolin and a lute, with five double strings. I listened as he tuned up into a modal tuning with the two bottom strings as a drone. I asked him what the instrument was called and he looked at me strangely, as I might if someone were to come up to me at a gig and ask the name of the instrument I was playing. It was a ludan, he informed me.

The three conferred for a while, agreed on something, and started off with a fast and lively air in 7/8 time, something between a Hungarian folk tune and klezmer music. The woman playing the fiddle was outstanding, playing increasingly more complex variations at each go-round. The songs they played, not surprisingly, were all unknown to me. But not entirely.

The music was familiar—an unusual blend of styles, but they were all styles I could identify. As I listened, I heard occasional phrases and even longer passages that reminded me of tunes of my own, long-ago half-done compositions, fragments of past tunes I'd started to write and then abandoned for one reason or another. It was a disconcerting feeling. Maybe Malcolm had been straight with me when he'd asked for a drop of my blood—this was certainly music that was in my blood.

But at the same time, it wasn't my music at all. Surprising twists, clever rhythmical shifts, and unconventional harmonies all played a part. It was as if they'd taken musical ideas from me but altered them and made them their own.

That gave me an idea. Perhaps this wasn't another world, but it wasn't a mere construct, either. Maybe a little of both—a world that Malcolm had accessed, but at the same time managed to change and make it somewhat his own. And a little of mine as well. He'd taken a drop of my blood and woven it into the ritual. So part of me had gone into making it what it was—and thus the almost familiar music.

Jackie had moved over beside me and was listening raptly. For a while, we ignored all the other stuff between us, the conflict and magical strife. We were two musicians appreciating a wonderful set. Every so often, after a particularly neat turn of phrase, we'd look at each other and smile, and she leaned into me occasionally in a way that made me think she wished our relationship were different.

They played for about an hour, and after they put down their instruments I sidled over and plied them with technical questions about the music. I had assumed they were mostly playing by ear, the way most folk and bluegrass players do, but instead found a wealth of musical knowledge, especially from the red-haired woman. She was delighted to talk theory and asked me what instrument I played.

"Guitar," I told her.

"Guitar?" she said. "How great is that. No one plays the guitar anymore, but I actually have one. I'm not even sure how it's supposed to be tuned. Do you think you could show me?"

Okay, so here guitarists were a rare and honored breed, as opposed to being a dime a dozen back in San Francisco.

There seemed to be a bit of wish fulfillment operating here. I told her I'd see what I could do.

"I'll be right back," she said, and ran out the door.

Five minutes later she brought back a sweet three-quarter-sized guitar and a tortoiseshell pick—a real one, of course, not plastic. I showed her the standard tuning and how useful that tuning can be for chording.

"Play something," she urged.

If you're a player and have a guitar in your hand, it doesn't take much arm twisting to convince you to perform. I considered what to play. Something of my own? I had a flashy and complex piece for solo guitar that I sometimes used as a showpiece, something I was proud of, a piece that showed off all my technical abilities without being a sterile exercise.

I was about to launch into it when I remembered another time I'd wanted to make a good musical impression. I was young, and had been lucky enough for the chance to play a tune with the late Joe Pass. I pulled out all the stops, and was rather proud of myself, truth be told. After, he looked over at me and smiled gently.

"You clearly can play," he'd said. "But there's nothing wrong with simple once in a while, you know."

Best musical advice ever. Not so bad for other things, either.

I stopped thinking and started playing, just a few random chords and runs. My ego fell away, and I was in the moment. Before I knew it I was playing a song, an old Mexican folk tune, "Blue Dove," something I hadn't played for years. A simple version, with some harmonized melody lines and chord voicings that brought out the beauty and heart of the melody. I forgot where I was and who my audience was. I just played and got lost in the music.

It was short, no more than four or five minutes. When it came to an end I looked over at Jackie, almost surprised to see her sitting there. She silently clapped her hands in gentle approval. The red-haired woman took me by the hand and smiled.

"My goodness," she said. I'd rarely received a more heartfelt compliment.

The rest of the bar had mostly ignored my playing, or listened with half an ear. That's the way it is with music sometimes, especially jazz. For most people it's background noise, so you play for the two or three people who are really listening, and that's enough. Not enough to pay the bills, however.

The other two musicians were getting antsy, as was the crowd.

"Time for us to play," the woman said. "Why don't you sit in? It'll be fun." Jackie looked at me in envy.

"I'd give a lot for a keyboard about now," she said. "But you go ahead. That's the first I've heard you play, you know."

I didn't even politely demur. I'd heard enough of their music to get a real feel for it and I was itching to join in. Not surprising, since it was also mine in a way.

They picked a tune that was clearly less complex than their usual fare, politely giving me a chance to get my feet wet. Jazz bands usually do the same, though I've heard tales of the old days when cutting contests were the rule. Even today if you show up as a stranger and push to sit in, the house band will often choose the most difficult chart they know, just to see what you've got. If you can't cut it, well, tough on you.

The woman played the theme, a catchy tune based on a harmonic minor mode. I kept things simple; this was not the sort of music that would benefit from exotic jazz phrasings. After she played a few variations, I played a few of my own, and then we traded back and forth, each time striving to outdo each other. I could have continued, using some even flashier runs and elaborations, but it's never polite to try to show up the house band. Not unless they're trying to make life difficult for you. At a certain point I gave up and nodded in surrender, picking up the changes and allowing the missing-teeth guy to show off his own chops while I held down the rhythm.

Carver kept coming by and refilling my cup. The cider gave way to wine, and then to something like mead. In my own defense, there are many cultures where it is unforgivably rude to turn down a drink, and how was I to know whether this was one of them? The longer we played, the wilder the music became. Jackie moved closer, happy and relaxed, smiling at the music. And at me. She'd been drinking almost as much as I had, and although she wasn't showing much effect from it, she had to be three sheets to the wind herself.

I also noticed Lou sitting quietly by the hearth and staring disapprovingly at me. He'd seen me drunk a few times in the past and it usually ended up with breakfast being late the next morning.

Eventually we wound down the music and all crowded around the fire. Jackie wedged herself up against me, more in a friendly manner than a seductive one. Malcolm had vanished, probably off to bed. We all talked music for a while, and then the musicians drifted away as well, leaving the two of us alone.

Jackie turned her back and leaned into me, sitting between my legs and resting her hands on my knees. It didn't feel simply friendly anymore. Not that it felt unfriendly.

"You know, I like you," she said, turning her head to look up at me. "I didn't think I would, but I do."

"I like you, too," I said. Not the most brilliant of comebacks, but I was pretty drunk.

"The fire's dying out," she said.

"We could put another log on."

"Or we could go to your room."

The firelight cast flickering shadows over her face, making her look sweet and innocent one moment and wise beyond her years the next. She was a beautiful woman in any case, and the firelight added another layer to her, making her subtle and mysterious, exotic and as fresh as the girl next door. The mugs of mead I'd consumed didn't hurt, either.

So on one level that seemed like an excellent idea, but

on another it most certainly did not. She was potential trouble, I didn't really know why I was here, I didn't know where here was, and the first rule in an unknown situation is to keep your head clear and your guard up. That first boat had already sailed, but the second part was still in force.

And she was young, almost a kid, really, though she wasn't acting like one. Jessie would probably kill me if she ever found out. What happens in Vegas stays in Vegas, but what happened here might have real-world consequences. No, tempting as this might be, it was a bad idea.

"Sure," I said. "Why not?"

We stumbled upstairs, clinging to each other. The room was cold, but there were quilts piled up on the bed. I pulled off clothes, hers and mine, and in seconds we were naked under the quilts. The length of her body was warm next to mine, and our kisses were a blend of passion, mead, and rum, all mingled together.

Alcohol has the well-known attribute of fueling desire while at the same time impairing performance. But when she put her mouth next to my ear and whispered what she wanted me to do, that was no longer a problem. She rolled over and pulled me on top of her, lips inches from mine, staring into my eyes. Her fingertips traced delicate patterns on my back, making me shiver in a way that had nothing to do with the cold. I pulled her even closer and lost myself in the moment.

My next awareness was of sunlight streaming through the window into my eyes. The shutters had been thrown open. I hadn't remembered sunlight being that horribly bright. I sat up and immediately regretted it. My head hurt, I felt queasy, a foul taste was in my mouth, and the sun hurt my eyes. Lou was nowhere to be seen.

A plain wooden table stood by the window with a jug on it. I jumped up, quickly ignoring my headache. I rinsed out my mouth with water from the jug and rubbed some on the day's growth of beard I now had.

Then I remembered. I looked around, but Jackie wasn't

in the room. I couldn't believe I'd been so reckless. Not for getting drunk and partying, but for letting down my guard. I was with two practitioners I didn't trust, in a place I didn't know and might not even be real, and I got blind drunk and fell into bed with one of them.

"I like you," she'd said, practically dragging me off to bed. Yeah, right. I'm irresistible. I'm no genius but I'm not that stupid, either, not even when I'm drunk. I'd been spelled, no doubt about it.

What was worse, in a way, was that I couldn't even recall exactly what had happened once we'd landed in the bed. I remembered kissing. I remembered the feel of her body next to mine. But that was about it. If I'm going to make a stupid mistake like that, at least I want to remember the good part. If there had been a good part.

I remembered Jackie's earlier trick with Lou and the piece of paper slipped under his harness. People, even practitioners, tend to stay in their comfort zones, to stick with what's worked before. I went carefully through all my pockets until I found a wadded-up scrap of paper with symbols scratched on it, and above, a large smiley face. She must have slipped it to me while we were listening to the music.

A smiley face. This had to be the most embarrassing spell directed against me, ever. But why had she done it? And although I do have my points, I doubt that Jackie had been seized with an uncontrollable lust for my body. When I tore up the note I felt no release of power. It had been a temporary spell and its work was done. Now it was just inert scribbling on paper. I examined my clothes again, more carefully, but found nothing.

So whatever she had planned, it must have involved getting me naked. I inspected every inch of my body that I could see, but again, nothing. A fleeting memory of fingers gently trailing across my back surfaced. I craned my head around as far as I could, but of course you can't examine your own back. And there were no helpful mirrors in the room, either—this wasn't the Marriott. But I had little doubt there was something inscribed on my back—and something that wouldn't wash off easily, if at all.

I smoothed out the top quilt on the bed and centered my talent on it, setting a basic attraction spell over it. It wasn't as strong as I would have liked since I had nothing outside to draw on. I picked up the jug of water that had been set out and balanced it carefully on top of the quilt. The idea was that the jug wasn't compatible—a full water jug does not belong on a bed. Again, rather weak, but better than nothing. I wove that difference into the quilt as well.

I lay back onto the quilt and triggered the spell. In theory, whatever didn't belong on my body would be drawn off of it and into the fabric. For a moment nothing happened, and I was starting to wonder if I wasn't just being paranoid when I felt it. A tearing sensation, just above my lower back, like a length of tape being pulled off or an old scab finally detaching from skin. So much for paranoia.

I sat up and studied the place on the quilt where I'd been lying. Three marks discolored the material, all dark red. Blood, or blood-based, I'd guess. Two of them were unfamiliar, though they reminded me of the glimpse I'd had of Malcolm's tattoos. The third one I recognized from the brief study of such things Eli had insisted on when I was younger. It was a binding rune, used for stasis or control. A simple triggering word and I'd either be frozen in place or compelled to obey on command, depending on how the other two marks interacted with it.

So. Jackie had installed an insurance plan. But now it was an insurance plan for me—when she tried to implement the spell, she'd be in for an unpleasant surprise.

It had taken a while to straighten all this out. By the time I went downstairs Malcolm was already sitting at a table in the front room eating breakfast, looking alert and rested. Lou was sitting next to him as if he'd found a new best friend. One with breakfast.

"Fresh baked bread," he said as I came in. "Have some." He held out a slice and my stomach lurched warningly.

"Maybe later," I said.

Malcolm handed the slice to Lou, who gobbled it up and pretended I wasn't there. Jackie came in from outside looking fit and happy. She looked me over critically, giving no indication anything had happened between us.

"My, but you look chipper this morning," she said.

"Please. Put me out of my misery."

She seemed to be considering it. I sniffed the air. At least this place had coffee. Carver the barkeep, now a provider of breakfast, appeared with a large mug of it, which I took gratefully.

"Ready to do some exploring?" Malcolm asked. The coffee was working its soothing magic, which was all that kept me from snarling at him.

"Where?" I asked.

"Nowhere in particular. I just want to get a feel for the place."

"You're in no hurry to get back."

"Nope. Why? Are you?"

I wasn't, especially since I still had no clue as to what he and Jackie were up to. One thing was for sure: they hadn't come here for a sightseeing tour, nor were they much concerned about my take on things. So far I'd played along, but now it was time for some hardball.

"Not really," I said. "Of course, I've got Lou. I don't have to worry about getting back. Unlike the two of you." Malcolm gave me a wary look.

"What do you mean?"

"I mean, this has been fun and all, but now I want to know why we're here. You're searching for something. You've been asking around. What is it, and why are you looking for it?"

Malcolm put on a baffled expression. He was good at it; if I hadn't known better, I might have bought it.

"I have no idea—"

"Yeah, you do. First of all, I don't understand exactly what this place is, but I don't think you created it—not by yourself. It's way too complex. I think you accessed it;

you knew it was here. I don't care how amazing that book of Richter's is; there's no way you simply read it and came up with this.

"Second, you've been hitting up everyone in the place, asking for information. So you're looking for something. Or someone.

"And third, if you don't tell me what this is really about, right now, I'll leave you here. I'll take Lou, go home, and you two can find your own way back."

"You wouldn't do that," Jackie said. "I know you better than that."

"No? You didn't have any problem leaving me in that singularity you devised, and that was a lot less pleasant than this one." I left out the trick she had pulled on me last night. "And if you did your due diligence, which I'd guess you did, then you know a little something about me. You know I've run up against dark practitioners before, and some of them are now dead. So don't try me."

I was being melodramatic, but neither of them knew me well enough to be sure of that. The stuff about dead black practitioners was true, but I'd only killed one of them. And that one had been doing his level best to kill me at the time. And the others weren't my fault at all, not really. I wouldn't actually leave Jackie and Malcolm stranded here, but they couldn't be sure of that. But Malcolm just shook his head sadly, determined to play it out.

"Mason, honest to God, you've got it all—"

I whistled at Lou. "Let's go," I said, and headed toward the door.

"Malcolm, tell him," Jackie said. "It's okay."

Malcolm looked at her with annoyance. Underneath that bland exterior was a tough individual and a good judge of character; I think he would have let me walk out and taken his chances that I was bluffing. But unfortunately Jackie had now let the cat out of the bag. Malcolm could no longer pretend to be wide-eyed and innocent.

"Come back," he said. "Sit down. This will take a while."

I was more than happy to return since I hadn't any

backup plan once I'd walked out. Plus, I hadn't had a chance to finish my coffee yet. I sat back down and waited.

"Okay," Malcolm finally said. "First of all, you're right about one thing. I didn't create this place; it's been here all along. Creating it from scratch would be impossible, even with the book. But I didn't just access it, either. I added to it—we all did, in a sense; that's what donating some blood was all about."

Score one for me.

"Almost like a wiki," said Jackie. "It's already in place, but anyone can make changes to it, and sometimes those changes can be extensive."

"So who set it up in the first place? Richter?"

Malcolm shrugged. "Who can say? It's complex enough so that it may have been created and then added to over the centuries, way before his time. But he put his own stamp on it, for sure; if you knew more about him, you would see that instantly. Richter was in love with an idealized concept of the 'old days,' of pre-industrial Europe. Although from our standpoint, his era was almost pre-industrial itself.

"So this jolly inn, the quirky innkeeper, the peasants, the casual acceptance of magic—these are all an idealized version of his own take on history. He was a great lover of tales, and a friend of Jacob Grimm, although Grimm was an old man before they crossed paths. Still, those stories of magic, ogres, and dark woods didn't all come from folklore—some of them came from Richter himself, things he'd seen or experienced, disguised as tales he'd heard in childhood."

That was what I'd been trying to put a finger on, why this world seemed not quite real, despite its detail and complexity. It wasn't Disney; it was the Brothers Grimm. That gave me a new appreciation for the place, and a warning as well. Those stories were seldom entirely benign.

"So does this place have its own reality?" I asked. "Does it continue merrily along when nobody's visiting, or does it only wink into existence when someone is in it?"

I realized that was the kind of question Eli would have asked. Not that I wasn't interested, but in practical terms it made no difference. And the answer was always the same, anyway. It is and it isn't. It depends on your definition of reality, and so on.

"Never mind," I said. "So why are we here, then? What are you looking for?"

Jackie leaned in toward me. "The book we've been using? Richter's book?"

"What about it?"

"It's only volume one."

"That implies a volume two."

"Yes. The second book is more advanced—there's enough information in it to change the world. At least the practitioner world. Richter was a brilliant man, but an odd duck and a paranoid. He was terrified the book would fall into the wrong hands and all his hard-earned knowledge would be appropriated by others."

"And by other hands he meant any hands but his own," Malcolm added. "But he couldn't bear to destroy the book, and besides, he needed it himself from time to time. So he found this place, or created it, and hid the book here."

"And now you want it."

"Of course. It's absolutely vital."

"Now we come to the crux of the matter," I said. I put down my coffee and leaned forward. "Vital for what?" Malcolm got a faraway look for a moment, then refocused.

"Well, in general, the knowledge in it is priceless," he said. Jackie interrupted, eyes bright and shining.

"With this book we can create a singularity that will make this one seem like a poorly constructed theme park. In effect, not a singularity at all. We can create a perfect world and move there—along with the brightest and best, the elite, the creative—not just practitioners, but everyone, everyone worthwhile. We can leave behind the pollution and crime and hatred that are destroying our own world, along with those who are responsible. Let them stew in the filth they've made. We'll be gone. We can make a fresh start."

"Sounds almost like the Rapture," I said. "But why didn't you just tell me about this? Why all the mystery?"

Jackie threw up her hands. "You're working for my mom, remember? What if you told her about it? What if, God forbid, you were to hand it over to her? That would be a disaster for everyone."

"She'd create her own singularity?"

Jackie snorted. "Hardly. She likes the world just the way it is. But if the legends are accurate, there's a lot of knowledge contained in that book—enough to make her the most powerful practitioner in the world. Has she approached you yet with her song and dance about changing practitioner society—using logic and persuasion?"

"She did mention something about that."

"I'll bet. Well, that's not her style. She's got other agendas, and if she ever got the book, you'd find out soon enough what she's really about. You wouldn't be pleased, believe me."

"Wouldn't the first book have been enough for her? To do what she wants?"

"Not her. She has bigger plans. Besides, she doesn't have it anymore. That's why I wiped her computer files and destroyed the original book. Why do you think she's been so anxious to find me?"

"But you gave it back," I said.

"Yes, but with some key pages missing. She won't realize that for a while."

She waved her hand at the room we sat in. "And the book is useful, incredible, in fact. But compared to the second book—well, it's the difference between a collection of folk songs and a Mozart symphony."

"I see. So you want to get your hands on the second volume and now you think you know where it is?"

"Yes," Malcolm said. "It's hidden away, but now I know its location. And we need to find it."

That was fine by me, not that I was going to let them

keep it. But getting hold of the book was a good idea—if the second book was that dangerous, it wouldn't be smart to leave it lying around. The next person who came along to pick it up might not be as responsible as me. And there would be a next person. There always is.

"One thing puzzles me," I said. "You found out where this book is pretty easily. So it's common knowledge, or at least not a mystery to anyone. This little world has practitioners in it. So why hasn't someone scooped it up already?" Malcolm gave a faint smile.

"I was wondering if you'd catch that. Well, it seems that the location isn't the main issue. It's the other obstacle."

"Which is?"

"There are guardians."

TWELVE

ON OUR WAY TO THE HIDING PLACE, WE PASSED fields of what Malcolm said were wheat and barley, with insects buzzing a pleasant chorus that made me want to stretch out and take a nap. Plenty of insects, but no biting flies and no mosquitoes. Richter's world might not be totally consistent, but that wasn't necessarily a bad thing.

Jackie chatted easily with me, acting as if the night before had never happened. Maybe I wasn't supposed to remember any of it, not even the parts that I did. Malcolm pointed out various things of interest, playing tour guide.

"Remember I told you Richter was friends with Jacob Grimm?" he said.

"What of it?"

"No one seems to know what's guarding the book. But given the fairy-tale aspect of this place, it might well be ogres or trolls or something else from folklore."

"Even a witch," Jackie said. "I don't mean a Wiccan; I mean a broomstick type."

"That, we could handle. A witch is just a type of practitioner when you get right down to it. Has anyone ever seen anything?"

"No," said Malcolm, "but that's not surprising. There are plenty of stories about those who have gone to collect the book, but no stories of those who returned. I don't think there have been any. I think whatever is guarding the book will turn out to be powerful and unusual. Richter was no simpleton."

After an hour without seeing anyone, we passed a big barn close to the road. A guy on the roof was hammering nails, but the sound was out of sync with the motion of his arm, as if he were a mile away. We were getting close to the singularity edge. As we crested a small rise, I looked into the distance and saw mountains, and they had the telltale blurring that indicates the limit of a singularity. Out on the edges, singularities start to unravel, losing internal integrity. Which also meant we were near where we needed to be, since we couldn't go much farther.

By this time the fields to the east had been supplanted by rolling woods, which grew thicker the longer we walked. About a quarter mile past the barn a path angled off into the woods. The day was bright and sunny, but the woods were dark and tangled, with trees that had grown into fantastical shapes, taller than trees should be. Fairy-tale woods. Out here on the fringes, reality was thinner.

Lou looked at the path leading off into the woods and immediately sat down. Not a good idea to go in there, he was telling me, as if I needed to be told.

"It's exactly the way it was described to me," said Malcolm. "This path leads into the heart of the woods, and then there's something in the middle. That's where the book is."

"Something?" I asked.

"Since no one who went into those woods ever came back out, no one could tell me exactly what's in there. A house, maybe. A cave. A hollow tree. Something."

I looked down the path leading into the dark forest.

More fairy-tale lore. But what had seemed like a reasonable idea back at the inn didn't seem so attractive now. Jackie wasn't put off, however. She stood impatiently, shifting her weight back and forth from one leg to the other.

"Well?" she said. I shrugged.

"Why not? We've come this far. Come on, Lou."

I took a few steps along the path and looked back. Lou hadn't budged from his spot.

"Really?" I said. "That bad?" He got up and walked ever so slowly to where I stood. He wasn't refusing; he was just making a point.

He took the lead, though. He clearly felt safer up front, no doubt figuring that the rest of us were liable to blunder into trouble that he could easily avoid. The trees crowded in closely, their bases covered with wet moss and their branches drooping over the path. No squirrels ran along these branches and no birds sang. A Grimm forest, to be sure. I'd half expected a long trek with uncanny creatures around every bend, but apart from the creepy atmosphere, nothing. And it couldn't have been more than an hour before a small clearing appeared, and in the middle, a house.

And not just any house. It was small, neatly constructed of stone and wood, looking very much like the illustrations I'd seen as a kid in the "Hansel and Gretel" story, except it wasn't made of candy and cake. A small window overlooked the area in front of the house. A plot of smooth, fine sand spread out from the front door, looking as if it had been carefully raked over and over until it was perfectly even. No footprints of any kind. Maybe Jackie had been right; maybe a grotesque witch would be appearing at any moment from around the corner, hovering on her broom.

"That's where the book must be," said Malcolm.

"You think?" Malcolm took a step forward. "Hold on," I said. "No one has come back from here, remember? Let's just cool it until we figure out what we're up against."

Nothing was visible, but that didn't mean there wasn't anything there. Lou stared fixedly at one corner of the house, then slowly turned his head as if following something moving across from one side to the other. Jackie noticed what he was doing.

"He sees something," she said.

"I would guess it's not a welcoming committee. Or if it is, it's the wrong kind of welcome."

"What is it?" asked Malcolm.

"I don't know," Jackie said. "But maybe I can find out."

She pointed in the direction of Lou's gaze and gestured subtly, too quickly for me to follow. At the same time, she sang two musical phrases, one up a Dorian scale, the other what I recognized as a Lochrian in the same key, but descending. Very elegant. Her method of spellwork made sense; like me, she was a musician after all.

A wave of pale violet rolled out from her fingertips and splashed against the front of the house, making it waver like a heat mirage. Nothing else happened; either she'd missed her target or it hadn't had any effect. She bit her lip unconsciously, disappointed and a little surprised. I had a feeling her spells did not fail very often.

"You must have missed whatever it is," said Malcolm.

She shook her head. "I don't think so. That was a broad energy wave—anything near the house should have been affected."

Lou was still watching closely, following what we couldn't see, so it was still there.

"Magical beings can be tricky," I said. "I've had some experience with them—being magical themselves, or sometimes created out of magic, they're often immune to the use of talent. Like Ifrits, but even more so. And if these are creations of Richter's, there's a good chance nothing we do will affect them."

"How do we get past them, then?" Malcolm asked. "We can't see them. We don't even know what they are."

"Talent may not affect them, but use of talent will."

"What's the difference?"

"Well, let me try something."

I wandered off the path, looking for just the right sort of tree—something like a maple or some type of conifer. I found a huge scarred pine tree not too far away, perfect for what I had in mind. I looked around for a rock to scrape off the bark. Jackie had followed me and saw what I was trying to do.

"Here," she said, offering me a sturdy hunting knife.

"You always carry one of those?" I asked.

"Always. You never know."

I scored the tree trunk with several long cuts, and waited for the resin to seep out. When it did, I gathered the essence of its stickiness, amplified it, and wrapped it up into a neat package.

"Now the sand in front of the house," I said. "Malcolm, can you break it up, make it finer?" He looked uncomfortable.

"Uh, I'm actually more a theoretician than an implementer."

"Jackie?" I said.

"Maybe. It might take me a while, though. I don't have anything handy for something like that."

Most practitioners aren't improvisers, so that was no surprise. Coming up with a spell to transform sand grains into even finer grains doesn't occur to them when preparing an arsenal of potentially useful spells.

"How about weather? Can you whip up a windstorm?"

Her face brightened. "Oh, sure. I'm good at that, if I do say so. I can even pull off a minor whirlwind, like a dirt devil."

"Perfect," I said. "We won't even need to mess with changing the sand."

She sat cross-legged with her back to a tree and prepared herself. I got the feeling she hadn't been in a lot of dicey situations before—no matter how strong you are or how good your spells may be, if you need to sit cross-legged and close your eyes before you can implement them, you're going to be in trouble.

Jackie got results, though. She sang a complex series of phrases, twisting her hands first one way, then the other. A breeze sprang up, mild at first, but turning gusty. The air thickened the way it does before a thunderstorm strikes. Then the wind picked up, swirled around, and sucked up leaves and small branches, gobbling them up into a miniature tornado. I'd done something similar at Cassandra's, but this was on a much larger scale. The tornado moved toward the house, growing stronger by the second. As it crossed in front of the house, it sucked up the sand in front like a giant vacuum cleaner.

I threw the packet of sticky energy I'd been holding back into the middle of the wind. Waves of sand blew across the house and the grains plastered themselves on the front wall like icing on a cake. I was taking a page out of the old *Invisible Man* movies, and it worked. The sand also stuck to everything else in the area of the house—including the invisible guardians, now invisible no longer.

The reason for the lack of footprints in the sand became clear. These guardians didn't walk; they slithered. Two enormous snakelike creatures, thirty feet long, thick and sinewy, writhed away from the sandstorm. They looked like gigantic sandworms, except for a couple of rudimentary appendages front and back. Nothing like this had ever appeared in Grimm.

The sand coating didn't allow for much detail, but their heads were blunt and massive, not snakelike at all. No apparent ears, but huge nostrils, now closed over with a flap of skin against the stinging sand. It took little effort to imagine rows of serrated teeth inside those bulging muscular jaws. Where there should have been eyes, nothing but smooth, sand-covered skin.

"How on earth do they see?" Jackie asked, staring. She was no longer so offhand about them.

"I don't think they do see," I said. "They can probably hear fairly well, or at least feel vibrations, but I think they mostly use smell—look at those nostrils on the front of the heads."

As if on cue, both heads turned toward us as if hearing or scenting us through the blowing sand. We all drew instinctively closer to one another, barely realizing we'd done so.

Lou alone was unfazed. He'd already seen them, and although they were massive and powerful, he knew if he kept his distance, there was no way they could catch him. He was too small and too quick.

The whirlwind died as Jackie ran low on energy, but the sand remained on the snakes, keeping them visible.

"Now that we can see them, what next?" Malcolm said, dropping his voice to a whisper.

"Whatever we decide, we don't have a whole lot of time," Jackie said. "Look what they're trying to do."

Both snakes were wrapping themselves around tree trunks, rubbing over the rough bark as if they were trying to shed their skins. The sand was stuck to their skins pretty firmly, but they were making some headway. Already I could see several sections where the sand had worn away, leaving gaps where you could see right through them to the trees underneath. It gave them an unsettling segmented appearance. Malcolm bent close and whispered again.

"If they use smell, can you block that in some way?"

"I doubt it," I said. "Remember, talent won't have much effect on them."

"How about overloading their sense of smell, then?" Jackie said. "Would that work?" I looked at her approvingly.

"Excellent idea. All we need is something with a strong scent. You wouldn't happen to have any perfume on you, would you?" Jackie looked at me in disbelief.

"You have got to be kidding. Jesus, Mason."

"Sorry. Just a thought."

I retreated along the path a ways looking for another type of plant. I'd learned quite a bit about herbal lore over the last couple of years from Campbell, my ex. I'm not sure what she'd learned from me, if anything. It took me longer than I would have liked, but I finally found something that looked right, sort of like a Copper Canyon daisy, but with broader leaves. I crumbled up a piece of a leaf and was instantly rewarded with an astringent odor, pungent and sharp.

"Hurry up," Malcolm whispered as I came up to them. "They're still trying to scrape off the sand." I crumbled up the rest of the leaves, inhaling the strong odor.

"We need to amplify the scent," I said. "Jackie, can you help?"

She nodded. "I can start with a simple melody and increase its complexity," she said. "Can you weave that into the odor?"

I could and I did. Surprisingly, we worked well together. She started out with a very simple tune and built on it, like a jazz solo. I got so interested in what she was singing that I almost forgot my part. Lou nudged me, and I used my own talent just in time, sending the increasing complexity into the crushed leaves. The odor grew stronger, at first pleasant if overpowering, then cloying, and finally overwhelming, strong enough to make Lou sneeze and retch and the rest of us gag. Unable to sing anymore, Jackie cut off the melody abruptly.

The air was still unsettled by the whirlwind Jackie had set in motion, and the pungent odor spread quickly. Soon the entire area simply reeked. Both snakes reacted at once, recoiling as if struck by a physical blow. It was bad enough for us; it must have been overwhelming for them. Stifling the desire to cough, I waved Jackie and Malcolm forward. We scuttled over toward the house like mice running past momentarily distracted cats.

"We'd better be quick about it," I whispered as we entered. I didn't know how well the snakes could hear, but I wasn't going to assume they couldn't. "That masking odor won't last forever."

Inside, the house was much like the outside promised—a fairy-tale setting, with bare floor, stone fireplace, heavy wooden mantel, a rocking chair, and even a spinning wheel in one corner.

A bookcase stood against the back wall, with leather-bound volumes crowding the shelves. Jackie rushed over and pulled out a book at random, thumbing quickly through it before putting it aside and going on to the next. Then she stopped and looked at Malcolm with something like awe.

"It's Richter's library," she said. "Everything. All his writings, things I've never even heard of. Incredible." Her voice rose in excitement, and I made a hushing motion with my hand.

"Not so loud. And we don't have much time, remember."

She stood, irresolute, book in hand. Malcolm joined her and started on the top shelf, methodically going through the books, scanning each one briefly before setting it aside and going on to the next. He was too focused to be awestruck.

I didn't think he was going to find it, though. It made no sense for the book to be there. If Richter had gone to all this trouble to hide that book, why would he then leave it out on the bookshelf for anyone to find, guardians or no?

But where could he have hidden it? The inside of the cottage was sparse, almost bare, without a lot of places to hide even something as small as a book. A practitioner has options, though, and if Richter had been the master of creating singularities, why not create another one? Something small, insignificant, folded into the larger one of the house and the world. Just large enough to contain a book, for example.

"Lou," I said, calling him over. "Can you find that book?" He glanced over toward the bookcase. "No, not there. I think it's hidden somewhere else—in the room, but not in the room." He looked doubtful. This was a pretty sophisticated concept to get across to him, smart as he is. "Just find the book," I repeated. "Not in the bookcase. Somewhere hidden. Somewhere special. Find the hiding place."

While Jackie and Malcolm continued to pore through the books, Lou darted around the perimeter of the room, then again, this time in the opposite direction about five feet from the walls. Finally he crisscrossed diagonally, back and forth. I'd begun to think I'd been mistaken when he gave a muted bark of triumph and sat down next to the spinning wheel.

Jackie shot a quick glance over at the sound, but then went back to her book search, ignoring him. When I walked over to where Lou sat, I couldn't see anything odd about the wheel or the area around it.

"Are you sure?" I asked. An annoyed bark was the answer.

I looked carefully all around and still saw nothing. I idly spun the wheel, and instantly Lou was on his feet, looking at me expectantly. Okay, I needed to spin the wheel for some reason. I gave it another whirl, slapping the top of it with my fingers to keep it going. Nothing. Lou sat back down, but continued to stare back up at me.

"What?" I said. "I'm spinning it, aren't I?"

Maybe spinning wasn't the answer. But it was a spinning wheel; what else could it do? Lou was looking more impatient by the second. He lifted one paw, then the other in succession, unable to sit still. Sometimes I get frustrated when I can't make him understand me, but he gets almost frantic when I'm the one who's clueless as to what he wants.

Then I saw the trick. It wasn't the spinning that was the problem; it was the direction. I stopped the wheel and reversed it, quickly getting it moving at a good clip. Lou jumped up and circled the wheel, nose to the ground. I still couldn't see anything, but he had no problem. He stopped dead, crouched down, and carefully extended his head out as if reaching for a treat offered by a stranger with unclear motivations. His head vanished, but the rest of his body remained visible. A second later he backed up and his head reappeared. Clutched in his jaws was a bound volume, so large it barely fit in his jaws and heavy enough so that he had to drag it across the floor.

Jackie and Malcolm hadn't noticed what we were up

to, focused as they were on the books in the bookcase. Jackie threw down the last of the books with something like a snarl.

"It's not here," she said.

I took the book from Lou's mouth and held it up. "Is this what you're looking for?"

Jackie stared at it, unbelieving. "Let me see," she said, walking toward me with outstretched hand.

"Sorry," I said. "Finders, keepers."

She smiled at me, with the knowing smile of someone holding a straight flush over your four of a kind. She walked up right next to me and sang a little trill, almost like a birdsong. I felt a faint twinge on my lower back where she'd inscribed her runes of control.

"Mason," she said with a lilt in her voice, almost as if she were singing her words. "Give me the book and sit down."

I acted like I was struggling against my own will, moving slowly and reluctantly, holding out the book to her. At the last moment, as she reached for it, I snatched it away.

"Psych!" I said.

This was childish indeed, but I didn't like being played, not to mention treated like a disposable tool. The look of pure bafflement on her face was satisfying, I must admit.

But I paid a price. When you indulge your pettiness, you almost always do. Malcolm took advantage of the byplay to bound across the room and snatch the book from my hand. He backpedaled, opened the book, and paged through it quickly.

"This is it," he said. "Let's get out of here." I held my hand out.

"Give," I said.

Malcolm's face changed subtly. His usual bland expression hardened, and I caught a flash of something.

"I think not," he said.

"You might as well give it back," I said, reasonably. "You can't get back home without me and Lou, and I'm not going anywhere without the book. We can always discuss what to do with it once we get back."

His face grew harder and he stepped back farther away. The pleasant, low-key demeanor he'd put on so far dropped away. He had the book and intended to hold on to it like grim death. Which might well be the ultimate outcome, since I wasn't going to let him keep it. Lou started up with a low growl, and I would have growled myself if I could have. I was pissed.

"Take it easy," Jackie said, moving up next to him. "This doesn't have to get nasty." But it did.

Malcolm relaxed for just a moment, and before he knew what hit him Jackie stepped back and punched him hard right above the kidneys, several times. The blows didn't seem that hard, but Malcolm staggered anyway. She ripped the book out of his hand and without a pause bolted for the door and threw it open. In her left hand she was holding the same knife I'd borrowed to cut grooves in the pine tree. She hadn't been just punching him; she'd been stabbing him. She stopped just long enough to direct a high-pitched shriek toward the snakes outside and then vanished through the doorway.

That shriek would be enough to alert the snakes to our presence in the house, even if they still couldn't smell us. And the odor that had permeated everything was fading away. I'd thought I was just getting accustomed to it, but it was definitely weaker. Those monsters outside would soon have little trouble zeroing in on us. Very soon. What in God's name had she done that for?

Malcolm staggered to the far wall and dropped heavily to the floor, propping his back up against the wall. His skin had gone gray and he didn't look well at all. I squatted down next to him.

"You okay?" I asked. He mustered up a faint smile.

"What do you think?"

Outside I could hear a loud slithering sound, like a street sweeper passing outside my flat. We needed to get out of here, and quick.

"Can you walk?" I asked.

"Maybe. Slowly." The slithering grew louder, and Malcolm noticed. "Slowly's not going to cut it, though, is it?"

No, it wasn't. Of course, I could just leave him here. You don't abandon a friend in times of danger; that goes without saying. But he wasn't exactly a friend; he'd been using me, or at least trying to. Still, I could hardly leave him to be consumed by giant snakes.

Lou had no problem with the idea of leaving Malcolm to his fate, though. He ran over to the door and danced around in a flurry of impatience. Lou's loyal to his friends, vicious toward his enemies, and neutral toward most others. Life's pretty black and white for him, and he's either selfish or practical, depending on how you look at such things. He's not the type to risk his life for a stranger, and as far as he was concerned that's exactly what Malcolm was. Unfortunately, I don't have Lou's clarity of purpose. Malcolm surprised me, though.

"You'd better get out of here," he said. "Those things aren't going to wait much longer."

"Very noble," I said. "But I don't think those snakes are coming in. I'm not sure they can. The inside of the house was neat and clean when we got here. If they'd ever been in the house, we would have found the door off its hinges and smashed furniture. I think they're programmed not to enter—just to prevent people from getting in."

"Or eating them when they come out."

"Yes, there is that." The sounds outside lessened, then ceased altogether. Lou stopped jumping around and listened, head cocked. I listened for a while longer and relaxed, if only marginally. "I think we've got some time to figure out what to do."

I had time, but I wasn't sure that Malcolm did. A knife to the kidneys is not a minor wound. I could help some with a healing spell, but that's not my forte. It would be first aid at best.

"How are you holding up?" I asked. "I might be able to help, though I'm not great with the healing arts."

"I've been better. But I don't think there's much you

can do for me—I don't react to spells of any sort."

"Really? Why not?"

"That's a long story."

"Make it shorter." He sighed.

"Well, first of all, I'm not a practitioner like you and Jackie. I have no talent."

"None at all?"

"Not a speck." This wasn't much of a surprise to me.

"So what are you?"

"By profession? A theoretical physicist." That *was* a surprise. "Both my parents were practitioners—but I myself don't have a trace of the talent. Not a whit. It was a sore disappointment to them."

"I can imagine," I said. Just like Bill Gavagan.

"Eventually I became depressed. I felt I didn't fit anywhere—I didn't connect with normal people, but with no talent I wasn't a practitioner, either. I withdrew, found a place of my own to live out by the zoo. I used to go there all the time—the sight of all those animals trapped in cages made me feel less alone—that my own situation was a universal of sorts. The animals weren't happy where they were, but they couldn't survive in the wild, either. Stupid, I know." He stopped talking for a moment as a spasm of pain hit.

"Not really," I said.

"So I finally decided to do something about it. I thought, maybe if I could understand how talent actually works, I could devise a way to acquire some for myself. So I studied theoretical physics, and believe me, once you've worked on string theory for a few years, understanding the workings of talent doesn't seem quite so impossible."

"But you didn't succeed, did you?"

"No, not entirely. I still have no talent. But I did learn an awful lot about it." He waved his hand weakly around at the room. "I got us here, didn't I? Even if Jackie had to supply the actual push."

"True," I said. "How did you hook up with her, anyway?"

"I'd developed a way to find the thin places, the areas where dimensions overlap, or where singularities exist. I used science and math to do what Lou there does naturally, though it's not nearly as effective. I started exploring, looking for answers about what they are and how they're constructed, but then I got trapped in one. I couldn't get back—everything I tried just took me farther away. I finally wandered into one that was brand-new—the one Jackie created. It was circular, with no way out I could find. I thought I'd be stuck in there forever—until you suddenly appeared."

"Oh," I said, catching on. "You're what followed me out of there."

"Yes, that was me. And once back, I was able to trace the maker of the singularity—Jackie. I figured if she was skilled enough to create that place, maybe she could help me as well. And maybe I could help her. When she told me about the Richter book, I was interested, and when she mentioned the second one, I was hooked. I saw my chance."

"Chance for what?"

"Richter was a scientist as much as a practitioner. With the information in that book, I'd be able to finally have talent of my own. I'm already close. There's no doubt I could do it, if I had that book."

"But something else came out of that singularity, too," I said. "Following you." A spasm of pain crossed his face, whether from the wound or the memory.

"Yes, I'm afraid you're right. One of the Shadow Men."

I'd never heard that term. "Shadow Men?" I asked

"That's what I call them. I've run across them before in my explorations. I don't think they have a home, not exactly—they're interdimensional beings of a sort. I don't know exactly what they are, honestly, but they can be dangerous, especially at night. Sunlight robs them of their power; moonlight feeds into it."

"Ah," I said. "Like vampires."

"You joke, but not a bad analogy, actually. They're not entirely corporeal, and they feed off life force—one of them caught me once and if I hadn't been ready for it, I'd have been dead—or at best, left to live out a short life as an eighty-year-old."

"And it was following you?"

"It was, across dimensions. And now that it's crossed paths with you as well, you might want to be careful. It can home in on specific living things once it encounters them, although it had a hard time with me. I think it's drawn more to magical ability." Another complication. How lovely.

"So Jackie hooked up with you, and decided to help you out, just because she's a good-hearted woman?" I said, skeptically.

"No, of course not. She wants the book for her own reasons, naturally. But she needed my expertise in dimensional matters, just as I need her talent to actualize spells, so we formed a partnership."

"Which she just dissolved."

Malcolm started to laugh, but it quickly turned into a coughing fit. I thought I was going to lose him right there, but it subsided, and he was quiet for a moment, catching his breath.

"Yes, indeed," he said. "She was afraid I'd take the book and get someone else to help me instead of her. We never really hit it off anyway. Of course, she had all the power, and I didn't trust her—I'm not a very trusting sort in the first place." He pulled up his sleeve to show the intricate design of symbols on his arm. "So I designed these and made Jackie implement them with her talent in exchange for my help—they keep me immune from spells and magical attack." He sighed painfully. "Never occurred to me to worry about a knife."

"An understandable oversight."

"But it has an unfortunate side effect as well." I saw what he meant.

"Healing spells are also spells," I said. "You're now immune to magical healing."

"Exactly. Ironic, is it not? Unfortunately, Jackie thinks

she knows enough now to no longer need me."

"Need you for what? What is she going to do with the book?"

"She told you. She believes she can create her own complete world with it, equal in complexity to the real thing, and move all the worthy people and practitioners there."

"Oh. So she's nuts, then?"

"Possibly. That doesn't mean she can't do it, though. Or something like that, at least."

Another slithering sound outside made us stop and listen again. I still didn't think the snakes could come inside, but that didn't prevent my heart from skipping a beat every time I heard them move. The door shook with a sudden blow, then silence again.

"But how does she expect to get back home without Lou to guide her?" I asked. "I thought that was the whole point of bringing us along."

"It was—in the event we didn't find the book. But now that she has it, no problem at all. She'll just follow the instructions." He waved a weak hand toward the pile of books that had been dumped on the floor. "And speaking of which, maybe I can find something about those snakes in one of the other books."

"Maybe. If we had a few days to sift through them. I'm not so sure those snakes will wait forever, no matter what their programming." Another blow hit the door as punctuation.

"Why can't you do the scent thing again?"

"It would be hard without a template, like those plants, and even harder without Jackie's help. And they know we're in here now—I think they hear well enough to crunch us the minute we walk out that door, even with their scenting messed up. Especially you—you're not going to be very quick on your feet, are you, now?"

But that did give me an idea. Lou was quick enough to avoid the snakes, and he could draw them away from us. They'd still be having trouble with the masking scent, but if an odor was strong enough, they couldn't miss it. What if I made him irresistible?

"If I let you out the door, do you think you could draw those snakes away?" I said to him.

Usually Lou's not thrilled at being used as a decoy, but he was pretty sure of himself on this one, so he just wagged his tail.

I didn't need help to prepare him, like I had with the leaves. I just intensified his own faint doggy odor until he was rank, like a wet dog who'd rolled in something nasty. Even my dull senses could smell him now from ten feet away. It didn't bother him, though. He seemed rather taken with his enhanced odor, as if I'd put a glamour on an average-looking man or woman.

I helped Malcolm to his feet and over to the door. When he got up he left a rather large pool of blood on the floor. He'd been putting on a good face, but he wasn't all right. Not by a long shot. He leaned heavily on me, but at least he was able to walk.

"Ready?" I said to Lou.

When I pushed open the door he flew out like an arrow. It was just as well he moved quickly, because something huge hit the ground right behind him, and another thump struck right as he dodged left.

Most of the sand had been rubbed off the snakes, but a few patches remained, enough to provide a bizarre quilt of floating patterns that were hard to make head or tail out of, though they did give a sense of where the snakes were.

Lou of course could see them, or at least sense them in a fashion. If not, he would have been toast. He lit out for the edge of the clearing, but just before he reached it, stumbled and fell. Malcolm drew in his breath with a hiss. It was an instinctive reaction, one of concern for Lou's safety. I started to think a little better of him.

"Don't worry," I said. "It's his standard wounded-duck routine; he doesn't want them to get discouraged and give up, so he pretends he's injured himself. Right before they reach him, he'll miraculously recover just in time."

The bits of sand floated through the air and the grass flattened down as the snakes glided toward him like giant sidewinders. Lou was now hobbling desperately toward the cover of a thicket, and his pursuers were gaining rapidly.

"Time to go," I said, pulling Malcolm along.

We headed in the opposite direction, Malcolm hobbling like Lou, except for real. The snakes, fixated on catching Lou, so tempting and close, didn't even notice us as we slipped away.

As we reached the far side of the clearing I heard a hiss of triumph from the snakes as they closed in, then a series of mocking barks as Lou evaded their final lunge and disappeared into the safety of the dense underbrush.

Malcolm and I stumbled in the opposite direction, with me taking up most of his weight as he leaned heavily on me. We'd managed a fair distance when Lou appeared from out of the bushes, stinking worse than ever but looking very pleased with himself.

"Nice work," I said. "Now get us home."

He looked at me for a moment, making it clear that in his opinion it would be just fine if Malcolm collapsed and we left him to rot, but he gave the canine equivalent of a shrug and trotted purposely down the path. Then, just as suddenly, he stopped and cocked his head sideways. A moment later I heard it, too, a snapping of bushes in the distance, along with a scraping sound like a road grader run amok.

Of course. I'd enhanced Lou's dog smell so the snakes would go after him. He'd lured them away from the house, as planned, but once they were free of the overpowering scent of the place, their senses were as sharp as ever. They could probably smell Lou from a mile away. No problem for him; he was quick as ever. But pretty soon they'd be close enough to scent me and Malcolm as well, and we weren't quick at all. Malcolm heard the crashing in the distance about the same time I did.

"Problem?" he asked. His tone was light but his voice was weak.

"There's always a problem," I said. "Haven't you learned that?"

It usually takes Lou a while to trace a path out of a singularity, and at the speed those things were traveling they'd be on us long before then. I could remove the enhancement from Lou, but the snakes were close enough now that it wouldn't matter. Or I could leave it on and he could lead them away from us again, but by the time we finally got out of here it would be too late for Malcolm. He needed to get to a hospital, and soon, to have a chance.

And now it was getting dark. Evening was closing in, and as difficult as it might be to avoid invisible monsters in the day, it's worse at night. They can still accurately locate you by smell but you can't even see where you're going. The chances of your getting away then approach zero.

Time for another plan. Fifty feet off the trail I spotted a deadfall: tangled branches, logs, and a new growth of tough-looking vines. It might work. I called to Lou.

"That way," I said, pointing. "Into that pile of logs, and wait."

He dutifully trotted off. He was getting used to my seemingly pointless directions by now. When he was younger he would have at least given me a questioning look, but these days he had more faith. He usually won't balk unless I ask him to do something that might result in unfortunate consequences if something goes wrong. He's not stupid.

He wormed his way into the middle of the brush, and as soon as he did I pulled the odor enhancement off him and focused it into a tight knot. Which I then buried in the middle of the deadfall.

"Back here," I yelled. "Backtrack on your trail."

This was something he understood. He followed his path back exactly, even the little twists that kept it from being a straight line. When he reached his starting point; I said, "Okay. Jump now, as far as you can. To me."

He gathered himself and leapt upward and outward, traveling a good eight feet before his paws hit the ground again. So now the snakes would follow his trail into the deadfall, where the intense odor that remained would convince them he was hiding in there, like a rabbit gone to earth. They'd tear the deadfall to pieces, spurred on by the overpowering odor that was concentrated in the brush, with a trail that dead-ended. Convinced that Lou had to be in there, it would take them a good while before they gave up.

We started off again and by this time I was half carrying, half dragging Malcolm. We hadn't gone far before I heard a thrashing commotion behind us. The snakes had found their prey, or so they thought.

Lou followed his usual routine when slipping between interdimensional spaces—turning, backtracking, speeding up and slowing down, as if he were weaving a silent musical pattern in space and time. I was having trouble keeping up. Malcolm could barely stay on his feet, totally out of it, and by now I was actually carrying him most of the time. My shirt was splattered with his blood and I was getting seriously worried.

The foliage and the weather started changing, bit by bit. We cut through some bushes after one final turn and I recognized the path we were on. We were back in San Francisco, on the side of Mount Davidson.

"We made it," I said, hardly able to believe it.

Malcolm didn't answer. I slipped his arm from over my shoulders and laid him down carefully. He flopped over bonelessly, head lolling to one side. I'd made it, but it didn't look like he had. Lou came over, took a brief sniff, and walked away, sitting down about ten feet away and turning his back. He doesn't like death.

I checked Malcolm for vital signs. Nothing. Then I searched with my talent for any spark of life, but I knew it was hopeless.

"Fuck!" I said. "Fuck."

Lou glanced over and yawned. None of his business, he was telling me. You mourn your friends, not your enemies.

I pulled Malcolm off the trail, covered the body with leaves and brush, and threw some dirt over it all to keep the leaves from blowing away at some inconvenient time. I laid an aversion spell over it all. If the body was found, as it surely would be just lying there unprotected, there'd be questions. I didn't need any extra complications, or anyone in authority looking for his acquaintances.

But there was no reason for anyone to be tromping through the damp and muddy brush off the trail, and even a mild aversion spell would cause eyes to avert and glide right over the area. With any luck, it would be a year before the spell wore off totally, and by that time, hopefully, there'd be nothing but a bunch of worn bones. I looked down at the mound of leaves and dirt. A sad ending for a man who had once traveled through dimensions, buried under a bunch of scattered leaves, alone and unremarked on a prosaic hillside. But I guess to him it hardly mattered.

THIRTEEN

I DROVE HOME, MORTALLY DEPRESSED. TRUE, Malcolm wasn't really a friend, but death is death, and it drained all the joy out of making it back safe and sound. It had been a fine adventure, a tale worth telling, but it's all fun and games until someone gets an eye put out. And I could hardly believe what Jackie had done. Sure, she was a black practitioner, but she was a musician, for God's sake. Musicians don't stab people without a moment's hesitation or remorse. Which is a silly thing to say; of course they do, as much as anyone else. But I still thought of her as being like me, in a way. That kind of sloppy thinking could get me killed, though.

A quick stop at a newspaper rack told me it was only the next day, so for once the time flow in the singularity had run parallel to the real world. By the time I got home it was fully dark. I checked to make sure my wards didn't show any signs of tampering and opened the front door.

Instead of going in, Lou stopped and looked around warily. I listened, but didn't hear anything. For a minute we both stood outside the door, like unwanted guests. Then he shook himself and trotted inside.

I was hungry, but the fridge didn't hold much of interest. I dug around and came up with some cheese, so I made a couple of grilled cheese sandwiches, the old-fashioned way, in a frying pan with a plate on top of them to provide the proper weight for grilling.

I usually made two, cut them in half, and gave Lou one of the halves with the other three halves for me. It's one of his favorite treats, certainly more interesting than kibble even if processed cheese isn't good for him. Or for me, I guess.

But instead of hanging around the stove, he hopped up on the table by the window and kept watch, on the alert. I opened it a crack to help his senses of hearing and smell. When I slipped the sandwiches on a plate and he didn't even acknowledge it, I knew something serious was up. He cocked his head again as if not sure of what he was hearing, but he was hearing something. I listened as well, but heard nothing.

Sometimes I use a trick where I can see through Lou's eyes, though it's disorienting and leaves me with a violent headache afterward. In fact, it's so disorienting that it can render me incapable for a while, so it's only a last resort. But I'd never tried it with his hearing. That shouldn't be so bad.

Another problem with the vision spell was that I could only see whatever Lou was looking at, and occasionally he'd be scanning the treetops for invading squirrels when I wanted to check out something very different. But sound is not dependent on a sight line like vision; I'd be able to hear anything he could, far beyond my own dull sense of hearing.

I put down the plate and concentrated, trying to focus on sounds I could identify, like the noise of traffic barely audible in the distance. Then I shifted my consciousness into the psychic realm, ran a feedback loop through Lou, and felt the familiar dislocation as his sense of hearing became mine.

It wasn't as bad as the vision spell. It didn't make me sick to my stomach, but it wasn't as useful as I'd hoped, either. I could hear amazingly well, not just better, but a quantum leap in ability. I could have heard a squirrel rustling a branch fifty yards away. But there was a problem—hearing is not accomplished just by the ears; it's also done by the brain. Babies can hear perfectly well, but they can't make much sense of the sound waves coming into their ears. Like sight, hearing takes interpretation as well as a perceptual filter to focus and block out irrelevancies—we're constantly ignoring things we hear unless they have importance to us.

So what I heard was astoundingly clear, but it was also a cacophony of sounds from all directions, some soft, some loud, but none of them identifiable or even comprehensible. It was worse than useless.

I tried to focus on the familiar traffic sounds I'd heard before, hoping to find purchase. At first I couldn't distinguish them from the wind blowing through tree leaves, but eventually I got a handle on it. I blocked out the myriad distractions until I could distinguish the sounds of engines revving and tires hissing on pavement.

I narrowed my concentration, ignoring farther-off sounds and listening only to those right outside my window. I fine-tuned, until I could hear footsteps going by, not pausing. A can rolling in the gutter. Branches rubbing together in the bush near the window. And an odd sound, not quite a rustle, familiar but hard to identify. Movement of some sort, something large, but with no footfalls, and a steady, smooth quality like a wave on sand.

When I suddenly recognized what I was hearing, it was enough of a shock to break my connection to Lou. My hearing went back to normal, and although Lou now had his lip curled back in a snarl, I no longer could hear a thing. But I knew what I'd heard. A snake.

How was that possible? There was no way either of

those things could have followed us back into our world, much less have tracked us to our home. But then again, what did I know about it? Anything was possible.

We'd probably be safe inside—the flat was protected by excellent wards, and if the snake was unaffected by them, there was still a strong front door and a back door as an escape hatch if worse came to worst. But if it tracked me here, it could track me anywhere. And waiting for it like a rabbit in a bolt-hole was not an attractive option.

Then I came to my senses. This was absurd, a fantasy constructed from nothing more than weariness, paranoia, and a peculiar sound I'd heard. There was no giant snake waiting outside for me. But that didn't mean there wasn't something out there.

I eased quietly over to the closet and took out the katana Victor had given me. I was sure it couldn't be the snakes, but even so, I still had a faint nagging doubt. I'd seen impossible things before. And magical talent might not work on them, but a sharp blade certainly would. Besides, there was something elemental and satisfying about the feel of the sword in my hand.

I motioned to Lou, turned out the lights in the house so I wouldn't be backlit, and cautiously opened the door. Lou slipped out silently, an invisible shadow. I closed the door behind me and stood there until my eyes adjusted to the darkness. The light streaming from windows of houses along the street provided enough illumination to see fairly well. Lou pressed up against my leg in warning before he crept toward the tangle of bushes that crowded the side of the house. I moved in behind him, sword held at the vertical. Anyone passing by who saw me would be sure to call the cops.

We made it all the way to the back of the house without incident, but Lou didn't relax so I didn't, either. He turned around and headed back toward the street, more slowly this time. He stopped and half crouched, every muscle quivering.

"Mason!" a voice called.

I glanced up and saw Jessie standing on the sidewalk fifteen feet away. She took a step forward, and as she did there was a flurry of movement by the side of the house as something moved and Lou pounced. A sudden thrashing, and then Lou was out in the open, jaws clamped down on the neck of a huge snake. Naja. So I hadn't been entirely mistaken. I'd just had the wrong snake in mind.

For a moment Lou had her, but he's only twelve pounds and Naja weighed as much, if not more. And she was reptile strong, a cord of banded muscle. She twisted around and threw him off his feet, and as he went down his grip loosened just enough for her to sink her fangs into his shoulder, just above the harness.

Lou gave a yelp and let go, springing back out of range momentarily. For a moment he faced her defiantly, and then his legs buckled and he staggered drunkenly sideways. Naja reared up in the iconic cobra posture, towering over him, almost as tall as I was, preparing to strike again.

I sprang forward, turning the edge of the katana blade toward her as I moved, drawing it back for a strike of my own. Naja was no rope hanging from a beam, but I'd still slice her in half if it was the last thing I ever did.

I heard Jessie's footsteps running toward me but paid it no attention. She'd never get to me in time. Then she yelled again, louder.

"No! Don't!"

If it had been a threat or a cry of anger, it would have had no effect on me. But it wasn't; it was a scream of fear and anguish, raw emotion and desperation. That made me hesitate a fraction of a second and that was all it took for Naja to pull back just enough so I couldn't be sure of a clean strike. Victor always says I'm too soft and that it will end up getting someone killed someday. Maybe he's right.

"Don't," Jessie cried again. "It was an accident. She didn't mean it." By now Jessie was almost on top of me.

"I can still save Lou, but it's got to be right now. He's only got seconds before he's gone."

It might be a ploy, but I didn't even have to think. Any chance was better than none. I lowered the sword and knelt down next to Lou. He tried to walk to me but his legs wouldn't work anymore and he toppled over in slow motion. His tongue lolled helplessly as he lifted his head and stuck out one feeble paw in hopeless supplication.

"Goddamn it," Jessie said, bending down next to me.

She muttered a few words and ran her hands over Lou's body. His eyes glazed over as he went limp. She'd thrown a stasis spell over him, effectively suspending his entire metabolism as well as the working of the poison, and her spell was a lot better than mine would have been. Mine tends to create a cold, brittle hardness; hers left him warm and still soft.

Naja had backed off a good ways, looking apologetic, if a snake can be capable of showing emotion. My first thought was to get Lou to Campbell; she was probably the only one with the ability to heal such a mortal wound. But Campbell was a thousand miles away, dealing with a sick mother again. I didn't hold out much hope Jessie could help—black practitioners are not known for their skill and dedication to the healing arts.

"What happened?" I said. "What the hell are you doing here, anyway?"

Jessie sighed. "You didn't answer any of my messages again, so I left Naja to keep an eye on the place and let me know if you showed up. I guess Lou saw her as a threat, and when he went after her she reacted."

"By trying to kill him?"

"It's instinct. She's an Ifrit, but she's also a snake. Snakes strike when they feel threatened."

I knew what she meant; in the same way, Lou's very much also a dog, but that didn't excuse what happened.

"We need a healer," I said. "Do you know anyone good?" Jessie shook her head.

"A healer won't help, although I've got some skill in that area myself. A cobra the size of Naja has enough venom to kill a full-grown man in fifteen minutes. Something the size of Lou? Sixty seconds, at most. I'd guess about half that time elapsed before the stasis spell, so when I bring him out of it, he'll have only thirty seconds, not nearly enough time to help him."

I got a cold feeling in the pit of my stomach. Jessie was still kneeling next to Lou, now reaching into her purse, searching around until she found what she was looking for, a compact brown leather case. She opened it and took out a syringe and a small vial of clear liquid.

"Antivenin," she said.

I'd seen that case before. So it wasn't drugs after all.

"You seem prepared," I said.

"It's not the first time something like this has happened. Naja's not aggressive, but she can be skittish."

She said this matter-of-factly, as if it were the most natural thing in the world. She really was a black practitioner.

"Has the antivenin worked?" I asked.

"No one's died yet." That was reassuring. "But then, no one as small as Lou has ever been bit before. And I don't know how an Ifrit will react." Less reassuring.

She filled the syringe and found a spot on Lou's foreleg. With the skill of a trained vet, she eased the needle in. She paused just long enough to take off the stasis spell, and as soon as Lou took a long, shuddering breath, she pushed the plunger home. For long seconds, nothing happened; then Lou gave a weak cough and managed to stagger to his feet. Jessie passed her hands over him again, doing something subtle. It must have been some type of healing work, because he took a couple of steps before he sat down again, exhausted. She looked at him closely.

"He'll be all right, I think," she said. "He's amazingly tough, which is no surprise. He'll need at least a day to recover, though."

I picked him up and carried him inside, being careful

not to cut off his tail with the sword in my other hand. He hates being carried and even struggled feebly, which was a good sign.

Jessie followed me inside, but Naja didn't. Mistake or not, that would have been a bit much. Lou climbed shakily up on the bed, where he immediately curled up and closed his eyes. Jessie saw my worry.

"He'll be okay. Honest, I know what I'm talking about."

I cleared off the uneaten grilled cheese sandwiches and put on some water for tea. My nerves were too shaken for coffee. Jessie wandered around, looking but not touching. At least she had the sense for that.

I handed her a cup of tea without asking and we sat down at the little kitchen table, facing each other. Then I got back up and took the disks out of the bedside table drawer.

"I got Richter's book back," I said, handing them to her. "And another disk."

"How?" she asked.

"Not important. Jackie has a copy, of course."

"Where is she?"

"That, I don't know. But she also has volume two now."

Jessie snorted. "The famous second volume? Sorry; that's a myth, a holy grail for black practitioners. It doesn't exist."

"I've seen it."

"Impossible. Where?"

"Again, irrelevant. But I held it in my hand."

"Did you look through it?"

"No. There wasn't time."

"So you don't actually know what the book you held was. It could have been a cookbook for all you know."

"I highly doubt that."

But I did have a moment's doubt. She was right; I hadn't so much as cracked it open for a peek. It might have been anything. Then I remembered where and how it had been hidden. Jessie was silent for a moment.

"If this is true, then things are even worse than I thought," she said.

"Why? Is this second book all it's cracked up to be? Would it be that much more dangerous?"

Jessie was staring off into space, her tongue flicking in and out of her mouth in an unconscious imitation of a snake. She did not look happy.

"That would depend," she said, slowly. "If I had such a book, or Victor, for example, we'd instantly become the most powerful practitioners on the planet. On the other hand, if someone less experienced got hold of it, it could spell disaster."

"Disaster for who?"

"Anyone who had hold of it."

"Like Jackie?"

"Or you." She smiled to let me know she was joking, but of course she wasn't. "But also, disaster for everyone else. Any object of great power is always dangerous; that's inherent in the very nature of power. And unintended consequences can be dreadful, as I'm sure you know. Remember what I said about thin places. Imagine what would happen if those places ruptured completely."

"Okay," I said. "Not a good thing. I understand. At least you have your own book back, sort of."

"I need Jackie back as well. She doesn't know what she's playing with."

"And the second book?"

"Screw the book. It's Jackie who's become the danger. You seem to be doing a good job of locating her, but not such a good one at holding on to her once you have."

"I'm not much of one for kidnapping," I said. "Even if it's a family affair."

Jessie looked at me sourly. "I was wondering when you'd find that out."

"I'm smarter than I look." She didn't make the obvious comeback, being in no mood for banter. "Why keep it a secret, though?" I said.

"It was irrelevant." She stared down at the floor, showing some embarrassment for the first time since I'd met her. "Besides, it's no one's business. How would it look? I run a corporation, I run much of the black practitioner community, but I can't even control my own daughter?"

I shrugged. "Whatever. But I'm still not comfortable simply handing her over to you, just on your say-so."

"You don't have to hand her over," she said. "Just let me know where she is; that's all." She looked at me shrewdly, then turned her head to stare at Lou, who was out like a light. "I know you have reservations. Who wants to rat someone out and turn her over to an angry black practitioner, no matter what she may have done? But it's for her own good, believe me. And ours. Can I count on you, Mason?"

"Sure," I said. "I can always be counted on to do the right thing."

She didn't like that answer, but then again, if she didn't, she shouldn't have asked that question.

"You know," she said, "maybe you're not the best person for this job after all. You don't seem to work that well with other people."

"I work very well with people. I don't always work well *for* people."

"That's a shame; you have potential." I'd heard that before.

"Sorry," I said. "I'm like Popeye the Sailor Man." She looked at me blankly, not getting the reference at all. "Never mind." She shrugged and opened the front door to leave, then stopped.

"I hope Lou will be all right," she said. "I'm really sorry about that."

"Yeah. Me too."

After Jessie left, I was ticked off. It was weird—I wasn't even working for her; I was spying on her. But I still was annoyed at her criticism. It was like finally deciding to ask out a woman you weren't even sure you were that interested in and having her turn you down. Or auditioning for a band, realizing they sucked and you didn't really want to play with them anyway, only to have them choose someone else.

I checked on Lou, who was sleeping deeply, though every once in a while he'd twitch and moan in his sleep. Morning had to bring a better day. It could hardly bring a worse one.

FOURTEEN

NEXT MORNING LOU WAS BETTER, BUT STILL NOT his old self. I had expected him to bounce right back; he's done that so many times that I unconsciously think of him as being invulnerable, which he's not. In fact, it's a miracle he's still alive, considering some of the fixes I've gotten us into. So when Campbell called, it was like a gift from the gods.

"I'm back," she said. "Did you miss me?"

"More than you know," I said. "Lou's hurt. He's okay, sort of, but he's not really right."

"What happened?"

"He was bitten by a cobra." There was a moment's silence.

"What?"

That one word accused me of all kinds of things. Or maybe I was projecting; most of Lou's injuries have been due to me when you get right down to it.

"A cobra," I repeated. "He got some antivenin, but he's not doing so well."

"I'll be right down."

"No, I'll come up there. He's well enough to travel." Campbell's healing powers are strongest on her own home turf.

"Okay," she said, "but you'll have to stop by Mama Yara's botanica and pick up something there."

"Will she sell to me?" The only time I'd been there, Mama Yara had treated me with great suspicion, like a dope dealer faced with a suspected undercover narc.

"She will if you tell her it's for me. Have her call me if there's a problem. I need something called Devil's Tongue, and if she doesn't have any of that, some Madras Thorn. A couple of ounces of either."

After I hung up I sat down on the bed next to Lou. He looked up without much interest.

"Campbell's back," I said, with false heartiness. "We're going to visit her. Pancakes!"

Lou's favorite food in the world is bacon, but Campbell's pancakes run a close second. Besides, he really likes her. Usually he'd be jumping in the air with excitement, but all I got now was a polite half wag of the tail.

"Come on," I said. "You can sleep on the way up there."

We stopped on the way at the botanica over on Church Street. Lou showed no inclination to leave the van, so I left him to sleep. The botanica display windows hadn't changed a bit, except for being dustier, perhaps. The same odd mixture of Miracle candles, religious icons, dolls, and African art sat in their usual places. The pale blue floor, covered with astrological signs, was still faded and patchy and hadn't been swept in a while.

Not a customer in sight. The tinkling of the doorbell brought Mama Yara out of the back room, and when she saw who it was she stopped short. She was wearing the same baseball cap she'd had on the last time I was there, and I still couldn't begin to guess her race or age.

"I'm Mason," I said. "A friend of Campbell's?"

"I remember you," she said. She gave no indication if that was a good thing or not.

"I need something. It's for Campbell." She waited silently, not helping. "Something called Devil's Tongue?"

"I have none," she said.

"What about Madras Thorn?"

"Snakebite?" she asked, showing some interest for the first time. I nodded.

"My dog, Lou."

She gave a slight smile. "Ah, I see. Your *dog*."

I didn't know quite what to make of her, but I knew Campbell held her in high esteem. She adjusted her cap and walked toward the back room she'd just come out of.

"I might have some Madras Thorn," she said, stopping in the doorway. "How much?"

"Campbell said a couple of ounces."

"Wait here," she said.

It took a while and I wandered around the store, finding something that hadn't been there the last time, or that I'd missed. A glass display case with perfectly bleached little skulls, ranging in size from what I assumed was a mouse up to that of a fox. At least, I hoped it was a fox. It was just about the size that Lou's skull would have been.

Mama Yara came back in carrying a large plastic baggie filled with dried, broad leaves. She glanced toward the front door as if to make sure no one was coming in. Again, the dope dealer vibe.

"Madras Thorn," she said, handing it to me. "Tell Campbell Live Oak can also be useful."

"Thanks," I said, taking the baggie. "How much do I owe you?"

"Five hundred dollars," she said, without blinking.

This was looking more like a dope deal every second. I got the feeling I was being ripped off, but then again, I don't know the going rate for Madras Thorn.

"I don't have that much on me," I said, trying to act unsurprised at the price. "Do you take credit cards?"

"No," she said. Impasse.

I thought about just walking out with the baggie, and if Lou had been in immediate danger, that's just what I would have done. But I didn't want to ruin Campbell's relationship with this woman.

"I can go to the bank and get the money," I offered. I thought I had enough in my account.

Unexpectedly she smiled again, and this one was genuine.

"I'm just messin' with you, dearie. That'll be twenty dollars, and say hello to Campbell for me."

CAMPBELL LIVES IN A SMALL CABIN UP IN SODA Springs, close to Donner Summit off of I-80, about three hours from San Francisco in a good car. Closer to four hours in my van. She's the best healer around—not a practitioner, but she has definite talents. She has personal power, and in addition knows more about the healing properties of plants and herbs than anyone.

We'd been together for a while, but it hadn't worked out. Bad timing. We were both different people back then, and if we'd met now, I think it would have worked. But it's hard to recapture that sort of thing. It feels like you're going backward instead of forward. Still . . .

When I finally pulled up in front of her cabin I barely recognized it. I hadn't been up here for a while. It was the same familiar place, but plants of all varieties had grown up around it, right to the very door. A definite fire hazard, should a forest fire sweep through the area.

There were plenty of plants I recognized, but a lot I'd never seen before, too. It had become a virtual arboretum. Campbell heard my van, stepped out on the front porch, and waved a cheery greeting.

Instead of bounding up to her as usual, Lou climbed slowly out of the van and walked slowly over to greet her. A look of concern crossed her face as she bent down next to him.

"Not feeling so good, eh?" she said. "Not to worry—we'll get you back to normal in no time, good as new."

Lou looked at her hopefully, like when you have a terrible case of the flu and the doctor tells you you're going to be fine. You believe it, but you can't really comprehend such a thing actually happening. I handed her the Madras Thorn.

"Perfect," she said, examining the leaves. "Did Mama Yara give you any trouble about it?"

"No, not at all."

"Hmm. She must like you. She's not usually the welcoming sort unless she knows someone well."

"I'd hate to see what she'd be like if she didn't like me."

Campbell ducked inside and came out lugging a small hibachi grill and a squirt bottle. She placed the leaves where the charcoal usually goes.

"No potions?" I asked. Usually she steeps her herbs and comes up with vile concoctions that need to be swallowed.

"Not with this. Remember the first time we met? I need to burn the leaves, and Lou needs to inhale the smoke, as much of it as he can. Can you get him to do that?"

"The way he's feeling, I think he'll go for anything."

Campbell stirred the dried leaves around until they were loose, with plenty of air in between, then lit them in several places. They caught immediately, turning red, then white around the edges, and curling up as the flames consumed them. She waited until they were burning strongly and misted water from the squirt bottle over the grill. A cloud of smoke plumed up, astringent but not unlike the smell of autumn bonfires.

"Lou!" I said sharply. "Breathe the smoke."

He looked at me doubtfully and turned to Campbell for confirmation. It's not that he trusts her more, exactly; he just has a good idea about who is the expert in these procedures.

"Do it," she said.

He bent over the grill, took a whiff, and not surprisingly immediately started choking. He backed rapidly away, but Campbell spoke in a sharp tone, totally unlike her usual voice.

"Again," she said. "Now!"

He dutifully stuck his muzzle back in, this time taking a considerably larger whiff. He backed off again, coughing and retching until Campbell swept him up in her arms, holding him tight. A surge of energy flowed from her into him. She believed strongly that the specific plants she used were responsible for the healings she performed, but I still thought it was more about her and her abilities than about any vegetable matter. The truth probably lies somewhere in between.

She put him down and he staggered away, sneezing uncontrollably. I went over to him but he dodged away, apparently blaming me for the ordeal. But I noticed he dodged, and rather quickly at that. Campbell noticed it, too.

"I think it worked," she said. "Come inside. He could use some water, I'm sure."

After drinking almost half a bowl of water, Lou wandered back outside. He might not be back to normal quite yet, but he was well on his way. Campbell made some tea, and handed me a cup.

"How's your mom doing?" I asked.

"Okay, I guess. I got her through a rough patch, but she's losing the battle. Cancer is a nasty, nasty thing."

"That it is."

"I feel so helpless. It's ironic, isn't it? I've dedicated myself to becoming the best healer possible, and now she's dying and there's nothing I can do for her."

"I find that hard to believe. I'm sure you help a lot."

"I do, some. But here's the thing—my abilities are based on enabling the body to heal itself, like any holistic discipline."

"Only your abilities are stronger and quicker—you have a gift, and it goes beyond the purely natural."

"Maybe, although our definitions of what's natural differ, if I remember. But anyway, here's the ironic part—I need a basically healthy body in order to heal someone effectively. The stronger and healthier someone is, the easier it is to work with. Like Lou and the poison—I've just returned him to his natural state.

"But with cancer, the whole system is compromised. There is no natural state to return to, unless you could go back in time. I can help, I can extend her life and her good days, but the absurd truth is that the vile chemo she's getting does her as much good as anything I can do."

She shook her head sadly and stared out the window for a moment.

"It's a mess," I said, using one of the meaningless phrases we all speak when there's nothing really to say. She stared out the window awhile longer, contemplating, then took a deep breath and came back to the here and now.

"Enough of that," she said. "Want to tell me how Lou ended up getting bitten by a cobra? I mean, even for you two that is just out there."

"You'd think," I said. "But that's actually the most normal thing that's happened lately."

"That can't be good."

"It's not."

I went through the whole saga of the last couple of weeks, starting with the day Jessie called me into her offices and offered me a job. Campbell settled into her familiar listening position, elbows on table, head resting in the vee her hands made. She'd finally cut her hair, not short, but shorter than I usually like on a woman. It looked good on her, though, accentuating her features and emphasizing their strength. She'd put an almost white streak in her blond hair, a fashion statement that softened her usual outdoors persona. She was in better shape than I was, and always had been.

"Wow," she said when I was finished. "You've been a busy lad."

"But as usual, not getting very far."

"Hmm. First of all, I think you underestimate Jackie."

"Tell me something I don't know."

"I don't mean it quite that way. She's young, attractive, and female. So I think you assumed that she's basically a decent sort—that's one of your blind spots, you know."

"I do know. So how can it be a blind spot?"

"You forget. Over and over. But here's the thing: I've known people like her. The Wiccan community is very focused on the health of Gaia, Mother Earth. No surprise there. But as things have gotten worse, ecologically speaking, there's been some real anger developing. And a desire to do something about it, whatever the cost."

"I thought Wiccans were all about peace and compassion and balance."

"Yeah, just like Christians. People are people, no matter what their beliefs. And when those beliefs are strong enough, concern and compassion can morph into something very different. Look at the jihadists—they're capable of doing the most vile of acts, totally convinced that their actions are not only justified, but blessed. Same goes for any religious zealots. And there are people in the eco movement—mostly not Wiccans, thank God—who are just as fanatical."

"You mean 'thank goddess,' don't you?" I said, resurrecting an old private joke. It got me the same look of exasperation that it always had.

"So you get the tree spikers, and the ones who set fire to housing developments, and the ones who trash animal research labs. I'm not so sure I disagree with that last one, but you get the point."

"Sure. But eco warriors aren't blowing up thousands of people."

"No, but some of them would if they thought it would help their cause. What are a few thousand people compared to saving the entire planet?"

"Well, that's all academic. She's not going to be doing anything like that."

"You think not? That's because when you see a jihadist, you view them as dangerous, even if it's unconscious. Bearded men, speaking a strange language, with strange motivations."

"Sounds kind of like Eli." She ignored me.

"But Jackie, now, is one of us. She's part of our own tribe, so to speak. She's us, not them. She could be just as dangerous as any terrorist, but emotionally, you don't see her in that way."

"Maybe, but what's your point?"

"My point is that you need to take her seriously, and be very careful. She's already killed someone, remember? I'd say she's capable of almost anything."

Lou interrupted, sticking his head back inside the cabin door, looking much like his old self.

"We should go," I said. "Thanks for your help—I don't know what we'd do without you."

"Well, it was good to see you, anyway. Try stopping by sometime just for a visit."

"I will. And I do see what you're saying about Jackie. I'll keep it in mind."

IT WAS GETTING DARK BY THE TIME WE GOT back, but I randomly drove around with Lou anyway, trying to get a whiff of Jackie. I didn't have much hope; she knew Lou was a tracker, and she knew I'd be looking for her. But maybe she thought I'd met my sad demise back among the giant snakes, and was no longer worried or shielding. But no such luck.

Until we were headed home. I took the Third Street route from downtown, trying to cover as much territory as possible, just in case. I was about to turn onto Cesar Chavez, heading back to the Mission, when Lou snapped to attention and barked, staring straight ahead. I continued on, throwing glances at him, and when I passed Cargo Way his head swiveled around, all the while keeping his gaze on an invisible point somewhere down that street.

I flipped a U-turn and turned into Cargo Way, following it until it dead-ended at a parking lot at the edge of the bay. A long and broad jetty, maybe a half mile in length stretches out from the parking lot. The jetty itself is a mini park of sorts for the adventurous. A dirt path nestles between the rocks piled up on either side.

Nobody went there after dark, of course; it was secluded and dangerous in the nonmagical sense. Magical creatures are not the only predators in San Francisco by any means, or even the most common. In any large city you have a lot more to fear from someone who wants your wallet than from something that wants to drink your blood.

I got out of the van and walked over to where the jetty stretched out into the darkness of the water. The parking lot had no lights, but the streetlights from Cargo Way behind us provided some illumination. And the moon was up, not full, but it helped. Lou sat down next to me, facing the jetty.

How interesting. Apparently Jackie was wandering around on the fringes of the city, away from anyone and everything, not bothering to shield herself even though she knew I'd be looking for her. Maybe she thought I was dead. Maybe she needed the water or this specific place to actualize her intentions. Maybe finding her was random luck. But I didn't think so.

Not that it mattered. If she had lured me down to this secluded spot with bad intentions, so what? What was I going to do, go home? I hated playing out a game on my opponent's home field, but if you go looking for someone, you seldom have a choice.

I jerked my head at Lou and started off down the long path that leads into the bay. The temperature remained constant, but it seemed colder the closer I got to the end. About fifty yards from the end of the jetty, I stopped. I could barely make out a figure standing there, waiting. I assumed it was Jackie, though from this distance I couldn't even tell if it was a man or a woman.

The moon had risen over the water and its weak glow was in my eyes, making it even harder to see. I stopped out of reflex before I moved forward again, trying to keep an eye on what I could see of Jackie as well as everything else around me. She was expecting me and I'm sure she was prepared, probably with some nasty surprise. The path had narrowed and the water was now only a few yards away from me on both sides. It wouldn't have been much of a surprise to see some ocean denizen launch itself out of the deep, flop onto the narrow path, and seize me in powerful jaws.

She'd chosen this place for a confrontation, and that didn't bode well. The jetty ended in the waters of the bay; there was nowhere else to go from there, no escape route. Which meant Jackie wanted to end it here and now, and also meant she was confident in her ability to do so. Richter's book must have given her something special, an edge that would prove decisive. I wasn't that worried, at least not about the book. Knowledge and power are useful tools, but they're not always the deciding factor. I'd fought practitioners and other things more powerful than me before this, and I'm still walking around. I got within thirty feet of her before she spoke.

"That's close enough, Mason," she said.

"Good to see you, too, Jackie. You know, if you wanted to talk, you could have picked a more pleasant spot. A warm café, for example."

"I have no interest in talking," she said.

I didn't believe her. If she hadn't wanted to talk, she would have launched an attack at me as soon as I was close enough.

"Why did you have to kill Malcolm?" I said. "He wasn't a bad guy—he certainly didn't deserve that."

"Malcolm's dead?"

"Yeah, that sometimes happens to people when you stick a knife into them."

She seemed genuinely taken aback, though it was hard to tell at that distance by nothing more than the light of the half-moon. Then she shook her head.

"I don't believe it," she said. "You don't know anything

about it. It was just a distraction—he's far too tough to die over a little stab wound."

"I was there when he died."

She looked at me blankly. "I guess I was wrong, then."

"Yeah, and what now? You kill me, too, so you can keep hold of that stupid book?" I paused. "Gosh, and I thought we meant something to each other." She almost smiled.

"Yes, you were very clever about that. You had a good time, though, didn't you? But you don't understand. I'm not a bad person. I don't like doing some of the things I have to do. But it's the survival of the planet we're talking about. Even if some people have to die. That's a horrible thing, but sometimes it's necessary."

"And then what? You and your friends enjoy a pristine world without the rest of humanity's fuckups to ruin it?"

"Yes. Clean air, clean water, mountain streams teeming with silver fish. All of the creatures of the goddess living—and dying—in harmony with nature. It's not about us; it's about Gaia. I can do it; I really can. I have the book now. All I need is some time to study it. But I won't be around to enjoy that new world anyway, any more than you will."

"Why not?"

"Richter was a black practitioner, remember? Something this big requires more than a simple drop of blood. It requires a blood sacrifice, a willing one; in fact, the enabler of the spell that creates it has to give up her life.

"And why wouldn't you just let me have the book, anyway? Why won't you leave me alone? I don't want to hurt you. I like you, honestly. It's not like what I'm doing is anybody else's business. They'll still have their miserable world to destroy, just like always."

She did have a point. If what she was saying was true, why not leave her alone? Except, she was willing to kill to achieve her goals, and that's never a good basis for a fresh start in life. And the law of unintended consequences would surely kick in. I wasn't sure exactly what would happen if

Jackie were left alone with her precious book, but I was willing to bet it wouldn't be good.

"Sorry," I said. "I just don't think things are as simple as you think they are."

"I know. And you'll keep hounding me until you get the book back. That's why you have to go. I'm sorry. I really am. I hate this."

This sounded like she was screwing up her courage to the sticking point, about to launch an attack. I set myself, ready for anything. I liked having the water so close; water is fluid and powerful, and makes a great metaphor for movement and transformation, applicable to many uses of talent. I gathered in the essence of the rippling, ever-morphing waves, and waited patiently.

Jackie crouched down and I tensed, but I couldn't detect any burst of talent coming from her. A small glow flared, as if she had struck a match, and a few seconds later a trail of fire arched into the night sky and explosions of color blossomed out. She'd set off a skyrocket.

At first I thought it was a diversion, meant to distract my attention away from the real attack, but there was no attack. She slipped away over the end of the jetty, disappearing behind the piled rocks. I didn't understand what she was doing; there was no way out from there.

Except of course there was. A moment later I saw a sea kayak moving away from the rocks, heading out at a good clip, with Jackie paddling strongly. How utterly simple—I pride myself on coming up with elegant nonmagical solutions to conflict, but this time I'd had the tables turned on me.

But what point was there in luring me here only to escape at the last moment? Lou couldn't have even found her in the first place if she hadn't wanted him to. And what was the point of the skyrocket, for that matter?

Lou whipped his head around at the same moment the answer dawned on me. It hadn't been just a random firework; it had been a signal. Now I saw the point of the jetty.

There was no way back except the way I'd just come, and without a doubt there was something waiting there for me.

The moon was a little higher and at my back as I looked toward the shore, making it easier to see. I could barely make anything out, but Lou was focused alertly, so I followed his sight line and looked where he was looking. Not too far from where we stood, the reflections on the water of the bay vanished momentarily, a blank spot in the dark night. It moved slowly as I watched, like an enormous shadow.

A shadow. Night. Moonlight. A Shadow Man.

She had learned how to call them. That book must be a useful one indeed. What had Malcolm said? That they fed on life force, and how he'd driven one off, but nothing about how he'd done it.

It moved in closer, black as ink, blacker than the night, and it did indeed have a vaguely manlike shape. My first thought was to fight it with light—that was the logical thing. But I was far away from the city lights and didn't have much to draw upon. I need to work with my environment; I'm not much good at creating things out of nothing. Victor could have whipped up a blinding fireball, I'm sure, but Victor wasn't here.

I used the power essence of water that I'd stored up while facing Jackie and temporarily turned a section of the jetty into a liquid mass, incapable of supporting weight. The shadow flowed over it without hesitation, the way a shadow can move over any one surface as easily as any other. It was closer now, and I tried setting up an energy shield. I hated to do that since it takes so much out of me to keep it going, but I needn't have worried. It flowed through the shield as if it weren't there. I hadn't really expected it to work; previous encounters had taught me that otherworldly entities are rarely directly affected by talent, and this thing was no exception.

Fifty feet from us, it stopped, assessing the situation. It liked what it saw. I thought about enhancing the far-off streetlights on Cargo Way to provide illumination, but the light would be weak and I had no reason to think it would act as a defense anyway. Not that I had time to do anything.

Once it had made up its mind, it moved, and it moved fast. Watching it glide slowly toward me, I had foolishly assumed that was its natural mode. But it was on me in two seconds, covering the last fifty feet between us in no time at all.

I automatically threw up my left arm to block its rush, and it latched onto me. Immediately my arm went numb, like it had fallen asleep, and I felt weariness creeping into my bones as if I'd just finished a twenty-mile hike. I grabbed at the creature with my free hand, trying to dislodge it, but there was nothing solid to get hold of. Not entirely corporeal, Malcolm had said. I wished I'd thought to ask him how he'd driven it off. It was like trying to fight a chocolate pudding; there was some resistance to its flesh, but my hand passed right through it and its substance closed up behind as my hand traveled through.

Of course, it couldn't hurt me, either, not physically, but it didn't have to. All it needed was to hold on to me in its unpleasantly sticky fashion and I'd soon be drained of life.

I panicked. I had no time; the longer it held on, the worse it would be for me. Even if I managed to ultimately defeat it and beat it back, I'd have lost years off my life, with what was left of my youth stolen away forever. I tried to tear my arm away from it, at the same time ineffectually beating at it with my free arm.

About this time Lou decided to sink his teeth into the thing's leg. It may have presented a pudding-like consistency to normal folks, but Ifrits are not your everyday folk. He got a firm grip with his teeth and shook his head back and forth. The creature didn't make a sound; I'm not sure it could. But it let go of me and reached toward Lou, although I can't imagine what it thought it was going to do to him. That doughy consistency it possessed couldn't hurt him, and I don't think it could suck any of the life out of him, either.

But Lou certainly possessed the ability to hurt the Shadow Man. He gave a vigorous shake and then suddenly fell back, losing his balance. I thought he'd lost his grip, but instead he'd managed to tear off a good-sized chunk from the creature's leg. He spit it out onto the dirt path and it lay there like a sticky bit of black felt. But not for long. It started to move, oozing back toward the creature, a grotesque inky amoeba trying to rejoin its parent.

At the same time, Lou went into a violent paroxysm of coughing and retching, just short of convulsing. He might have been able to hurt the thing, but in its own way it had hurt him as well. He was out of commission for a while. It looked like I was going to have to deal with it on my own after all.

The sight of the crawling piece of protoplasm reminded me of something. Amoebas react to stimuli. In the lab, the easiest way to demonstrate this is with a mild electric current. And the streetlights I'd dismissed were powered, of course, by electricity.

The creature had temporarily abandoned its attack on me, concerned more with reabsorbing its missing part. I reached out to the distant lights, almost out of my range, and felt the trickle of current that powered them. I gathered it up, and looked around for something to push it into. But we were out on the jetty, with nothing but rocks and sand and water, and I needed metal. The Shadow Man had finished reattaching and turned back toward me.

I dug in my pocket and came up with three quarters and a dime. Not the ideal metal to hold an electric charge, but this wasn't precisely electric—like all my workings of talent, it was an analogue and a metaphor. I didn't have much of the current, but I concentrated everything I had into those coins. They vibrated in my hand, the pent-up power waiting to escape.

Before the Shadow Man could close with me again, I flung one of the quarters at him, unleashing the power at the same instant. It hit him squarely in the chest and sizzled when it did, sparking like a live wire. It jumped back, confused, and I threw the dime. The coins weren't lethal, not by any means, probably not even dangerous to it, but they hurt the creature and that surprised it. They were something completely outside its experience.

I had only two quarters left, but I walked toward it confidently, and as the Shadow Man backed away I threw another. It sizzled satisfyingly again as it struck. The Shadow Man moved farther away, more quickly this time. I pushed forward; in selling a bluff, confidence is essential.

I ran toward it as if eager to get as close as I could, and threw the last coin. I almost missed, which would have been a disaster, but it struck it right in the head, or what passed for a head. I actually got close enough to almost touch it before its nerve failed. At the last moment it turned tail, gliding back toward the parking lot at top speed. I made a show of chasing it for a few more steps before stopping and turning my attention to Lou. He had stopped coughing and was sitting with his head down.

"You okay?" I said.

He coughed a couple more times and got to his feet. I don't know what that thing tasted like, but I'll bet it was disgusting. It must be a problem when your only weapon is your teeth and things you run into are made of stuff you don't even want to touch, much less eat.

Right where we'd been struggling, an oily black residue coated a small area of the path. I kicked some dirt over it, kneaded it into a messy paste, scooped it up, and dumped it into my jacket pocket. It might not be of any use, but it couldn't hurt. Victor or Eli might be able to use it to extract some information about the thing.

We walked back down the path to the parking lot. Lou acted unconcerned, which was a good indication the Shadow Man was really gone, but that didn't keep me from peering suspiciously at every dark and shadowed area. Two minutes later we were headed home. Another fruitful and productive evening.

FIFTEEN

IT TOOK ALMOST AS LONG TO RELATE THE EXPERIENCES of the last few days to Eli and Victor as it had to experience them. It didn't help that Eli interrupted me after every sentence with a question, which led to another question and so on until I finally didn't know the answer.

"Part of my arm is still numb," I said. "I can use it fine, but it feels weird."

"Have you called Campbell?" Eli asked.

"Not yet. I thought it might just go away."

"Or maybe get worse and spread," Victor said.

"Point taken. In the meantime, what are we going to do about Jackie? I'd just as soon forget about her, though she did try to kill me. But with the second book, she's liable to start really messing with the edges of our reality."

Eli nodded. "She doesn't appear to be amenable to reason, does she? She'll be trying experiments, and experiments can have unintended consequences. Like the Shadow Man. And have you forgotten Rolf's attempt to create an Ifrit? That had quite an effect on us all, did it not?"

"True."

"And that experiment was on a much smaller scale than what she's contemplating. Think about the implications of that for a moment. Things could easily get worse, far worse."

"I get that. But if this is dangerous, why hasn't Jessie been straight with me? She's still holding back, I can tell."

"Maybe she's trying to protect her daughter. Maybe she wants that second book for herself."

"And what am I going to do about this Shadow Man? If it's zeroed in on me, I don't want to be looking over my shoulder every time I go out at night."

I pulled out a paper bag. In it was the dirt and residue I'd collected from the Shadow Man. A paper bag is better than a plastic one if what you're dealing with is damp or sticky. A plastic bag traps organic compounds as they break down, and whatever is in it eventually becomes a useless, foul-smelling sludge.

"What's in the bag?" Victor asked.

"I collected some of the Shadow Man's leavings. Maybe we can use them to make a protective shield."

"Good thinking," Victor said. "You're learning." Victor could make even a compliment sound condescending. "But I think I've got something simpler that will work just as well."

He walked over to the huge safe that sits in the corner of the study, placed the bag inside, and rummaged around in it for a moment. The safe is where he keeps magical props, rare crystals, elixirs, arcane volumes of magical lore, and pictures of his family for all I knew. As well as firearms of various types—Victor likes to be prepared for any and every eventuality.

"I don't think a gun would be of much use," I said. "It would be like trying to shoot silly putty."

"Agreed," he said. "Take this." He handed me a slim black object the size of a cigarette pack. Two silver prongs jutted out of one end. "You slide the safety switch forward and push the button."

"A stun gun?"

"Exactly. It doesn't like electricity, you said."

I held it at arm's length, pushed the button, and was rewarded by a bright arc between the terminals and a satisfying electrical buzz. This was just the ticket.

"All right," said Victor. "Now that's out of the way, we can concentrate on finding Jackie. Eli?"

"If she's gone to earth, I doubt we can locate her. She's a strong practitioner, and if she's shielding, we're not going to find her. But we can make a device that will alert us if and when she tries to implement a major spell." Eli joined Victor by the safe and peered inside.

"Did you get the idea from Richter's book?" Victor asked.

"Exactly. We'll need to modify it some, of course—Richter used blood for everything, sometimes quite a bit of it. Blood was more available back then." He stuck his head in a little farther. "We'll need some mercury, copper filings, a battery, of course, for an energy analogue . . ."

His voice grew muffled as his head poked in deeper still, and when he backed out he had several items in his hands. I watched with interest as Victor and Eli proceeded to assemble a makeshift magical energy detector. The crux of it was a thin shim of metal, pointed at one end, floating on the surface of a bowl of mercury. The bowl itself had crude runes drawn around the rim on the outside, just below the lip.

"That's done it," Eli said. "All that's needed now is to sensitize the metal. It needs to be balanced in a state of tension, between opposing forces."

"That will take Mason's assistance, then," Victor said.

"Glad to help," I said.

I always felt a bit intimidated when Victor and Eli were busy whipping up a complex spell or operation that was beyond me, like I was a slow child who could only watch in wonder. And I was sometimes envious of Eli's knowledge and intellect.

But I also wondered if Eli ever felt angst of his own, though he never shows it. He hasn't got the intrinsic power to implement the spells he crafts—he has to rely on others to carry out that part. Like a basketball coach who plots out the strategy, sets the defense, and knows just where everyone should be and exactly what they need to do in order to win, he's invaluable. He can even teach proper stance and footwork, helping players reach their potential. But he has to rely on those players, because he can't do any of those things himself. It would be hard to avoid some measure of envy and even jealousy as he watches those amazing athletes fly through the air and knock down the shot.

Victor, now, was a player coach. He could do it all, but I wasn't jealous of him in the slightest. Maybe that's because he's not a very happy man and I wouldn't want to be him.

"The easiest way to do it will be for Victor to try to move the metal shim, while you try to keep it in place. Or vice versa."

"I'll move it," said Victor.

That was fine with me. Victor's natural inclination is toward action, while I'm more comfortable playing defense, thwarting things. I reached out to the safe, something with the absolute essence of holding things in place, and bound up the metal of the shim with the metal of the safe.

"Anytime," I said.

Victor nodded and concentrated on the bowl, subvocalizing. He put his hands together and unexpectedly sent out a bolt of force, visible as green light. That was just for show; it had nothing to do with the efficacy of the spell. It hit the metal, which trembled but stayed resolutely fixed in its spot.

The whole point was to balance the opposing forces; if he had managed to flip the shim out of the bowl, we'd just have to start over again. But he hated to "lose" at anything. He muttered something and a slight smile appeared on his face as he raised his hand again.

"Victor," Eli said warningly. "That's perfect. Fix the balance in place."

Victor nodded again and spread his hands apart, speaking words aloud this time, as if that was what he'd had in mind all along. A different sort of energy rolled off his fingers and splashed over the shim.

"Okay, ease up," he told me, and I released the binding energy. Eli bent over to examine it.

"Perfect," he said. "Any release of magical energy within a radius of fifty miles will cause it to react. The faster it moves, the more energy has been detected. An ordinary spell will only move it at about the speed of the second hand on a watch; the energy involved in accomplishing a major shift such as what Jackie plans will cause it to spin like a top."

"When's the last time you saw a second hand?" I said. "You need to join the digital age. And what about direction?"

"A simple energy pulse will stop its motion, and the shim will point to the source."

I smiled. "Very neat. So you've established a device that shows the direction and scale of a powerful release of energy, based on a design by Richter. In other words . . ."

"Please, Mason," said Victor. "Don't always go for the obvious."

"Sorry. But you say this can't locate Jackie, not precisely. So I'm not sure how useful it will be."

"That's true," Eli said. "But it will give us some warning and an idea of the scale involved. At least we won't be caught unawares. It's better than nothing."

"I guess."

"Also, I imagine Jackie won't try anything too complicated at first. She'll do a few practice runs—I know I would, and from what you say she's not dumb. So it might give us some additional opportunities to locate her."

"And in the meantime?"

"In the meantime, we wait."

I WOULDN'T HAVE BEEN THAT SURPRISED IF WE never heard from Jackie again. It would be easy to screw up on a spell from the book, especially now that she didn't have Malcolm to help her. Powerful spells that get out of hand can kill a practitioner, which would solve our problems. But no such luck.

Meanwhile, I still had a life, or a semblance of one. I finally got off my butt and scored a corporate gig with Novasca, one of the big Bay Area biotech companies. When I was young and foolish I looked down on corporate gigs. I was an artist. Well, I'm still an artist, but corporate gigs pay five times what you'd make in a club. During the dot-com boom when money was pouring out of spigots, it was more like twenty times, but those days are gone forever, and getting a corporate gig these days is a coup.

But my arm wasn't getting any better, worse if anything, and it could end up affecting my playing. I finally went up to see Campbell, which I should have done right away. She examined the arm and listened with interest as I told her about the Shadow Man.

"I've heard of this before," she said. "Not exactly the same, but close, part of the old legends my grandmother used to talk about. They steal your life, and even if you get away, they leave their mark."

"Old legends are often based on real things," I said. "I never used to believe that, but I do now."

"Better late than never," Campbell said. "We'll make you into an expert in ancient wisdom yet."

"Doubtful."

She held up my arm where the sunlight lit it up. "Look."

At first I didn't see anything, but when I viewed my arm at a certain angle I saw what she meant. There were five faint marks on my forearm, like shadows of fingers, almost unnoticeable.

"Hmm," I said. "The mark of the beast."

"Not so far off. But the cure is simple, once you notice them. You just have to clean them off."

"I have showered in the last few days, you know."

"Yes, you're delightful. But soap and water won't do it."

"Steel wool?"

"Don't tempt me. No, it's rather simple, as I remember. You need . . . Well, I can't quite remember, but I know someone who will." She pulled out her cell, made a quick call, and talked briefly to the person on the other end.

"Yes, now I remember . . . No, it's not just academic interest . . . Yes, I'll tell you all about it later." She put the cell away. "Just as I thought. Very simple, and very logical, actually. Ginger, cayenne pepper, horseradish root, thistle, sea salt, and lavender."

"Lavender?"

"I know, that doesn't make much sense. The lavender might be unnecessary, a holdover for an old recipe, but there's not much point in experimenting. I'm already doing one substitute—I don't have any horseradish root, but I do have some powdered wasabi, which should work just fine."

As she gathered together the ingredients I asked her what else her grandmother had told her about the Shadow Men.

"Not much. She called them the darklings—creatures of the night, bogeymen of a sort. But there was one thing—whenever they appeared it was supposed to be a sign of a change coming."

"Like what?"

"She wasn't clear about that. I don't think she knew, just repeated what she'd heard. 'A big change,' she'd say. 'An ending and a beginning.' "

That made sense. Jackie was screwing around with dimensions, and if the Shadow Men were interdimensional beings, the very presence of one could be a predictor of a coming upheaval.

Campbell scrubbed my arm with the paste she'd made, the marks faded, and sure enough the feeling started to come back almost immediately.

"Thanks," I said. "I owe you. Again."

"Anytime. How are you feeling, other than that?"

"Okay," I said. "I've been having a lot of headaches lately, though. That's not usual for me."

"Let me see," she said.

She walked behind and put a hand on each side of my head. Her hands were warm and pulsing with energy as her fingers probed gently. I closed my eyes and concentrated on the feel of her hands.

"Hmm," she said. "You're just fine, as far as I can tell."

"Why the headaches, then? Stress?"

"I doubt it. You've had stress before—lots of it. Have you ever had headaches?"

"No."

"I think it's something outside you, not inside. Something's affecting you."

"You mean like a trigger?" I asked.

"Not exactly. All sorts of things can trigger a headache, but that just sets off what's already there. I'm thinking something more direct, something you have no control over, like if your furnace was leaking carbon monoxide."

"I don't have a furnace."

"You know what I mean."

"Yeah," I said. Campbell grabbed me by the arm.

"Oh, and I almost forgot. I want you to take a look at something. It might interest you."

She led me over to the garden of plants that had grown up almost to the front door and pointed toward the middle of them.

"What am I supposed to be looking at?" I asked.

"You see that plant in the middle, there? The one that's peculiar?" I gave her the kind of look she usually gives me. She laughed, bent down, and showed me which one she meant. "Look at this."

"Looks like a plant," I said.

"Yes, but it doesn't belong here. It's like a yarrow, but it's not, and it just shot up overnight. I've never seen anything like it and I've seen a lot of plants."

That was an understatement. But this was significant.

A plant that wasn't quite normal, like an odd squirrel or a peculiar cat. Whatever was going on, it was spreading.

"Interesting," I said.

ANOTHER BONUS OF A PRIVATE PARTY GIG WAS that I could bring Lou along. Which was important; with all the magical mayhem going on lately, a problem could crop up anytime.

The company had rented a downtown club called Park Place for the evening, and since the head honcho was that rarest of creatures, a jazz buff with money, I was in. Originally it was just going to be my trio: me, Dave from Oakland, and Roger Chu on drums, but at the last moment I called Bobby, the organ player. A three-way split is better than four, and he's basically an asshole even if he can really play, but I knew he was hurting for money and hadn't been playing much. He'd burned too many bridges with too many people the last few years. But I felt bad for him even if it was his own fault, and anyway that B3 sound is a big hit with crowds—maybe we'd get another gig out of it.

We set up early, and even by that time half the crowd had a good buzz on. There must have been four hundred people there, with an open bar. Even in a down economy Novasca had had a good year—they'd patented some new drug, or discovered a virus or something.

Park Place is basically a rock club, and they have a raised stage, a large semicircular space with all kinds of room. For once Bobby's Leslie speakers wouldn't be blaring in my ear, drowning out Dave's bass. A tiered balcony runs all the way around, from almost over the stage to over the bar in back, with stairs at each end.

"This is more like it," said Dave. "No more tiny little clubs for us—we've hit the big time."

"Yeah," I said. "Just don't give up your day job."

Actually Dave's the only one of us who doesn't have a day job. Roger works at a skateboard shop, though he's getting a bit old for that—all of nineteen. Bobby's been fired from as many jobs as he has from gigs, due to his sparkling personality and congenial demeanor. I don't think of working for Victor as a day job, but without the money it brings in I'd have trouble making rent each month.

Dave, however, is a fine player who's as comfortable playing electric in a funk band as he is playing stand-up in a jazz setting, and good bass players are always in demand. There just aren't enough of them. Guitar players, on the other hand, are a dime a dozen.

Plus, he has the look—urban black hipster, ready to get down and party at the drop of a hat. The right look is important to a band's success—an unfortunate truth. People who see him grooving up onstage don't know he's a family man with two kids and a wife who keeps him on a short leash.

We played mostly jazz standards for the first set, nothing too out there, and mostly up-tempo tunes with a swing: "Well, You Needn't"; "Four on Six"; "Straight, No Chaser"—stuff like that. Toward the end of the set, people's alcohol intake had risen along with the party mood, so we played some jazz/funk tunes like "Walk Tall," taking full advantage of the B3. We couldn't play any real funk because Dave hadn't brought his electric bass, but we got the crowd dancing anyway. And Roger was my secret weapon. He could get people dancing with nothing but a drum solo.

During the break, I altered the set list to include more tunes people could dance to, including some tunes not usually seen as jazz. Jazz purists may scoff, but they sometimes forget jazz was originally dance music. Which doesn't mean you can't play ballads; it just means that after you strip away all the altered chords and clever riffs, the heart and soul of jazz is all about movement. Duke said it better: "It Don't Mean a Thing If It Ain't Got That Swing." A deceptively simple statement. Bobby of course was annoyed at the changes.

"What is this crap?" he said, poring over the list. "I

thought we were here to play jazz. This shit is way boring, way uncool."

Dave shook his head and flashed a grin at me. He was used to Bobby.

"Cashing his check for the evening might mellow him out a little," he said.

"I doubt it."

You'd think after the financial and creative mess Bobby had got himself into, he'd be slobberingly grateful for the gig instead of carping about the set list. He'd never change. I couldn't complain, though. I know what he's like, but I'd hired him anyway. People are who they are. But his complaining gave me an idea.

"You want interesting?" I said. "Tell you what. I'll write out a chart for us." I scribbled for a few minutes and handed him the chart. "Chords are simple, but the time's a bit tricky."

It was indeed. I'd written down a variation of one of the tunes I'd heard back at Carver's tavern in Richter's singularity. It was in simple 7/8 time, but divided oddly and switching every eight measures to a differently accented rhythm. Bobby was a great player with real heart and soul, but technically a bit weak. He'd have to scramble to keep up. Dave would have no problem, and Roger has ears the size of elephants—one pass through and he'd be grooving with it and adding his own spin.

I saved the tune for the last of the set. If you get people engaged with the music, they'll listen to anything, at least for a while. When we started off with it, people stopped dead in midswallow, put down their drinks, and looked up at the bandstand. They'd never heard anything like it and couldn't decide if they approved or not. But the melody was strong, and when we settled in, people started nodding their heads and smiling. Bobby was lost at first, which served him right, but he caught on after a while and found a repeating riff that really worked.

I was having a great time until I started feeling queasy. The room blurred, like I was experiencing double vision.

Bobby lost the time completely and even Dave, who's rock solid, stumbled. So it wasn't just something happening to me; it was something happening to the room.

My vision blurred even more, and the faces in the crowd flickered and shifted. The room shrank and became smoky. In the back of the room I now saw a fireplace with brightly burning logs superimposed over the bar that I knew was really there. Shadowy figures dressed in heavy wool shirts moved languidly through the mist.

I was back in Carver's tavern, back in the singularity, except I wasn't, not entirely. But it was growing stronger every second, and Park Place was receding into memory. The music ground to a halt as we all stopped playing and the singularity receded for a moment, then strengthened. My attention wandered as I stared into the fire, now closer and more real, giving off waves of heat. The party crowd noise dimmed, replaced with the quiet hum of conversation.

A volley of sharp barks brought me out of it. I looked down with some surprise and found Lou up onstage, angrily barking his head off. Everything rushed back into focus—Park Place, the bandstand, Dave and Bobby and Roger, the crowd.

A roar of laughter surged up from the audience as Lou continued his barking, not sure if I was all the way back yet. One of the crowd yelled out, "Everybody's a critic," and almost fell off his chair at his own wit. Actually, it was pretty funny. I bent over the mike.

"We'll be taking a short break so I can beat my dog."

That got another laugh from the crowd, this one kind of nervous. They weren't entirely sure if I was joking or not. Besides, some of them had experienced that same dislocation. Not as bad as ours, because they were on the floor of the room looking up at the stage. From their vantage, all that had happened was that the music got weird for a moment and the band suddenly grew dim. But they just attributed it to the lights and the alcohol consumed. What else could it be?

When we sat down for our break Bobby wasn't laughing, though.

"Some motherfucker dosed my drink," he said. "I almost wigged out in the middle of that tune."

"You too?" said Dave. "I thought I was having a stroke or something."

"You guys all right?" I asked. "How are you feeling now?"

I knew the answer, of course. Dave stretched carefully and turned his head from side to side.

"Okay, I guess. That was weird, though. You didn't feel anything?"

"Just a little woozy for a second. Maybe it was a gas leak or something."

"Maybe." Dave looked dubious.

"That was no fucking gas leak," said Bobby. "We got dosed."

"Maybe it wore off."

Bobby looked at me as if I was nuts, but didn't pursue it. He'd seen a couple of things he shouldn't have in the past, things involving me, things he couldn't explain. So he's understandably a bit wary of upsetting me. I'm probably the only one he feels that way about, which is why I can keep his antisocial tendencies in control most of the time.

"I didn't notice anything," Roger said.

That figured. Roger lived in a world of his own, one made up almost exclusively of drums, gigs, and skateboards. He didn't do any drugs. It wasn't that he had anything against them; he once explained that he didn't see the point. They didn't have much of an effect on him; that was all.

"Dave, can I borrow your cell phone?" I asked.

When Victor picked up I asked him if the Richter meter had shown anything.

"Definitely. There was a huge surge about twenty minutes ago. How did you know?"

"Things suddenly got a bit thin. I might have helped trigger it, at least as far as it concerned me specifically."

"How thin?"

"The veils of reality as we know it were lifted from my eyes."

"Yeah, I hear that can happen. Keep an eye out. When things get thin is when visitors push their way through, remember."

We played one more set, but our heart wasn't in it. My head was pounding again and both Dave and Bobby were nervous, waiting to see if anything else odd was going to happen. Luckily by this time the party was in full swing, and we could have been playing kazoos for all they cared.

After the gig I handed out the checks and loaded up my van. I was a bit on edge, not exactly jumpy, but close to it. I'm not much of one for superstitions, but over the last few years a lot of unfortunate complications had occurred immediately after gigs.

It wasn't until I'd unloaded my gear at home that I realized there was nothing to eat in the house. I didn't feel like going out again to eat, so I walked the couple of blocks to one of the ubiquitous corner markets that dot the city. Half of their shelf space is devoted to alcohol, and fresh fruit and vegetables are scarce and not all that fresh. But it's fine for emergency rations, though about 50 percent higher than supermarket prices. That's how they stay in business. I didn't begrudge them their markup; they provide a service for stoners and other late-night denizens, for which you pay a premium. That's all.

On the way back to my place I felt a sudden twinge in my head. Mildly painful, but more than that it was weird, like a soundless explosion. It was like what I imagined a small stroke would feel like. I stopped, a bit worried, but it seemed to have passed with no effect. Still, it was unsettling. Especially after the incident at Park Place.

When I started walking again I saw two pigeons in the middle of the sidewalk, aimlessly pecking. Not an unusual sight, but uncommon after dark—pigeons, like most birds, roost after dark.

Lou edged over to the curb, giving the birds a wide berth, so he thought there was something odd about them, too. I stopped about ten feet away and examined them carefully. As far as I could tell, they were pigeons.

I started to feel foolish. Staying alert is one thing; descending into paranoia quite another. And not a useful survival skill; one of these days I'd be focused intently on some peculiar-acting pigeons and something large and angry would come up behind me and take my head clean off.

I continued on, and just like every pigeon in every city in the world, they scuttled out of the way, their little legs speeding up like clockwork toys as they hurried along. But at the last moment, like a squirrel that almost makes it all the way across the highway and then unaccountably turns back, the fatter one reversed course and darted back under my feet. I tripped and stumbled, accidentally kicking the bird at the same time.

It uttered a most unpigeonlike squawk and fluttered off to the side. Its mate saw this as an attack and flew at me, flapping its wings and going for my eyes like a scene out of Hitchcock's *The Birds*. It would have been funny, except that as it did so, its beak lengthened and sharpened, so that I was no longer facing the weak weapon of a pigeon. It was more like the bill of a woodpecker.

I threw up my arm to protect my face, and the bill gashed my forearm, leaving a long shallow groove. The first bird circled back and attacked from the opposite direction, pecking me on the back of my head, just below my right ear. I clawed at it, but it easily avoided my clumsy hand, veered off, joined its mate, and both disappeared into the darkness.

The back of my head was now bleeding, as well as my arm. The wounds were minor, but it was disturbing. Things were escalating. A minor dislocation, to be sure; mutated pigeons weren't going to bring down civilization, but it wasn't a good sign. If Jackie was experimenting, starting off small, the dislocations would be hardly noticeable. But once she got some confidence and tested her limits, things might get truly weird. The next things that slipped through might be worse than pigeons, even ones with razor beaks. Finding her was no longer just a hope. It was a necessity.

SIXTEEN

NEXT MORNING I WAS BACK AT VICTOR'S ONCE again. If I spent any more time there, I'd have to think about renting a room. Timothy was making breakfast and Sherwood was helping out, so that was one good thing about hanging out there.

"How are we going to find Jackie again?" I asked. "For all we know she's already left the Bay Area."

"I don't think so," Eli said. "She's comfortable here; she has friends. She doesn't want to leave. If she were planning to, she wouldn't have bothered to try and get you out of the way."

"That still doesn't tell us where she might be. Maybe I should just call her cell and ask her. At least that would stir things up, to find out I'm still alive."

"You've got her cell number?" Timothy said. "You can ping it, you know, and find out her approximate location within a couple hundred feet. Well, *you* can't, but the cell provider can."

"Of course," said Victor, slapping his head in annoyance. "You didn't happen to notice what kind of phone she had?"

"It was an iPhone," Sherwood said. "I noticed it when we first met at Thinker's Café. Why?"

"Because the newer phones have GPS chips in them," Timothy said. "The cell providers can narrow down those phone locations ever further. You don't even need to be talking on the phone as long as it's turned on."

"Don't you have to be a cop for that, or get a warrant or something?" Sherwood said. Timothy laughed.

"Um. We're talking about Victor, remember? He has friends."

"Well, contacts, at least," I said.

"Let me have the number," Victor said, and when Sherwood gave it to him he pulled out his own cell and retreated to a corner of the room. It didn't take long before he rejoined us.

"She's at Sixth and Mission," he said. "At least her phone is."

"What would she be doing there?" Sherwood asked.

"I don't know," I said. "But I'll bet she's back at the Hotel Carlyle. She must have friends there—I never thought to look for her there again."

"Let's get down there," Victor said. "Mason, we'll take your van. "

Even with the prospect of the world slowly unraveling, Victor had no intention of risking his beloved Beemer. If he parked it in that area of the city, unpleasant things were bound to happen to it. An eighty-thousand-dollar car acts like a beacon for street people, and peeing on it is the protest of choice. I may not approve, but I do understand where they're coming from.

On the way over, we worked out a plan, such as it was. If Jackie was in the Hotel Carlyle somewhere, still shielding, it wouldn't be easy to locate her position among all those close-together rooms. The tenants at the hotel weren't the forthcoming type, and randomly poking around in rooms could lead to trouble, as my previous experience had shown.

But if Lou and I went in unshielded and wandered about asking questions, we'd come to her attention quickly enough. Just our presence there would unsettle her, and rather than confront us again she'd most likely bolt. Victor, Sherwood, and Eli would be waiting outside for her and the three of them together should have no problem scooping her up.

"Are you okay, Mason?" Sherwood asked. "You look drawn out."

"Just tired, that's all. I've been having a lot of headaches lately."

"Me too," she said.

Eli's head snapped around. "What?"

"Headaches," Sherwood said. "I've had quite a few in the last couple of weeks. Why?"

"Because I've had some as well, and so has Victor," Eli said.

Okay, this was no coincidence. But we didn't have time to discuss it; we were almost at the Carlyle. I parked the van a couple of blocks away and we set off toward the hotel. But once again things didn't go quite according to plan. Who could ever have foreseen that?

When we were halfway to Sixth Street, I noticed a group of people on the corner. Nothing unusual there; hanging around on street corners is a long and honored tradition, especially for those who have no real place to call their own. But I recognized one of them, a small, light-skinned black woman with freckles across the bridge of her nose. She saw me about the same time I saw her. I stopped and grabbed Victor by the arm.

"That's Cassandra," I said, pointing her out. What the hell? Had she known we were coming? How could she have?

She fumbled for something in her pocket, got it out, and stabbed frantically at it. An amulet, a power object? No, but something equally effective. A cell phone. It was no coincidence Cassandra was down here; she was acting as a lookout for Jackie.

"Let's get a move on," I said. "Cassandra's warning her, and Jackie will be gone in half a minute."

We all broke into a trot, although only Lou can actually trot since you need four legs for that. Cassandra stepped toward us and raised her hand. She had ability, I knew, but there was no way she could face us all. But she didn't have to face us; all she needed to do was delay us, and that was a lot easier. Instead of attacking us, she turned and spread her hand out toward the street.

The wave of cold and damp that came off her hand was palpable, even at a distance. The street glistened where she'd cast out her talent, and then a thin layer of black ice, invisible and unexpected, covered the asphalt. A cab came by, speeding along and taking the corner a bit too fast even if there hadn't been any ice. The driver lost control, skidded, overcorrected, and the cab slid sideways. It jumped the curb right where the group of street people had gathered. They scattered as the cab bore down on them, barely getting out of the way, and one slower-moving individual was saved only by an old-fashioned iron lamppost that the cab slammed into. The horn went off and its blare kept up a constant wail, drawing onlookers like a magnet. People crowded around the cab, blocking the sidewalk. Most rushed over to help; some were undoubtedly looking for a way to profit off the situation.

"Fuck!" Victor yelled as another car rolled down Mission Street, headed for the ice patch. He thrust out his hand in a gesture very much like the one Cassandra had used, but this time I felt heat rolling off. A second later, the driver of the oncoming car hit the brakes, having seen the accident on the corner, but this time the car came to a screeching halt on dry pavement.

Meanwhile Cassandra had melted into the crowd and disappeared. She'd gained all the time she needed. The four of us stood in the middle of the sidewalk and looked stupidly at one another.

"An unfortunate setback," said Eli.

"Can you get your people to ping her cell phone again?" I asked Victor. "We can still trace her."

Victor nodded, and stepped into a doorway away from the noise of the street. The rest of us waited impatiently. A few street people approached us with the intention of hitting us up for spare change, but they all veered off at the last moment and walked on by. Maybe their street sense told them there was something a little off about us, or maybe our impatience and bad mood told them it was a hopeless proposition. Victor finally came out from the doorway shaking his head.

"The phone hasn't moved."

"So she's still here?" Sherwood asked.

"Hardly. The phone hasn't moved at all. She ditched it. She must have finally realized she could be tracked by the phone, or maybe one of her friends reminded her of that fact."

"Whatever," I said. "She's gone now, so we're back to square one."

We trudged back to the van in silence, discouraged. As we were about to climb in, Lou's ears perked up and he stood up on his hind legs like a meerkat, the way he does when he wants to get a better look at something.

I followed his gaze to see what he was looking at and got a glimpse of someone turning the corner, not enough of a look to recognize anyone but enough to get a sense it was someone familiar.

"Hold on a sec," I said. "I want to check something out."

I walked rapidly to the corner, but when I got there the sidewalk was crowded with pedestrians. By the time I sorted through the various random bodies and focused in on the figure I'd glimpsed, he was almost at the end of the block. I picked up my pace, but a second later a Muni bus pulled up to the bus stop and he climbed aboard.

His back had been toward me, but as he boarded the bus I got a good look at him in profile. I wasn't positive, but he looked an awful lot like someone I knew, although it was someone I'd never expected to see walking the streets of San Francisco again.

Malcolm.

THE FIRST THING I DID AFTER DROPPING OFF everyone back at Victor's was to head back to Mount Davidson. Neither Victor nor Eli had any explanation for Malcolm's reappearance; in fact, Victor basically dismissed the idea.

"Lots of people look alike," he said. "He was dead, you say. So it seems highly unlikely it was actually him."

"Don't be ridiculous," Sherwood said, coming to my defense. "If Mason said he saw him, he saw him. It wouldn't be the strangest thing that's ever happened to one of us, would it, now?"

After that, Victor shut up for a while.

I found the place where I'd left Malcolm without any problem. There was no doubt it was the right place; the leaves and brush I'd carefully piled over him were scattered over the hillside, and there were traces of blood, still not dried in the dampness of the soil. But no Malcolm.

I could accept that Malcolm had fooled me, though I didn't know how. Or why. But it was a good thing I hadn't had the time nor the inclination to bury him in a grave six feet deep.

He'd been hanging out near the Carlyle, looking for Jackie, obviously. But was he hunting her or was he working with her again? Had they patched things up? If I could find him, I could get the answer, and maybe even find Jackie as well. But there was a problem—those tattoos that rendered him immune to spells might screw up Lou's tracking ability as well. I needed an edge, and luckily I had one. Malcolm's blood, smeared over the dirt and leaves. I gathered up as much of it as I could and rolled it into a ball. I wasn't sure this would work, but it was worth a try.

Now I needed a location, somewhere for Lou to start

tracking. What had Malcolm told me after he'd been stabbed? Something about having found a place to stay, out by the zoo, where he could commiserate with the animals. He shouldn't have revealed that. Even if you're not planning anything at the time, it pays to be paranoid and secretive when dealing with adversaries and magical practitioners, and doubly so if they're both. Bits of information given away that seem innocuous at the time have a way of coming back to bite you.

The zoo is no more than a ten-minute drive from Mount Davidson, so I headed over there. Malcolm might not be around, but the bus he'd boarded was headed away from downtown, away from the city, so maybe he'd been headed for home.

I parked outside the zoo gates, which are located just a few blocks from Ocean Beach, and let Lou out of the van. I took the dirt and leaves I'd collected at Mount Davidson and fashioned them into a crude stick figure. Voodoo lite. Lou watched with interest.

"This is Malcolm," I said, pointing at the dirt. Lou looked at me calmly. He was used to humoring me when I started talking crazy. "Not the real Malcolm. Part of him. We need to find the rest." I pushed the figure toward him and he backed off. "No, idiot," I said. "I'm not crazy. Track him. Can you track him, using this?"

He sniffed delicately at it, then sat down and looked up at me.

I pantomimed looking for someone, putting my hand over my eyes and staring off in one direction, then another. Lou continued to gaze calmly in my direction. I started to feel that maybe he was just screwing with me; I'm never quite sure with him.

"Malcolm," I repeated, inanely. "Use this to find Malcolm."

Either he finally got it or he decided he'd had enough fun, because he grabbed a small bit of a leaf and ate it, lips pulled back as if it were some particularly nasty-tasting medicine. Then he stood up on his hind legs again and sniffed the air, ears back, questing. He doesn't actually use his scenting abilities, of course; it's just his own personal metaphor to make it easier to locate whoever it is he's seeking through his own methods. That's the way I read it, at least.

He stayed facing that direction for a while, then did a quarter turn. Then another and another until he'd made a complete circle. At the end of his ritual he sat back down and faced me.

"No-go, eh?" I said. "Not close enough, I guess." Or maybe my bright idea just hadn't worked.

I was about to climb back into the van when I felt another twinge, just like the one I'd felt the night before, only this one was stronger and hurt more. It passed quickly again, but this was getting more than worrisome. What if it was some sort of progressive thing? It would be ironic after surviving all manner of violent supernatural creatures to end up dying of a brain tumor.

Lou gave a short bark to alert me. At first I thought he'd caught a whiff of Malcolm, but he was focused on the entrance to the zoo, and I could hear a commotion in the distance. The ticket taker stepped out of her booth and stared down the path leading to the interior of the zoo, so it wasn't anything normal. Lou barked again in a peremptory tone, so whatever it was warranted attention.

I put a small masking on both of us and strolled past the ticket taker, who wasn't paying that much attention anyway. It wasn't that I was too cheap to pay; I just didn't want to waste a lot of time getting her back in the booth and buying a ticket.

People were running now, some toward the commotion and some away from it. I wondered if there had been another big cat escape. A few years ago, just at closing time, three teenagers had been throwing things into the tiger pit, young primates teasing the Siberian tiger from their perch of safety behind a moat and fence.

But the tiger got annoyed, and then enraged. No one is really sure how the tiger did it, but it managed to scale the thirteen-foot wall and killed one of the boys and injured the other two before being shot by police.

Opinion was divided between those who believed it to be a horrible tragedy and those who felt the boys got what they deserved—that it was more a tragedy for the tiger than for them. I thought it was both. But even as victims, the boys didn't make very sympathetic figures. One scenario was that the two who apparently teased the tiger escaped with their lives, and ironically it was the other boy, the one who had done nothing, who died trying to help his friends. They say justice is blind, but karma seems a bit skewed as well sometimes.

But after a few moments I dismissed that idea. People were excited, but not scared. Whatever it was, there didn't seem to be danger involved. I moved down the sloping path, past various enclosures of deer and antelope, until I came upon the scene I'd been looking for.

Several zookeepers were gathered around a bench, and underneath was a medium-sized brown animal about the size of a small golden retriever. The keepers all held long sticks, trying to keep it at bay until someone could get a net or a tranquilizer gun, or whatever they were going to use to recapture it. Another keeper was trying to push the people back who were trying to get a look at what was going on. He saw me, glanced down at Lou, and said, "You can't have that dog in here, you know." Talk about misplaced priorities.

"Not my dog," I said, falling back on my default excuse to avoid confrontation.

Lou wandered away as if he'd never seen me before in his life. The keeper was distracted by a young Asian couple with a camera trying to get closer and forgot about me.

The animal under the bench snapped at one of the keepers that had gotten too close and I got a good look at it. I don't know what I was expecting, but it wasn't this. It was an otter, probably a sea otter from its size.

It poked its head out from under the bench and focused at something it saw across the path. When I followed its gaze, I saw it was looking at Lou. Then it snapped its attention back to me, staring up with a quiet intensity. I could see its eyes, and they didn't look like the eyes of an animal, even as clever a one as an otter. Another thing odd about it—it had ears, floppy ears like Lou's. I'm not an otter expert, but I've seen plenty of pictures and nature films. Otters have tiny ears, not ones that flop over like a beagle's.

It stuck its head out farther and barked at me, sounding very much like Lou asking for help before ducking farther back to the relative safety under the bench. Which was fine—I was sure by now this was no ordinary otter, and I had no desire to leave it in the hands of zookeepers who were bound to notice before long that it wasn't an otter at all. But how to go about abducting it out of there?

An aversion-type spell would help, but wasn't sufficient. All it does is make the eye disinclined to rest on an object, to glide over it. That wouldn't deter the keepers who already knew there was an otter under the bench and were focused on it.

But the two keepers on either side of the bench offered something I could use. The two of them quite resembled each other, much like brothers, and wore identical uniforms as well. I used that similarity to craft a spell. Their identical appearance provided a template where I could create an illusionary twin for the otter.

If I threw an aversion spell over the original creature and at the same time created an identical-looking illusion and sent it charging off, the real one might then slip off unnoticed in the ensuing chaos. The only problem was the timing; I'd have to set the two spells in motion simultaneously, like playing two separate lines on the guitar at the same time. I might not be able to pull it off on the guitar, but I thought I could do it here.

I sent the spells flying in, one on top of the other, and for just a moment there were two otters there, but with both of them huddled close it was hard to tell that. When the two spells kicked in, every eye avoided the real otter and focused on the illusion. I sent the illusion running out in a mad dash for freedom, ignoring the keepers' sticks. One of the keepers poked his stick right through it, but since that obviously wasn't possible his mind told him he'd simply missed.

It was across the path and heading away from us in seconds, heading for a large bush, keepers in hot pursuit, not noticing there was another figure still under the bench, protected by the aversion spell. As soon as the copy of the otter dived into the nearby bush, I'd release the illusion and for all intents and purposes it would vanish. The keepers would be sorely puzzled about where it had gone, but at least they wouldn't have the physical evidence of a lop-eared otter to examine.

The otter cautiously stretched its head out again and I gestured to it urgently. If I'd read things right, it would come bounding out. If not, and it was nothing more than an unusual animal after all, it would ignore me and hunker down in place.

No worries there. It was out of its temporary lair and moving toward me in less than a second. I turned and ran toward the front gate, otter close behind and Lou on its heels ready to nip if it changed its mind.

I glanced back to make sure it was following me, noting that it wasn't running with the normal otter gait, bouncing and somewhat goofy. Its long body stretched out and it moved with ease, almost like a large cat. People looked at me curiously as I ran by, and even the aversion spell couldn't keep them from noticing a large furry creature bounding along right behind me. But they wouldn't be able to describe it if anyone were to ask them later.

I didn't have a plan, apart from getting the otter out of the immediate area. Maybe I could convince it to get into the van, though what I would do after that wasn't so clear. I couldn't very well take it home; my landlord was back in town. Victor wouldn't take kindly to the idea of having a super intelligent otter as a permanent houseguest, though I'd bet Eli would be thrilled at the prospect.

The otter solved that problem as soon as we exited through the gate. It stopped, pulled itself erect like Lou searching for a scent, and faced Ocean Beach. Two seconds later, without a backward glance, it bounded down the sidewalk and across the Great Highway, the road that runs along the edge of the ocean. I could hear the screech of brakes as drivers tried to avoid it. Then it was gone. I looked at Lou.

"It could have at least said thank you, don't you think?"

Lou ignored me. He was back on his hind legs, sniffing the air. I looked around to see if the otter had returned for some reason, but that wasn't it. When he gave a short bark of triumph, I got it. Malcolm had returned to the area, and Lou hadn't forgotten about him. When I opened the door of the van, instead of jumping in, he passed it by and set off across Sloat Boulevard, which meant Malcolm was close by, close enough so that tracking him down would be easier on foot.

We hadn't gone more than a block when Lou stopped in front of a small, ratty-looking house painted a nauseating pink and sat down. I thought about what to do, and finally decided on simply knocking on the front door. Steps approached from inside, and after a slight hesitation the door swung open and Malcolm stood there in front of me. He didn't seem surprised to see me.

"I figured you'd show up eventually," he said in a tone of resignation. "You might as well come in."

SEVENTEEN

"GOOD TO SEE YOU LOOKING SO WELL," I SAID. "Having been dead seems to agree with you."

"I wasn't dead," he said.

"Obviously. How did you pull that trick off?"

"It wasn't a trick. It's the tattoos. I included a healing provision in the template; I can survive most any injury unless it's really severe. What I didn't count on was that it didn't work in the singularity—but it kicked in the moment we got back here, where it was originally implemented. It took a while for me to recover, since I was inches from death. A close call—I guess I've got you to thank for bringing me back. I freaked out when I woke up and there was dirt thrown over my head, though. I thought you'd buried me in a deep grave, and that's just where I'd stay."

"Maybe I should have," I said. "Your convenient death gave you the opportunity to freelance, didn't it? Like tracking down Jackie on your own? What were you doing down by Mission Street, anyway?"

"So you did see me there, then. I was afraid of that."

"And?"

"I was there to meet Jackie, of course. Your untimely arrival prevented that, so I came home."

"How did you know where she was?"

"No big mystery there. She called me. Since she's the one who powered up the tattoos, she knew I wasn't dead, despite what you told her. She's been having trouble implementing any of the spells in the book on her own—every time she tries one, it goes wrong. She discovered she still needed my expertise, and I still need the book, of course, so we decided to re-form our alliance."

"And when you help her, more little rips in our world's fabric takes place, and things leak through."

I told him about the otter I'd just seen at the zoo, and the pigeons as well.

"Exactly," he said. "You've got it. And it's not just a temporary glitch in the fabric. It's all cumulative; every opening stays open and each opening reinforces the others."

"And that doesn't worry you?"

"Not in the slightest. It won't affect me much, personally."

"Maybe not, but it will hardly help you. Why are you so interested in helping Jackie?"

"Well, I'm not anxious to help you; that's for sure. When Jackie's done with the book it'll be my turn, and I'll have it. You certainly wouldn't ever let me have the book, would you, now? What if I were successful in using it to gain talent? If I were, then anyone could be a practitioner—anyone with my scientific background, at least. You guys would never let that happen."

"Probably not." He laughed, bitterly.

"There's no probably about it. Because then you guys wouldn't be so special anymore, would you, now? No, if you ever get your hands on the book, that's the last I'll ever see of it."

"I see," I said. "Be that as it may, it's too dangerous to let Jackie run around trying out things from that book. It's already causing trouble, and it could get much worse."

"You have no idea. But that doesn't affect me at all—my head's as clear as a bell."

"What does that mean?" An expression of annoyance flitted across Malcolm's face, as if he'd let something slip.

"Nothing. Just an expression."

I thought about how I'd felt pain and that odd dislocation just before the appearance of the otter in the zoo. And how I'd felt something similar when I'd run into the pseudo pigeons. Not to mention the corporate gig we'd played. And the headaches we'd all been experiencing.

"You got a phone?" I asked.

"My cell."

"Let me borrow it a sec." He looked at me warily, obviously not wanting to.

"I don't think so," he said.

"Don't push me, Malcolm. You've caused me enough grief already." He stepped back, a bit unsure of himself but still defiant.

"Don't push you? What are you going to do? Your spells can't affect me. What—you're going to have Lou bite me?"

What an excellent idea.

"Bite him, Lou," I said.

Before the words were out of my mouth, Lou had him by the meaty part of the calf and was shaking his leg like it was an unfortunate rat.

Malcolm howled in surprise and reached down to get hold of Lou. As he bent over, I pulled out the stun gun Victor had given me, jammed it into his neck right below the ear, and flipped the switch.

He forgot all about Lou, doubling over and screaming in a high-pitched voice. I lifted the stun gun and he crumpled to the floor, more in shock than anything else, I suspect.

"Lou!" I said. "Enough."

Lou gave the leg one last shake and backed off, looking

satisfied. He seldom got an opportunity to bite anyone, and I think it pleased the dog part of his nature no end. I waited a moment and then held out my hand.

"Phone, please," I said.

Malcolm reached shakily into his pocket and handed the cell to me. He tried to glare, but all that did was make him look like he was about to cry. I punched in a familiar number.

"Victor? I got a question for you. Did you feel anything weird about a half hour ago? Like one of those headaches, but different?"

He was silent for a long moment, which usually means I've hit on something, and he was considering the implications.

"As a matter of fact, I did."

"Was this the first time you felt something like that?"

"No, the same thing happened yesterday, but this one was stronger."

"Figures. Is Eli there?"

"No, but Sherwood is. Just a moment." I heard him asking questions and then he was back on the line.

"Timothy didn't feel a thing, but Sherwood did. A twinge, and a feeling like something slipping."

"That's what I thought, and I think I know what's been causing it. I'll call you later when I know more," I said.

I hung up before he could ask any more questions and handed the cell back to Malcolm. He took it sullenly.

"You didn't have to do that," he said.

"Maybe not, but I did. And I want to know what's going on. Why are we all getting headaches every time something odd turns up? What's the connection? I mean, I see the connection, but why? And don't tell me you don't know what I'm talking about."

"How would I know—" He broke off as I lifted the stun gun suggestively. "All right. It doesn't matter anyway—there's not much you can do about it. Richter developed a method for creating complex singularities; that much you know. And some of those same principles also allowed him to rip open the fabric of the world and access other worlds, other dimensions.

"But he focused on singularities and didn't bother to pursue that other aspect of things, because his methods, though effective in bridging dimensions, created an unfortunate side effect. A psychic wave that ripples out from the point where worlds intersect, and that wave affects practitioners in a painful fashion. The stronger the practitioner, the worse the effect. The closer you are, the more it resonates, and the larger the rift, the more powerful the wave."

"Interesting, if true," I said. "But how would you know all this?"

"It's all in his book, the first one, but it's presented as theory. The second one describes the science behind it, the actual process and methods."

"Like the energy pool," I said.

"No, that's different. That energy pool was constructed in an entirely different way. It's like a door that connects rooms. It can be opened and closed, with no effect on anything else except for what might come through. What's happening now is more like taking a sledgehammer and busting a hole in a wall. It's violent, and the hole stays open permanently. And it weakens the wall, as well."

I'd gotten some answers out of Malcolm and they sounded plausible, but there was no way for me to tell if it was really true. He was afraid of me, which was the only reason he was talking, but that also meant he could be inventing it all out of whole cloth. The idea that Jackie was experimenting with the book, and that every time she made a breakthrough the rest of us could feel it, rang true, though.

"So Jackie's been taking little baby steps," I said. "She makes a little tear in the fabric, things slip through, and we all get these headaches. What happens if she goes all out, trying to create her new world?"

"Well, that's a moot point. You saw the singularity

Richter helped create—it took him years, with many additions by many people. And yet it's still a pale shadow of the real world. Jackie thinks she can create something a thousand times more complex in a single day, but of course she can't."

"So what happens when she fails?"

"That depends. The most likely thing, if she can find a source with enough power, is that by trying she rips apart the world fabric on a scale that's never been seen before."

"That doesn't sound good. God knows what might pour through."

"No, it's not good, not for you. But don't worry—you won't be around to witness the aftermath and neither will any of your friends. It will kick off a wave so strong that every practitioner within a fifty-mile radius will stroke out—if she figures out a way to harness enough power, it could take down every practitioner in the world, theoretically. That's why Richter went to so much trouble to hide the book, although he would have been better off destroying it. I guess he couldn't bear to throw away his life's work."

"So we all just keel over? Sorry; I don't buy it."

Malcolm shrugged. "Oh, I doubt it will kill everyone, or at least I don't think so. But those who survive will find every trace of talent they ever possessed has vanished. There won't be any more practitioners, dead or alive. None at all. And good riddance, if you'll pardon a personal opinion." He smiled, with a great inner satisfaction. "But talent won't be lost to the world entirely. Because I'll have it, even if nobody else does. I'll use my knowledge and the book to get it. And I might even let a few select others have some as well. It's going to be a different world, a very different world."

King of the world. A modest ambition. This was getting too heavy for me. I needed Victor, and especially Eli's expertise. They might be able to separate fact from fiction; Lord knows I couldn't.

"Okay, stand up," I said. "It's time for us to go."

"Go where?" he asked, regaining some of his former belligerence.

"You're going to help us, whether you want to or not." A slight smile appeared on his lips.

"Really? Are you positive about that? Because I'm pretty sure Jackie's going to be trying another little experiment anytime now."

I never got a chance to answer. I started to feel strange, and my head began to ache in that familiar way. But this time it wasn't a brief, transient pain. It grew until I could barely stand upright, and I staggered when I tried to take a step. Soundless cannons were going off in my head, and the color leached out of the room, then the light, as everything grew dim. I vaguely heard Lou whine as he realized something was wrong with me, and then my legs gave way and I toppled to the floor. My vision narrowed until I could only see directly in front of me, like I was staring down a tunnel. Then all vision faded and the world vanished.

EIGHTEEN

SOMETHING KEPT BATTING AT MY FACE, BOTHering me. I tried to push it away, but it kept up, raking my cheek and almost drawing blood. Finally I opened my eyes, but they wouldn't focus. There was something there, though, insistent and annoying. Then I came to, just enough to realize it was Lou, pawing at me, scratching me with his long nails, trying to wake me up.

"Enough," I said, and closed my eyes again.

The pawing stopped, only to be replaced by high-pitched barks right next to my ear, slicing through the haze and making the violent headache I had even worse. I opened my eyes again, and this time tried to sit up.

I succeeded on the third try, feeling an immense sense of accomplishment. After resting awhile, I managed to make it all the way to my feet. I stood there, propped against the wall for support, until I felt well enough to walk. Which was a whole other experience.

Malcolm was gone, of course. If I'd been a movie hero, I could have quickly shaken off the effects, figured out where he'd gone, and tracked him down, but real life is a little different. I could barely walk, and I was having trouble remembering where I'd parked the van, much less figuring out where Malcolm might be.

I tottered outside, walking like a very old man. My head felt too heavy for my body, which felt fragile enough so that a good sneeze would break bones. Jackie must have tried a more powerful incantation from the book, and that must have made a significant rupture in the world's fabric. God knows what might have slipped through this time.

I looked up at the sky, wincing from the light. Gulls swooped and circled overhead. I watched one that was riding a current with enough skill to keep it stationary, like a hawk scanning a field for an unwary ground squirrel. It dipped and hovered, making constant subtle alterations as the wind ebbed and surged. It looked as normal as could be.

Halfway back to the van, I remembered the other part of Malcolm's explanation. Those who were not killed might well lose their talent. If true, that would be a change of epic proportions, and I wasn't sure how well we'd all handle it. Victor would be hit the hardest. In his own mind, being chief enforcer of the magical community, unofficial though it might be, defined him. But maybe not. He was rich, after all, and had many talents, one of which is facing reality unflinchingly. Maybe he'd just shrug and start a new life and career, as a captain of industry or something.

Eli would care the least. He loved teaching, he loved academia, and his only real regret would be that of having an interesting area of knowledge closed off, as if an earthquake had destroyed a priceless archaeological dig.

Sherwood? I didn't know. In many ways I didn't really understand her, which says a lot about me since we'd been together for almost a year before it fizzled out.

And myself? A sick feeling came over me. I've always liked to think of myself as a musician, first and foremost, with my magical talent a sideline. A wonderful thing, to be sure, but not intrinsic to who I am, not the thing that defines me.

But my gut told me that was a lie. The thought of living out my life devoid of talent was unthinkable, horrendous. As many times as I've denied that to myself, it is who I am, as much as any of the others if not more so. And what about Lou? Ifrits find practitioners, and only practitioners. If my abilities vanished, was I still a practitioner? Would he stick around or would he slip away forever?

When I reached my van I leaned up against it for a few minutes trying to gather myself enough to try a spell. My head was still muzzy, but I was beginning to be able to think again. I thought at first about a simple illusion to test if I still had my talent, but that wouldn't tell me enough. Illusions take little skill and even less energy, and I wanted to try something more complex, to see if I still had all my power.

Overhead, the gulls were still circling, riding the wind. I focused on one that was surfing in place, took the energy of the wind and the bird, and transferred it down to the sidewalk next to my van. I poured energy into one square, and waited. So far, so good; at least it felt right.

A young couple, deep in conversation, passed by the van. As they entered the square I'd prepared, their forms wavered momentarily. Their legs kept moving but they no longer made any progress; instead, they remained in the same place like the gull overhead. For them the sidewalk had become a giant treadmill.

They walked along, oblivious, but they were bound to notice sooner or later. I diverted the power and they passed by me, still talking. "I'm just going to wait him out," said one. "After all, time is on my hands." It looked like their conversation wasn't going anywhere, either.

At least I still had my talent. I climbed into the van, thankful to finally be sitting down, and drove slowly and carefully down the Great Highway until I reached Victor's house.

He greeted me at the door, looking terrible, one eye bloodshot with half the white turned red from a burst blood vessel.

"You too?" I said. He nodded.

"Passed right out. Sherwood, too. Eli fared better—for some reason, whatever it was didn't affect him as much."

"That makes sense," I said. "Are they both here?"

He nodded again and looked at me impatiently. Usually it's Victor or Eli who have to patiently explain what's been going on, but this time it was the other way around. Timothy was hovering in the background, plainly worried. He of course has no talent and hadn't felt a thing.

"You look like you could use some coffee, Mason," he said. "Come in the kitchen."

Coffee was exactly what I needed. I followed Timothy and Victor into the kitchen, and gave a weary wave to Sherwood and Eli. Maggie trailed behind us, giving me the feline version of the evil eye. She didn't care for me much—it wasn't personal; it was just that every time something unpleasant happened to Victor, I was usually involved. She ignored Lou and jumped up on the kitchen table, a favored spot.

"Was Lou affected?" Victor asked.

"Nope. Not as far as I know. Then again, I was passed out for a while."

"Maggie didn't seem to be bothered, either. But since you called me right before it hit with a question about headaches, I'm guessing you have a theory about what's causing this."

"Not so much a theory as some information," I said. "How much of it is true, I'm not sure, but evidence is piling up."

I relayed what I'd seen at the zoo, and everything Malcolm had told me, right up to the point where I'd passed out.

"What do you think?" I asked Eli. "Truth or dare?"

"It all hangs together," he said. "The type of thing Jackie is trying to do opens rifts, and the way we've been reacting each time is not a coincidence. And the headaches? I have less intrinsic power than any of you, and indeed I've been less affected—so yes, I think what Malcolm told you is accurate."

"What about the otter?" I said. "Or whatever it was?"

"Clearly it slipped through a rift—as did those pseudo pigeons you ran into."

"But if the rifts stay open, why aren't there more things coming through?" I asked.

"I don't think it's easy for them. Relatively few things will come through, even with an open pathway. But the bigger the rift, the more traffic there will be—that stands to reason. And this last one worries me. If it affected us so badly, it's got to be major." Sherwood looked thoughtful.

"And this last one affected us ten times as badly as the others," she said. "But if Jackie has been flexing her muscles, and the resulting rift is huge, *something* is bound to have slipped through. So why haven't we noticed anything?"

Before anyone could answer, Maggie arched her back and uttered a low growl, almost exactly like Lou does to warn me of approaching trouble. Immediately after, there was a knock at the front door. Victor put out a hand to quiet Maggie and stood up.

"It seems we have company."

Apparently so, but no one unexpectedly drops over to Victor's house except the very people sitting around the kitchen table. He walked out of the kitchen, leaving us sitting there.

"Any guesses?" I said.

"A friend of Timothy's?" Sherwood said. Timothy laughed.

"Not a chance in hell."

Victor reappeared at the door of the kitchen with the visitor. I realized it was the only person it could be.

Jessie.

NINETEEN

AS VICTOR STOOD IN THE KITCHEN DOORWAY, I saw something rare indeed. Victor, acting indecisive when faced with a situation. The logical thing to do was invite Jessie into the kitchen to join us. But on the other hand, the kitchen, like many kitchens, was also a refuge—informal and relaxed, speaking of hearth and home, a place for friends and trusted acquaintances to gather.

Jessie was neither of those things, and bringing her into the kitchen felt wrong, like a violation of trust. She belonged in the study, a place suitable for friend and foe alike, as well as those who were neither. A place where civil formality ruled and where the conventions of manners work to keep things from getting out of hand. But what could he do? We were already assembled in the kitchen—should we all get up and troop upstairs to the study? Eli rescued him from his dilemma.

"Jessica," he said, standing up and pulling out a chair from the table. "So nice to see you again."

Jessie appeared to be exhausted, looking older than usual. I knew the reason why. She took the proffered chair and Timothy asked if she'd like a cup of coffee. She looked at him with puzzlement, since he clearly wasn't a practitioner, but had other things on her mind.

"Where's Naja?" I asked.

"At home."

After that exchange not another word was uttered. Eli kept up a steady gaze coupled with an inquiring expression, but Jessie was tough and didn't lose her composure.

"I guess you're wondering what I'm doing here," she finally said.

"Could it have something to do with headaches?" I asked. Her expression didn't change.

"So you do know what's going on, then."

"Most of it," said Eli.

Jessie rubbed her temple with one hand. "Well, I need help," she said. "It turns out that not only has Jackie gotten herself in over her head; she's become a real danger to the rest of us."

"So it would seem."

"I met with Jackie earlier today," Jessie said. "Downtown."

So that was why Cassandra had been keeping a watch out. She didn't trust Jessie, not in the slightest.

"Jackie told me what she's planning—tried to make me see her side of it. Still wants her mother's approval, I'd guess, despite everything. She's doing something very dangerous. I couldn't talk her out of it, and I was just about to take stronger measures when she got a call. She dropped the phone, jumped up, and ran out of the room. She thought I'd set her up in some way—why, I don't know."

"I'm afraid that was our doing," Eli said. "We'd tracked her there, and she must have thought you had a hand in it."

"Oh, great. Well, whatever. But now she doesn't trust me and won't even talk to me. And we've got to find her. Those headaches you mentioned? They're just the start. It's bad, and going to be a whole lot worse."

"We know," I said. She looked at Eli.

"You know about the book she stole, of course?" Eli

nodded. "And the other book, the second volume?" Eli nodded again.

She stole a quick glance at Victor, trying to assess just how much we already knew. Even with this deadly situation, she was having trouble opening up. Black practitioners are paranoid by nature, or if they're not, they become that way. They eventually start to view others as untrustworthy at best, if not actively malevolent, and their guard is always firmly in place. Right now one of her worries was that Victor might discover information and use it to gain an advantage over her.

And she was still looking for an angle that would benefit her. It's hard to give up habits formed over a lifetime, no matter how dire the circumstances. She wanted our assistance, but didn't trust us enough to provide any of her own. I didn't think she was going to be much help until Sherwood spoke up unexpectedly.

"Jessie? You don't know me—I'm Sherwood."

"Yes. I know who you are," Jessie said, in a neutral tone.

"I suppose you do, but you don't know anything about me. But you do need to listen to me." A guarded expression smoothed out Jessie's face.

"About what?"

"Just listen," Sherwood said, in a matter-of-fact tone. "I'm pretty good at reading people." A slight smile of condescension appeared on Jessie's face and Sherwood picked up on it immediately. "No, that's not what I mean. It's part of my talent; it's a skill, just like someone who's particularly good at healing spells. And guess what—despite evidence to the contrary, I'd say you're basically a decent person."

"Why, thank you," said Jessie, and I couldn't tell if she was being serious or mocking.

"But I can see you've got your own agenda. You want to know how much we know, what Victor is up to, and how you might turn that to your advantage. I get that. But this is different. We don't know everything, but what we do know makes one thing very clear—if we don't handle this situation quickly, we're all in trouble. Every one of us, every practitioner, and that includes you and all your friends. Your honest help just might make the difference between success and failure, between living and dying, so it's time to stop holding back and simply pitch in."

When Sherwood started talking I didn't think she'd get through to Jessie. People like Jessie are impervious to mere words. Some patterns of behavior become so ingrained that they will die rather than change. Or maybe they just can't change no matter how much they want to.

If Victor had given the same lecture, it would just have put Jessie's back up, but something about Sherwood's speech was oddly compelling, even though it wasn't directed at me. I found myself unconsciously nodding as I listened to her, and then realized this wasn't just her common sense at play. Sherwood was using talent, a lot of it, but so subtly that it passed almost unnoticed. No compulsion, no emotional sway, but a total believability that made sense on a primal level. I picked up on it only because it wasn't being directed at me; I was off to the side, just catching the backwash. This was slick indeed; it had to be to get past Jessie's defenses.

Good for Sherwood. She was using a con on Jessie, with the noblest of motives. I'd have to get her to show me how to do that in the future. If there was going to be a future. Sherwood continued on, her tone reasonable, convincing, and compelling. Jessie took a deep breath, let it out slowly, held both hands out, and breathed a word I couldn't catch. Talent spilled out, and Sherwood's voice now seemed flat, lacking its former magic, like reverb on an amp suddenly cutting out. It had fooled me, but it hadn't fooled Jessie. Sherwood stopped speaking.

"Very impressive," Jessie said. "Delightfully subtle."

"It was worth a try," Sherwood said ruefully.

"Yes," said Jessie, giving her a chilly smile. "But I've been around a long time, and I've seen it all."

I didn't say anything. The moment Jessie put her talent

in play, I recognized where I'd run across it before. It was that distinctive. She'd been the second practitioner in the Carlyle when the dead body illusion was crafted. So she'd hired me to find Jackie and then tried to throw me off the trail. I was finally beginning to catch on, but as usual, a day late and a dollar short.

"But you know what?" Jessie said. "You didn't need the talent. You're actually right. It's that serious." She turned to Victor. "Just how much do you know?"

Now the shoe was on the other foot. Victor wasn't happy, either, about revealing his knowledge, and especially its limitations, to an enemy. He hesitated until Eli added his weight.

"Victor," he said.

Jessie listened to Victor's summary without interrupting. When he was done, she put her head in her hands. I don't know if she was tired or whether her head hurt worse than the rest of ours. She had a reputation as a powerful practitioner, so maybe that was it.

"You've got most of it," she said. "There's not a lot I can add, but if you have any questions, feel free."

"Something major just happened," Eli said. "That's why you're here, after all. Another rift, or something worse?"

"Another rift. Things have already poured through; we just haven't seen them yet."

"I've got something to ask you," I said.

She saw that I was referring to something specific, which made her regard me with a certain wariness, but she shrugged.

"Be my guest."

"The first time I tracked Jackie to the Hotel Carlyle, she pulled off an illusion that she was dead. To throw me off the track. But she had help. You. The question is, why? Why hire me to find her and then try to make sure I didn't?"

I expected her to deny it, but she didn't blink an eye. She really must be worried.

"Because I didn't want you to find her, of course."

"Yeah, but why?"

She hesitated, not so much because she had anything to hide, but more like she was embarrassed. Eli suddenly snapped his fingers.

"Ahh," he said. All heads turned toward him.

"Jessica's been agitating for a while now, insisting that it's time for practitioners to make themselves known, to come out of the closet."

"So?" Victor said.

"So, what if Jackie were to get hold of a book, and use that book in a way that opened up pathways? What would be the effect on society if a stream of bizarre creatures suddenly were roaming the streets? At first, denial and dismissal, but eventually ordinary people would have to accept that their past worldview has been severely limited—they could hardly do otherwise. And when the creatures became numerous and dangerous enough, guess who would need to come out into the open, to deal with them?"

"Practitioners," Victor said. "I see. And then the question of whether to remain in the shadows would become moot. And right in the thick of the new world order, guess who?"

"Precisely. Now, Jessica couldn't do it on her own, not directly—her political ideas are well-known, and if she were to do such a thing, the entire practitioner community would turn against her. She might achieve her objective, to out us all, but it wouldn't be very good for her personally."

"Of course," I said. "But if Jackie were to steal the book and go off on her own, Jessie would be in the clear. But Jackie's her daughter—people would still suspect she was involved. But not if she could point to the fact she was so worried that she actually hired outside help to prevent it from happening—me. Only, I couldn't be allowed to actually track her down."

Victor was looking disgusted, whether about Jessie or about the fact we'd all been conned, I couldn't tell.

"But you did find her," he said. "That threw a wrench in the works."

"To tell the truth I never expected Mason to get close that quickly," Jessie said. "I gave out too much information, and he turned out to be cleverer than I thought."

"Was Jackie in on all this, or were you playing her as well?" I asked.

"No, she was a more than willing helper. But she didn't care one way or the other if practitioners were outed—she had her own plans, obviously. I didn't think there was a chance in hell of her succeeding, but I underestimated the dangers. So no, I wasn't playing her. Quite the opposite, as it turns out."

"And all this other stuff we came up with, about you trying to recruit Mason to your side or turning him against Victor, was just a cover?" Sherwood asked.

"Not entirely," Jessie said, "I knew suspicions would arise eventually, when things started to get weird, so I did want him on my side. And if nothing else, it did provide a distraction. The more stuff you have going on, the more threads you can toss out; the more layers you have, the harder it is to see what's really going on. Victor knows that."

"And here I thought I had you conned," I said. She gave me a weary smile.

"You were quite good, actually. If I'd really been interested in co-opting you, I would have bought your entire act."

"So how did this get so out of hand? Weren't you aware of the dangers?"

"It would have worked. But then something unforeseen happened. She ran into this Malcolm. When he appeared on the scene and Jackie found that second book, everything changed. The first book could only cause trouble; the second is as dangerous as a nuclear bomb. Trust me, I've done years of research on this."

"Those headaches?" Eli said.

"Yes, and they're just the tip of the iceberg. They're going to get worse, much worse. And eventually . . ."

"We know that," Eli said. "So we've got to find Jackie, and soon. You're on our side, then?"

"I'm not on anyone's side. But you're right, she has to be stopped, and I can't find her. Maybe you can." She looked at me. "You managed it before, after all."

"One more thing," Sherwood said. "Things slipping through into our world every time Jackie uses the book. This last one knocked us silly—why hasn't anyone noticed anything yet?"

"Give it time," Jessie said, grimly. "Watch the morning news, for starters."

"If we're not all dead by then," I said.

"We have more time than that. That last one she tried must have taken a lot out of her. She'll need time to recover. And if she's planning a big finish, she'll want to prepare carefully. In the meantime, I've got all my people out looking for her, and I suggest you do the same."

She got up abruptly, apparently deciding she'd had enough of talking for one day. Without another word she left the kitchen and headed for the front door.

"Always a pleasure," Victor called after her. "Drop by anytime."

TWENTY

JESSIE PROVED TO BE RIGHT; MORNING CAME and we were all still alive and kicking. I turned on the early-morning news and she was right again. A very serious newsman dispensed with the usual chat and got right to the main story.

> A wave of unexplained deaths has struck the Bay Area, leaving grieving relatives and unanswered questions. Since only this morning, five people in the Richmond District, two men and three women, all apparently young and healthy, have died suddenly for no apparent reason. At this time, foul play is not suspected, but police and medical professionals are baffled. One paramedic, who did not wish to talk on camera, said one victim he treated appeared to be a very old man despite identification to the contrary.

There were a couple of interviews, one with an epidemiologist about possible links between the victims, and the standard reassurance there was nothing for the general public to worry about. Sure there wasn't.

More Shadow Men. One had already slipped through, and this sounded like a lot more of them were now out and about. I reached for the phone to call Victor, but then another story came on. This one was a puff piece, with smiles all around. A young couple, also in the Richmond, was claiming their house was haunted. They'd been woken up, their story went, by what they thought was an earthquake. There was a camera shot of cans lying all over the floor in the pantry.

Then they heard a horrific rending sound, like a thin sheet of metal being torn like cardboard, and at the same time, a gust of cold air swept through the house. The news anchor, grinning, pointed out this was San Francisco, after all.

Their two dogs, border collies, went berserk and frantically clawed at the front door, trying to get out. Fearing the house might collapse, the couple got out themselves, and afterward the dogs refused to go back in. One of them, described as "the gentlest dog in the world," bit his owner when the man tried to force him back inside.

Then, when the man glanced in through the front window, he swore he saw shadowy shapes moving around inside the house. Thoroughly spooked, the couple decided to spend the night at a friend's house—a decision that probably saved their lives.

Their house was on Clement Street, and although naturally the exact address wasn't given, it wouldn't be too hard to find. Once near, Lou could focus in on any dimensional rift like a homing pigeon.

Victor called almost before the segment was over.

"Did you catch the morning news?" he asked.

"I did."

"Shadow Men?"

"What else? And did you see the other story, the one about the house?"

"Yes. A haunted house. Very cute."

"You think that's where they came in?"

"Must be. We need to get down there."

"What for?" I said. "It's not like we can do anything about it. Unless you've learned how to repair rips in the fabric of reality since last night."

"Remember what you said about the Shadow Men? How they're weak in daytime, strong at night?"

"So?"

"So they'll need to have a place to hole up. And what better place than right where they came through the rip? They might even be hanging out there hoping to get back in for all we know. In any case, we need to do something about it before any more people die, and it's a place to start."

"And how do we accomplish that? Remember, talent won't work on them, and although that stun gun works fine, it won't kill them. And we'd have to get close enough to touch them with it, and if there are a lot of them . . ."

"I know. Come on over, and bring Lou." As if I would be leaving him at home. "And bring that sword I lent you. You're going to need it."

TWENTY MINUTES LATER I WAS SITTING IN VICtor's study. He'd already pulled a lot of magical props out of the safe: crystals, copper dishes, salt—the usual stuff. Another sword was lying on a cloth at one end of them, and he motioned for me to put my sword next to it.

"Where's Eli?" I asked.

"Doing research."

"Sherwood?"

"Tracking down a lead."

"So it's the two of us, then?"

"We should be able to handle it. If it were night, it might be a different story, but daytime will even out the odds." He busied himself arranging the objects he'd assembled.

"Swords?" I asked. "Why not one of your handy automatic weapons? You could cut them in half with one."

"Too noisy. Wouldn't have a lasting effect, anyway."

"I don't think these swords are the answer. They won't affect the Shadow Men much, either," I said. "Even if you spell them—if it were that easy, we could just directly use talent to stop them."

"But you're forgetting something." He held up the paper bag I'd brought back with the residue from the original Shadow Man attack. "We have this." He leaned over and pointed at Lou. "And we have Lou. Ifrits can affect them."

He fired up a Bunsen burner and slid it under a stand that held a copper dish. Bits of charcoal went in, a pinch of salt, a few drops of liquid from various vials, and the dirt mixture from the paper bag. Finally he took a large bottle and drizzled in what looked like olive oil, as if he were preparing a salad. While the mixture bubbled, he took a couple of strong magnets and used them to enable a simple attraction spell over the sword blades. He turned up the flame on the burner until the oil mixture began to burn and smoke.

"Can you run some energy through Lou?" he asked. "We need a bit of his essence blended into the mixture."

I'd done this enough times in the past so that it was now second nature. When I sent the surge of magical energy through Lou he reacted by immediately going into a sneezing fit, also par for the course. I don't know why it always affects him that way. As the energy flowed through him, I directed it into the mixture, which was now furiously smoking.

"Done," I said, and Victor picked up the swords and waved them in a circular motion through the smoke.

The combination of the oily smoke and the attraction spell Victor had created worked like a charm. Instantly both blades became coated with a sooty residue, turning them almost black. Victor laid them back on the cloth, clapped a lid on the copper dish, and turned off the burner.

"That should do it," he said. "With Lou's Ifrit essence bonded to that Shadow Man's residue, these blades will have a deadly effect on them."

"Won't that smoke ruin the blades?"

"No. It's not very good for them, but they'll still do the trick."

He sheathed both blades, handed me mine, and strapped on the little fanny pack, stuffed with useful items that he carries on all of his missions.

"Whose car?" I asked. He thought a moment.

"We'll take your van. We'll need to be inconspicuous, and the Beemer sometimes draws attention."

Like the van wouldn't. But if things got heavy, at least he wouldn't end up with blood on his pristine upholstery.

"LOOK FOR SOMETHING OUT OF PLACE," I TOLD Lou as we drove down Clement Street. "Like the pool under the bridge, Rolf's pool."

I wasn't sure he got it completely, but it didn't matter. Any rip in the fabric of our world would have enough energy coming through so he'd pick up on it immediately. Sure enough, we hadn't driven more than half a mile when he put his paws up on the edge of the window and gave several barks, high-pitched enough to make Victor wince.

"Couldn't he just raise a paw or something?" he said with annoyance.

I didn't think he was that annoyed by the barking. I think he was keyed up, which meant this operation wasn't going to be the breeze he was making it out to be.

I recognized the house from the TV news clip. Hopefully the couple hadn't changed their minds and returned; that would pose an entirely different set of problems, assuming they would still be among the living. But the shades of the front windows were only partially drawn, and there was no sign of anyone inside.

"Try not to use any talent," Victor said. "An aversion

spell might be useful to avoid curious neighbors, but it's likely any use of talent will alert the Shadow Men if they're here."

He strolled nonchalantly over to the small ground-level garage, casually carrying his sword as if it were a golf club, and peered through a tiny window on the sliding garage door. He motioned for me to come over.

"No car in the garage," he said.

He held up a hand for silence and we listened for a minute. Everything was quiet. I followed him as he walked up the short flight of stairs to the front door. By the time we reached the door he had a roll of duct tape in his hand.

"Right here?" I said, seeing what he was about to do. "Why not around back?"

"People messing around at the back of a house invite suspicion. They're always worth a second look. People in the front of a house are natural. You'd make a lousy burglar."

He knocked, waited, and knocked again. After a minute he tore off a number of pieces of the duct tape and pasted them against the small window toward the top of the door. Without hesitation he pulled his arm back and struck the tape-covered pane a sharp blow with his elbow. There was a muffled crunching sound as the window fell away and shards dangled from the tape.

Reaching through the broken pane, he stretched his arm out, then pulled it back.

"I can't quite reach the lock," he said. "Your arms are longer; you give it a try."

I reached through and felt around until I found the dead bolt lock. I could just reach it and snapped it open. Of course, the doorknob itself was still locked, but Victor took out a thin length of plastic from his pack and slipped the lock in a matter of seconds. I was impressed; it looks easy, but it isn't. I tried once to get the hang of it because I thought it might be a handy skill to have, but gave up after half an hour with no success.

It took only a moment to get safely inside with the

door closed behind us. Only one person had passed by during this entire time, and she had only glanced incuriously at us as she passed.

It was an extraordinarily normal-looking house inside—not shabby, not fancy, not clean, not dirty. Except for the streaks of oily black residue that marred the front room carpet. I had been expecting to see something like the energy pool, an area of shifting lines and colors, only larger. But nothing. There was something here, though; I could feel it like a pressure on my mind and on my skin as well, a psychic heat wave. I imagine it was what Lou felt, how he sensed it, but a thousand times milder. Like in the same way that I can smell the sea, but when he smells the sea it's a hundred different scents—fish, salt, kelp, birds, sand, wet rock, and even faint traces of oil leaked from ships. I was surprised he wasn't overwhelmed more often.

I'd had some notion that we could maybe close off the rift, but that was hardly an option if we couldn't locate it. And there were more immediate things to worry about. Victor held his sword at the ready and moved away from me. Lou moved away from him at the same time, to the far end of the room. He's not a fan of long, sharp blades, even if they're on his side.

"You should keep your distance as well," Victor said, looking at me. "I don't want to accidentally slice off your arm when I'm moving fast. And I sure as hell don't want to be anywhere near you while you're swinging away."

This was not the best way to build up confidence in a novice swordsman right before a fight, but now was not the time to point that out. I moved over to the other side of the room next to Lou and nudged him.

"Where are they?" I said.

He paid no attention, since he was already busy, nose twitching, every sense alert. I didn't see anything. Maybe the Shadow Men were all hiding in closets, like bogeymen.

"I can smoke them out," said Victor.

He snapped his fingers and colored lights appeared in

the air in front of us. Waving his fingers gently, he made the lights slowly coalesce into interconnected shapes and forms like a Kandinsky painting, then morph into not-quite-abstract images, almost recognizable: a mountain sunrise, a forest, a castle. It was what many practitioners do when they're young and just discovering their talent, a form of play as well as a way to learn about focusing magical energies. It was a rare look at Victor's artistic side, all the odder because of the circumstances.

Either the Shadow Men really were sensitive to the workings of talent or it was coincidence, but it succeeded with a vengeance. They didn't spring out of closets or creep out from under the floorboards, though. They oozed out of the walls, like a dark miasma. One second we were alone in an empty room; the next we were surrounded by nightmare creatures.

Victor went into motion instantly, slashing down and then down again in a figure-eight motion before I even thought to raise my sword. Lou snarled and headed for cover behind a couch. I don't think he was afraid of the creatures as much as he was of me with a sword in my hand. One loomed up right in front of me, reaching out, and I swung the sword without thinking. My stroke was awkward and the Shadow Man dodged away, but I still caught it partway down its arm. The blade sliced through the doughy consistency with ease, but this time the wound didn't close up like the first time I'd fought one. Victor's trick with the blades had worked. A section of the Shadow Man's arm fell away, cleanly as a plywood strip falling from a band saw.

It stumbled back, but another took its place. I swung again, but it jumped back and I hit a lamp on a tabletop instead, almost losing my grip on the sword. The lamp crashed to the floor, shockingly loud in the silence. The Shadow Men hadn't made a sound during the entire time. The only sounds had been the swishing of blades through the air, and the sound of my own breathing, harsh and shallow. I couldn't hear Victor at all; maybe he really does have ice water in his veins. Or maybe he's so conscious of his image that he'd never allow himself to appear tired or nervous, even if he were totally alone.

The silence was broken by a snarl and a scuffle behind me. I whirled around and saw that another of them had eased up behind me, but at the last moment Lou had left his hidey-hole and fastened teeth into it. I swung reflexively and caught it right at neck level, more from luck than anything else. Its head detached neatly and toppled off in a very satisfying fashion.

Lou backed away and disappeared behind the couch again. I glanced over toward Victor, who was standing amidst a virtual pile of black formless bodies scattered on the floor around him. He moved toward me with a series of quick sliding steps, his feet barely clearing the floor. He jerked his head, motioning for me to get out of the way, which I was happy to do. Instead of waiting for the two figures in front of me to close, he bounded toward them, sword flashing, and down they went.

I'd seen him fight before and had compared him to a ninja, somewhat mockingly. It was hard to mock him now. Maybe like a movie ninja was the best I could come up with. Then it was over. It was something of an anticlimax—one moment we were fighting for our lives; the next we were standing alone in an empty room. Lou poked his head from behind the couch and tentatively sidled out. He sniffed at the dark bodies for a moment before losing interest.

"Great job there, Lou," I said. "But try and join in a little earlier next time, okay?"

Victor was still standing with sword at the ready, not quite trusting that it was over. Finally he relaxed a bit, but kept the sword in his hand.

"Quite a mess," he said.

"What do we do now? We can't just leave it like this. When the people finally come back it'll bring some . . . unwanted attention, won't it?" He gave me a flinty smile.

"Very astute. Any suggestions?"

"We could burn the house down," I offered, not too helpfully. Victor's smile vanished.

"It might just come to that. But I'm hoping it won't be a problem."

"Nobody will notice?"

"Not exactly. But these things don't belong here, and they're not flesh-and-blood creatures, like some of the things that have come through. Remember the Gaki?"

Oh yes. I remembered it well.

"So we wait? How long—"

I didn't need to finish the sentence, because as I spoke I could see a change taking place to the figures lying on the floor. Already the bodies were losing integrity, looking more now like masses of black crepe paper than people. The black shapes grew softer, edges running like tar on a hot day. As the process accelerated they became pools of inky liquid barely holding together. Two of the bodies lying closest merged and became one, like two touching but separate drops of water when surface tension finally breaks down. Black oily steam began rising from the pools, and little bubbles formed on the surface like tea water starting to boil.

Before long the entire floor surface was covered with a bubbling, viscous sludge. Lou hopped up on the couch to avoid it, and Victor and I quickly did the same. I watched the progression with fascination until there was nothing left.

But not quite nothing. The sooty steam had blackened the walls and ceiling, and the floor was covered with an oily residue. Lou refused to step in it and I had to carry him outside.

"That couple's going to have a hard time figuring out what happened in there," I said as we climbed back into the van. "A broken window and a house full of black, greasy gunk?"

"It doesn't matter. They may even decide it's ectoplasm or some other ghostly residue. But nobody will care."

"What about the rift? Since it's still open we're eventually going to have the same problem, and if that couple comes back, it's going to be ugly."

"That's why I'm going to lay an aversion spell over the house."

"That's not going to stop them. Neighbors, sure. Jehovah's Witnesses, maybe. But people don't avoid their own homes. It'll make them uncomfortable, but it won't stop them from going in." Victor shook his head in disagreement.

"Of course it will. They're already spooked. They left because they thought their house was haunted, remember? They'll be nervous as cats about coming back anyway, and when the aversion spell kicks in they'll turn around and decide to give it a few more days. And if we don't have this mess cleared up by then, this house will be the least of our problems."

He was probably right, and anyway I didn't have a better idea. I waited in the van while he set up the spell. I couldn't really help; our methods of working with talent are very different, and if we tried to work together on the same spell, we'd get in each other's way and the spell would end up weaker than if either of us did it alone.

"Let's go," he said when he was done.

I drove back to the mansion with mixed emotions. We'd succeeded, but it was a small victory in a minor skirmish. The important stuff was still ahead of us.

TWENTY-ONE

VICTOR'S WAS BEGINNING TO SEEM LIKE A CLUB-house, and we the Hardy Boys, solving crimes and making things right. Those Hardy Boys seemed to have better luck with it than we did, though.

"So we took care of the Shadow Men," I said from a deep chair in his office. "Great. But if we can't find out where Jackie's going to try her final experiment, we're still screwed."

Eli had returned and sat staring off into space, head tilted back, eyes closed. He was obviously thinking hard. Or maybe he was daydreaming, since there wasn't much to think about. It was a simple equation—we needed to find Jackie in order to stop her, but we couldn't find her. If we couldn't find her, we couldn't stop her. A circular mental path.

Sherwood came in a few minutes later, shaking her head before Victor could even ask her a question.

"Nothing," she said. "The woman who thought she knew where Jackie was didn't even know *who* she was."

Eli finally stirred himself, got up from his chair, and started pacing.

"We've been concentrating on finding Jackie," he said. "That's the most logical avenue, naturally. But we've run into a dead end, so we need to find a different approach."

"Such as?" I asked.

"Yes, that's the question I've been asking myself. We need to find a way to prevent her from succeeding, even if we can't locate her."

"I don't see how," I said. Sherwood made a hopeless gesture with her hand

"Well, I certainly don't have the answer," she said. Eli cleared his throat, tentatively.

"There is one person that might be able to help—if he's willing." Victor looked up suspiciously.

"Who? No, don't tell me."

"Yes, you know who I'm talking about. Now, I understand how you feel about Geoffrey, but he does know more about the magical world and how it operates than anyone else around."

"For what that's worth," I said. I was with Victor on this one. "We'd never get a straight answer out of him, even if he wanted to help us."

Geoffrey was a "transcendent," a practitioner who had gone far enough down the path of knowledge and enlightenment that he'd abandoned all use of talent, much like those Indian holy men who reach satori, renounce their studies, and live the simple life of a man with a begging bowl. The difference was that I could never quite decide if Geoffrey was an enlightened being or a total loon. Maybe both.

Victor saw him as a fraud, Eli thought he was the genuine article, and I switched back and forth between the two. I have to admit he had been some help in the past, almost despite himself. He did possess knowledge, to be sure.

"Have you talked to him?" Sherwood asked.

"I called, but his phone is no longer in service."

That could mean he'd done away with yet another

modern distraction, or just as easily that he'd forgotten to pay his phone bill.

"Maybe we ought to pay him a visit in person," Sherwood said. Victor uttered a sound of disgust.

"A complete waste of time."

"As opposed to what?" Eli said. "Sitting here and wondering what to do? Maybe if the four of us show up together, that will impress him enough to loosen his tongue."

"Or his screws," Victor said.

"Hey, at least it'll get us out of the house," I said. "Half Moon Bay is nice this time of year."

"Yes, it's quite lovely there," Victor said, sarcastically. Then he surprised me. "But I suppose it couldn't hurt." Considering how he felt about Geoffrey, that showed he was as desperate as the rest of us.

Victor's BMW is too small for four adults and a dog, even a small one, and my van was acting up, so we ended up taking both. Eli rode with Victor and Sherwood came with me and Lou. Sherwood rolled down her window so he could stick his head out from his vantage point on her lap.

We didn't speak for a while; the day was gray and overcast, with occasional hints of rain on the horizon. It didn't help either of our moods, which weren't too cheery to begin with.

I hadn't seen Geoffrey in quite some time, although I knew Eli kept in touch with him. Geoffrey runs a small café in Half Moon Bay, forty minutes south of the city, and I hadn't been down there since the problems with Christoph a few years ago. On the way down Sherwood asked if I thought he really could be of help.

"I'm inclined to think he could," I said. "The question is, will he?"

"Why wouldn't he? Didn't he use to be a practitioner?"

"It's hard to explain," I said. "First, you know he doesn't do magic anymore—nothing that has anything to do with talent. He just won't."

"Won't or can't?"

"That's an open question."

"Have you asked him?"

"Several times, in several ways. But he thinks in such a convoluted way that he's incapable of giving a straight answer. I don't think it's on purpose; I think he's just incapable of grasping simple concepts such as cause and effect. Or maybe I'm too simple to understand what he means. Either way, it's frustrating, especially when you need to know about something.

"Second, you have to remember that what's important to us isn't necessarily important to him. If we tell him the world is about to end, he may well shrug and say that all things end eventually and that time is an illusion anyway, so what's the problem?

"On the other hand, he could well divulge a key piece of information that he doesn't even realize is important, or maybe he would help because it's time for him to practice his piano and you won't leave until he does."

"He plays piano?"

"Oh yes. Jazz, but not very well. Apparently he could be a master musician if he wanted to, but there's no point in it."

"Do you believe that?"

"Depends. What day is it today?"

When I pulled up in front of Lucinda's, Geoffrey's café, Victor's car was already there. Victor and Eli weren't, so I guessed they were inside the café. Lou jumped out, excited, as soon as we pulled up—Geoffrey was a favorite of his, almost too much so. He fawns over Geoffrey like the man was made of bacon. It's one of the things that makes me think there might really be something to Geoffrey, but at the same time it made me jealous in a petty way.

I'd never been inside the café—the last time I'd been here we'd talked at a table outside. Knowing Geoffrey, I expected the inside to be spare and minimal, like a Zen retreat. But it was nice—down to earth and homey, with large wooden tables and heavy straight-backed chairs. A few customers, locals, were seated in the front. Geoffrey was standing in the far corner next to an old upright piano, talking with Victor and Eli. Mostly with Eli; Victor was standing a little off to one side with a sour look on his face, body language disapproving and stiff.

Lou rushed across the room and threw himself against Geoffrey's body, bouncing off him like a toy windup dog.

"Lou!" Geoffrey cried. "What a treat." He ruffled Lou's ears, then glanced over and saw me. "And Mason, too. Well, this is just lovely."

"Geoffrey."

Before I could say another word, he grabbed me by the hand and pulled me over to the piano.

"You have got to hear this. My first jazz composition—not in your league, of course, but it's my first real one, if you know what I mean."

He sat down, took a deep breath, and started to play, a little syncopated riff with his right hand, then threw in some sparse Monk-like chords with the left. In half a minute he was merrily pounding away, and it wasn't half-bad. Clearly he'd been working on his chops these last couple of years. When he finished, he looked up for approval, beaming with pride like a child whose first performance has gone well.

If I hadn't been familiar with his quirkiness, it would have been bizarre. We'd come here for help, time was running out, the world we knew might be about to end—at least for practitioners—and here I was critiquing his musical efforts.

But I did understand him, at least a little bit. Trying to push him onto the important topic would be worse than useless, but a little musical talk might put him in the right frame of mind. If there was such a thing.

"Not bad," I said. "Great feel, and some interesting voicings. One little thing—right before the bridge, where you play that flat-nine chord? Instead of that, how about . . ."

I launched into a quick lesson on tritone theory and how certain substitution chords can not only add color but how the extensions should function to connect with the melody. Geoffrey sat rapt, ginger hair wisping around his head and his little mustache twitching like a rabbit's nose. I actually got interested, but the reason we were here was always on my mind. Geoffrey asked a number of questions, quite sensible ones.

Victor was understandably impatient, but Eli listened to us quietly with apparent great interest. When a momentary pause in our discussion occurred, he judged the right moment had arrived and slipped in smoothly.

"You know, Geoffrey, I'm sure you realize we didn't come all the way down here just to visit, no matter how delightful your company." Geoffrey's face fell.

"Yes, of course. I'm aware of that." He sighed. "But it's rare that I can get Mason's input on my music." He turned to me. "I do value your opinion, you know." I tag teamed and hit him from the other side.

"Well, I appreciate that. But you know we have other concerns, things that are really important that you could help us with."

"All things are important. In their own way."

I hoped Eli wouldn't let himself be drawn into a philosophical argument, but I needn't have worried. He just smiled.

"Yes, I know," he said, and waited patiently.

Geoffrey got the message, but he wasn't giving up so easily.

"Well, if it's important enough to discuss, we need tea." He clutched Eli's arm and steered him toward a table by the window, the rest of us trailing behind, rather hopelessly. "Sit, sit," he said. "I have some fresh Keemun, a new batch, and it's just wonderful."

He skipped off behind the front counter and busied himself, fussing with water and cups and strainers. The four of us sat there morosely, staring at one another. Victor broke the silence.

"You hear that?" he asked, holding up a hand.

"Hear what?" I said, playing the unwitting straight man.

"That faint ticking—the sound of the last moments that we have to actually do something slipping away while we wait for tea. You do realize Jackie's most likely going to try executing the final spell today—she could be preparing it this very moment."

Geoffrey finally returned to the table carrying a large tray with cups and saucers and spoons, and in the middle a beautiful teapot with a Chinese dragon on the side. He insisted on serving us all, deliberately and carefully. Then he flitted around the table, straightening napkins and spoons. I didn't see how Victor was going to be able to drink the tea with his teeth clenched so tightly. Eli just sipped his tea and regarded Geoffrey with a genial air. Eventually Geoffrey gave up and sat down with a sigh.

"All right," he said in defeat. "Tell me why you're here." Eli cleared his throat.

"Well, first of all, have you had any headaches lately? Dizziness, or even passing out?" Geoffrey seemed to be considering it carefully.

"No," he said. "Have you?"

"We all have," Eli said. "Have you noticed anything unusual at all, though?"

"Ahh, I think I know what you mean. Yes, I felt something and wondered what it was. Is this why you're here?"

Eli looked over at me. "Mason, why don't you do the honors," he said. "You've been closest to it."

The last time I'd related a story to Geoffrey, he'd spent the entire time playing games with Lou, seemingly not listening at all. He had been, but it was disconcerting, and I expected more of the same this time.

But for once he paid close attention. Maybe I'd improved as a teller of tales, or maybe, for whatever reason, this particular subject interested him more. In any case, he listened and even interrupted a couple of times for clarification, just like any normal person would.

"Ah yes, Richter's book. I spent a lot of time looking for it back when I was interested in such things. I think it's a good thing I never found it. If I had, I might be a very different person today."

This was a topic I knew Eli would have loved to pursue, but I recognized Geoffrey's deflection strategy—to get us talking about other things instead of the subject at hand. Which was troubling in itself—he really is fundamentally kindhearted, and hates to disappoint people. Which probably meant that whatever he was going to tell us was going to be something we didn't want to hear. Still, Eli forged onward.

"So you see our problem," he said. "We can't find this woman, so we can't stop her from opening another rift—and the results of that will be catastrophic. At the very least, we may well all lose our powers."

"Would that be such a bad thing?" Geoffrey said.

"Yes," Victor and I said in unison, on exactly the same page for once.

"Practitioner society has been built up over the centuries," Eli said. "If it's destroyed, it diminishes the world. Remember, you wouldn't be the person you are today if not for your talent and the society you grew up in."

"Oh, very true. I'd be someone else. Or would I? My circumstances wouldn't be the same, of course, but is that what really matters?"

Eli held up his hand. "Be that as it may, can the side effects of opening the rift be countered, even if we can't stop her from opening it?"

"Oh, I'm sure it could, if you knew how."

"But we don't," I said. "Do you?"

Geoffrey got more and more uncomfortable. I tend to ask direct questions, and he tends to avoid answering them. Whether he can't or just won't is something I've never been able to make up my mind about.

"I don't deal with matters of talent anymore; you know that."

"Yes, you've made that clear. But *could* you, if you had to?"

"'Could' is a tricky word."

I had a moment of déjà vu. This was word for word the same conversation I'd had with him a few years ago. This time I'd learned there was no point in pursuing it, though. It would only go around in circles. I tried a different tack.

"Well, if you were us, and wanted to prevent this, what avenues would you explore?"

"But I'm not you. So how can I answer that?"

I gave up. We weren't going to get anything useful here after all. But Victor, who hadn't said a word up to now, surprised me by speaking up.

"How could Jackie pull this kind of thing off? Even with the book as a guide, it would take impossible amounts of power. Even a power object, if she had one, wouldn't account for it."

Geoffrey's face brightened. Here was something he could talk about, something that wouldn't result in his getting involved in the problem.

"Well, she has Richter's book. And if I remember right, it's supposed to include ways to harness natural forces. That's what provides the power to institute the spells."

"Of course," said Eli. "There'd have to be a way to access huge amounts of power. But is that practical?" I expected Geoffrey to go off on the meaning of the word "practical," but Sherwood interrupted.

"Well, she's doing it, isn't she?" she said. Geoffrey beamed at her like she was a clever student.

"Now, see, there's a practical answer."

"What kinds of forces, exactly?" Eli asked, trying to get Geoffrey to focus again. He waved his hands in a vague manner.

"Oh, you know. Wind. Water. A tsunami would be useful. A volcano would be ideal."

"A tsunami," Eli mused. "A very big wave." Geoffrey said nothing.

"She'd need a lot of power for this last spell," Victor said. "Someplace where there are really big waves. Huge, giant swells would do it. Somewhere close by."

"Somewhere world famous for the power of its waves," Sherwood added.

We all stared at one another with the slightest dawning of hope.

Mavericks.

TWENTY-TWO

EVERY YEAR, A WORLDWIDE SURFING COMPETITION is held at Mavericks. The combination of an odd underwater rocky shelf configuration and the long Pacific stretch the waves must cross to reach it make for an ideal surfing venue. During storms, waves can reach heights of fifty feet, and twenty-five is routine.

Sometimes the waves are even too strong, and the competition has to be postponed. They crash on the breakwater with astounding force, plumes of spray shooting up hundreds of feet in the air. They wouldn't be that strong on a normal day like today, but there was a stiff breeze blowing and the waves would still be impressive.

Mavericks is right down the way from Half Moon Bay. Ironically, we'd passed it on the way up to see Geoffrey. Legend has it that it was originally named Maverick's Point, after Maverick, a white German shepherd that belonged to the first surfer to discover the area back in the early sixties.

The entry point is a small touristy town called Princeton, with a long pier and lots of little shops, many selling surf-related stuff. I pulled off the highway at the Princeton exit right on Victor's bumper, and we wended our way through the back streets until we reached the parking lot that is the jumping-off point for the Mavericks beach.

Strangely, there were only two cars parked in the lot. A light rain had started and the wind had picked up, blowing in off the ocean and churning up the waves, but even so, it was unusual to find it nearly deserted. Many couples visit the beach when the weather kicks up; the rain and wild surf and windswept ocean is viewed as romantic. Look at the personal ads.

As soon as I got out of the car the reason became clear. The lot felt deserted and unsafe, the beach stretching away toward the point dark and ominous. Another simple aversion spell. Not strong enough to raise any real concern, but enough to make the random beach walker decide it might be better to come back another day. This was good, in fact, wonderful. It meant we had guessed right, that Jackie was here, and that we had a good chance of stopping her before she completed her task. Lou was unaffected by the aversion spell, naturally, and the rest of us didn't waste any time in trying to counter it. We simply gritted our teeth and ignored it.

I examined the cars, one a black Civic and the other a gold Lexus. One car must belong to Jackie, probably the Civic, but what about the Lexus? A friend of hers, an ally? The hood on the Civic was cold, but the Lexus was warm. So whoever owned it hadn't arrived much before we had.

A wave of dizziness swept over me as I stood next to the car, bad enough so that I had to sink to my knees to avoid falling down. It passed quickly, and as I got up I saw Victor and Sherwood getting up as well, and Eli supporting himself by leaning on Victor's BMW.

"It's started," Eli said.

A bark from Lou alerted me to a lone figure that had appeared at the end of the parking lot where it led to the beach. A woman, small, delicate, and familiar. She stopped when she saw the four of us and made no move to run as we approached her. She put her hands out in a supplicating fashion, showing she was no threat to us—at least not for the moment.

"You're too late," Cassandra said, but without the air of satisfaction I would have expected.

"We'll see," I said.

Another woman came out from behind some large rocks at the base of the cliff and came toward us. It could only be Jackie—but it wasn't. She was wearing a small backpack over a light parka shell.

"Well, I'll be damned," said Victor. "We should have known."

It was Jessie.

"What's going on?" Victor said when she got close enough to hear him without shouting. He held himself ready, but I couldn't tell if he was getting ready to defend himself or if he was about to launch an attack of his own.

"Relax," Jessie said, wearily. "I'm here for the same reason you are."

"How did you figure out where she was?" I asked. Jessie pointed at Cassandra.

"She told me. Jackie finally confided in her about what was going to happen. All of it, including what would happen to the practitioners left behind. Jackie understands what the consequences will be, all too well."

"And she doesn't care?"

"She does care. It's tearing her up inside, I'd guess. But she's going to do it anyway. That's why she finally told Cassandra—she had to tell someone. But she believes she can create a better world, and any sacrifice is worth it. She doesn't care about practitioners; she cares about Mother Earth. She cares about a new beginning. She doesn't plan to survive the process herself."

"Yeah," I said. "She told me that."

"Lord save us from the righteous," Eli said softly.

"But Cassandra was appalled—I'll give her that. So she came to me, figuring I'm the only one who might be able to change Jackie's mind—or be strong enough to stop her. Unfortunately, neither one of those things has turned out to be true."

She pointed to the massive stone jetty that jutted out at an angle from the shore, acting as a breakwater. Waves crashed against it, sending spray flying. Farther out were rocks where the waves broke even larger, but these waves were still impressive. A sign at the base of the jetty warned that it was not safe for pedestrians to walk out onto it. That didn't take a genius to figure out.

Almost at the end of the jetty, legs braced against the wind, stood two figures. One was Jackie; she wore a long dark coat and her wiry hair was whipping in the wind. She held a large book in one hand and, although we couldn't hear her, was obviously intoning a ritual. Occasionally she would stop, crouch down for a moment, then straighten up and continue. It was either part of the ritual or the ritual was taking a lot out of her.

The other was no surprise, either; it was Malcolm. Jackie faced the sea and he stood behind, offering occasional words of direction. He turned his head and stared back at the shore, noting us and waiting. He was also there to make sure nothing interrupted her, or at least to do his best.

I turned to ask a question and caught sight of Cassandra hightailing it across the parking lot. She'd done her part. She didn't know what would happen next, but she knew she wanted no part of whatever it was.

"So why are we just standing here?" Victor said, and took a few steps toward the jetty. He stopped when he saw Jessie wasn't moving. "And why didn't you let us know where she was, anyway?" Jessie looked at him, defiant.

"What did you expect? She's my daughter, remember? I want her stopped, not killed, and I didn't trust you'd be mindful of that distinction. I only just got here, anyway. I thought I might be able to talk Jackie out of what she's planning, but she's set up a protective set of wards around her perimeter. I can't get close enough to her to even talk to her, much less do anything about it. I can't break the wards, either—she's strong, you know, probably as strong as I am. And she's had all day to work on them."

"Maybe between all of us we can break through," Eli said. Victor grunted in agreement and spun on his heel.

The jetty was broad and smooth, covered with ocean spray, but easy to navigate close to the shore. But as we got farther out, the waves picked up in force, crashing against the sides and occasionally washing over our feet. I kept a close eye on Lou—the waves weren't high enough yet to threaten the rest of us, but he's a lot smaller and closer to the ground.

We got to within a hundred feet of the two of them before the wards kicked in. It wasn't a physical thing; it was more along the lines of an aversion spell, but a lot more powerful. My head began to hurt, and at the same time the beginnings of nausea stirred. I took a few more steps and doubled over, trying not to throw up. A stabbing pain above one eye took over, like a migraine, but even more localized. I took another few steps and the symptoms doubled. I almost fell over from the pain as my legs suddenly became too weak to hold me upright. Victor was a few steps ahead of me, so he must have been feeling it even worse. We were now about ninety feet away from where Jackie stood, arms outstretched to the sea, but it might as well have been miles. There was no way we would be able to reach her.

Lou stayed right by my side, totally unaffected. It pays to be an Ifrit sometimes, even if you can't operate a can opener. I stumbled back toward the shore. A wave crested the jetty wall, and in my weakened condition almost knocked me off my feet. The good thing was that the effect didn't last; by the time I returned to where Jessie was waiting, I felt perfectly fine. But I wasn't about to try that again.

Victor staggered back a few moments later. He'd made it farther than I had but it was a hollow victory.

"Okay," he said. "That didn't work. We're a little far away, but we'll have to make the best of it."

He bowed his head for a moment, looked up, threw out his hands, and sent a wave of energy toward them, nothing specific, just probing. At the same time I reached into the power of the waves, taking a page from Jackie's book. I didn't try to attack her directly; with the power crackling around, nothing could touch her. And Malcolm had his own protection.

But while Malcolm and Jackie were immune, the jetty wasn't. Waves are ferocious eroders of rock and cliff. Those who build on the edge of the ocean often find that out, much to their discomfort a few years later when the cliff erodes and their homes plunge into the ocean. If I could do the same thing to the jetty, in fast forward, our troubles would be over.

But it didn't work. The energy I sent out toward the jetty flowed instead into Malcolm, as if he were a giant magical magnet. He seemed to glow for a moment, but other than that remained unaffected.

"This is bad," Eli said, seeing what was happening. "Jackie's used the power she's drawn to make him into a living shield—anything we throw in that direction he'll absorb, and it's not bothering him one bit."

"Can't we work around it?" Sherwood asked.

"Probably. But I doubt we can do it in time."

Jackie was still facing the ocean, back not entirely turned, but mostly. She had to be aware we were on the jetty, but hadn't yet acknowledged our presence with so much as a glance. Malcolm was on alert, but she remained entirely focused on the task at hand. She was drawing power from waves, not only the ones that were slamming against the jetty, but the larger ones crashing on the rocky breakwater farther out. Every time a particularly large wave broke, the booming sound was matched with a surge of energy that flowed into her and out again. We could all feel the energy coursing around her. The very atmosphere was charged, the way it is right before a thunderstorm breaks, but ten times stronger.

It didn't look like we could stop her, but maybe we could at least distract her. An interruption at a timely moment might be enough to send the invocation awry. That had its own dangers, but compared to the consequences if she succeeded, it was a minor concern.

"Lou," I said, bending down next to him. "We can't reach her. But you can. Distract her, bite her, anything. It's important. But watch out for Malcolm, okay?"

He looked down the expanse of jetty that separated her from us. It narrowed as it reached farther out, and waves were now crashing over it with increased force. Jackie must have used an attraction spell to help keep the two of them in place; otherwise they might have been knocked off the jetty themselves.

Lou looked back at me, then back down the jetty. A huge wave crested over the top, not far from where we stood, foam hissing and swirling. He licked his lips nervously; he doesn't like water at the best of times, and a violent sea was not his idea of a good time.

"I know," I said. "It's dangerous. But there's no choice."

I could almost hear him thinking, *Yeah, not for you.* But he shook himself, getting some of the rain off his fur, and started off toward Malcolm and Jackie with a determined gait. He had to stop a couple of times, dancing around to avoid the wash of some of the bigger waves. I don't know if Jackie never noticed him or if she was just ignoring him like everything else, but Malcolm was ready. He crouched down for balance, arms outspread as Lou got closer. Lou sprang at him, then at the last moment ducked under his arm and zeroed in on Jackie. There wasn't much room to maneuver, though, and when he got next to Jackie he was still within Malcolm's reach. Malcolm spun and caught him by a hind leg just before he could close his jaws on her leg.

Lou twisted around, quick as a snake, and sank his teeth into Malcolm's hand, but Malcolm didn't let go. He scrabbled at Lou with his free hand, finally getting a hold right behind the neck, lifted him up, and tried to cast him out into the roiling water.

Lou wasn't about to let go, though. He clamped down on the hand holding his leg like a crazed pit bull. After a few futile attempts to dislodge him, Malcolm figured out what to do. He raised Lou high above his head, with the idea of driving him hard onto the rock surface of the jetty. And that might have been the end of it, but as he stretched full length, Lou let go of his hand and tried to claw his way down Malcolm's arms to get at his face. Malcolm flinched and turned away, and just as he did, a powerful wave crested the top of the jetty and hit him full force.

He might have weathered it if he hadn't been off balance in the first place. But he was, and the wave knocked him off his feet and swept him off the jetty toward the sea. He let go of Lou as he fell, trying for a purchase on the rocks that formed the jetty lip. For a moment it looked like he was going to make it until a second wave crashed into the jetty, sweeping him off into the water. I thought Lou was going over as well, but somehow he managed to wedge himself against the rocky lip at the edge, and when the wave receded he was still there.

Malcolm's body type, thick and heavy, wasn't made for swimming. I don't even know if he'd ever learned to swim. It didn't look like it; his arms thrashed and he kicked his legs spasmodically, each limb working at cross purposes with the others. A wave rolled over him and he disappeared for a moment, then briefly reappeared before vanishing again. This time he didn't resurface. He was gone.

That in itself should have provided enough of a distraction, but Lou wasn't counting on it. He picked himself up and lunged toward Jackie, but by now she was ready for him. She stepped back and unleashed a solid kick to his midsection. I could hear the thud even from a distance, and the strangled yelp Lou uttered wasn't reassuring. The kick lifted him off the ground and launched him into the heaving water below. A huge swell picked him up and spun him back fifty feet, almost even to where we were standing.

His head popped out of the water, and I got a glimpse of legs whirling in a desperate dog paddle, paws scrabbling in a frantic attempt to keep his head above water before he sank out of sight once again.

It would have made an interesting ethical dilemma—did I ignore him and concentrate on stopping Jackie, who was in the process of killing people and destroying practitioner society, or did I try to save Lou and let our society dissolve? What's more important, loyalty to an individual or loyalty to the common good? But it was a moot question—before I could think, I'd dived headfirst off the jetty after him.

I hit the water next to him just as he surfaced again, and grabbed his harness as he was about to go back under. So far, so good. Luckily I'm a strong swimmer, and the summers I'd spent with my grandparents by the ocean had left me comfortable with waves and surf.

But this was different. Another wave hit the jetty and the backwash spun me around and I found myself underwater. The spinning around disoriented me, and for a moment I had no idea which direction led up to the sweet air and which headed down to the dark depths.

Another swell swung me around and popped me up like a cork, still holding Lou's harness in a death grip. I had a quick decision to make. I could get away from the jetty, strike out toward the beach in the slim hope I could make it. Or I could aim for the jetty, so very close, where Eli and Victor might be able to reach in and haul me out. But the jetty was made of rock and concrete, and at its base large jagged rocks protruded out. Even one of the less powerful waves would slam us into those rocks the moment we got close, breaking bones, rupturing organs, crushing skulls. We were between a rock and a hard place for sure.

I got a glimpse of Victor and Sherwood doing something by the side of the jetty using gestures and employing talent, I assumed. Eli was looking out at the water, gesturing frantically toward me, motioning with huge, sweeping arm gestures for me to come in toward him. The rocks underneath where they stood were particularly sharp and jagged; even if the waves didn't crush me, I'd be sliced up before they could pull me out. Still, it's not like he was unaware of that. I didn't know what they had in mind, but sometimes you just have to put your trust in friends.

I kicked and swam directly toward the jetty, aiming for where they were standing. As I feared, before I reached it a wave caught me and sent me hurtling toward the rocks.

The wave lifted me up and slammed me into the rocks full force. I thought that was the end of me, but instead of receiving the crushing blow I expected, I sank into the rocks as if being thrown into deep, soft foam pillows. Sherwood and Victor had done a neat job on them, transforming their hard essence and making my landing safe and easy. Eli reached down with one huge arm and grasped me by the collar, much like I had grabbed Lou by his harness. With one massive heave he had both of us out of the water and back on the jetty.

I collapsed on the ground, while Lou coughed and retched up quantities of salt water. But nobody paid us any further attention, which was odd indeed. You'd think a simple "Are you okay?" would have been in order. Instead, they all stared out to sea in rapt attention.

"Do you see what I'm seeing?" Victor said.

He got no answer. I struggled to my feet and followed their gazes out to the horizon where the water meets the sky. My eyes were still blurry and stinging from the salt water, so I couldn't see clearly, but I could see well enough to get a horrible feeling in the pit of my stomach.

"Holy mother of God," I said. "What is that?"

TWENTY-THREE

WE'VE ALL SEEN VIDEOS OF THE TSUNAMI IN Indonesia, an ominous line stretching across the horizon, inexorably pushing shoreward, an unstoppable natural force. This was similar, except there was nothing natural about it. It was huge, maybe a hundred feet tall, like an impossibly giant wave, but not made of water. It was a mass of seething, roiling, magical energy.

Only a practitioner would be able to see this; a normal person on the beach would notice nothing. And why should they—it would have no effect on them whatsoever. We weren't exactly seeing it, either—not with our eyes. It was like auras on the psychic plane or wards around a house, but the sight was none the less impressive for that.

Swirls of energy circled ceaselessly inside it, occasionally breaking out like lightning forking from a thunderhead. It was dark but shot through with color, with the texture of a desert sandstorm. Patterns shifted and recombined into images, real as life one second, gone the next. I saw faces, impossibly huge; Aztec-looking symbols glowing gold and red; armies on horseback led by the four horsemen of the Apocalypse; a brook in winter running through a snowy landscape under a pale moon that took up the entire sky.

I saw an antlered God sweeping through the forest on a hunt; Native Americans trudging over an endless prairie; Mayans toiling on their pyramids, like so many specks of dust.

I saw a beach with children playing and bathers bathing, looking like a pencil drawing by Picasso, frozen in space and time but with movement all the same. I saw creatures that once walked this earth, and others that never did, and dogs, and cats, and long-lost friends.

I saw . . . everything, all at once, all history and all possibilities, jumbled together and timeless, eternal and haunting. A moment later, I saw nothing but a gigantic energy wave bearing down on us, dark and ominous.

Malcolm had said that the energy wave produced could well strip every practitioner of talent. I had only half believed it; such a thing was impossible to conceive of. But now that I saw it, my only doubt was if any of us would be left alive after it passed through.

The wall was closer now, and as it neared it gained in power. It didn't seem to need Jackie anymore; it sucked energy straight from the ocean, feeding on it. The waves around the jetty slowly calmed as the energy left the sea until the water lapped gently at the rocky sides, and even the breakwater farther out barely caused the waves to crest.

Jessie had been staring at the energy wall as if mesmerized. Finally she tore her eyes away and called out to Jackie.

"Jackie! Stop, please. I'm begging you."

Jackie heard her, because she flinched just a bit, but she didn't hesitate for a moment. If anything, her gestures grew more expansive, and I could hear her singing with a high-pitched keening sound.

Our talent was useless now. Any energy we sent out

would be sucked into that maelstrom like so many straws into a hurricane. Jessie didn't try calling again. Her face was set and hard, and she stood motionless for a moment and then slipped off her backpack and knelt down. When she flipped open the top flap, Naja glided out, wrapping her tail around Jessie's ankle to give herself purchase against the wind and water. Lou made a hissing sound, much like a snake himself, and backed away.

"You have an idea?" Eli asked her.

She ignored him as if he didn't exist. Bending her head down close to the snake, she whispered to her at length. Naja reared up for a moment, almost as tall as Jessie, then lay flat and slithered toward the end of the jetty where Jackie stood. As she moved, her skin changed like a chameleon's to the color of wet sand until it perfectly matched the rough and sandy surface of the rock.

She was almost invisible as she wove her way, head inches from the ground. The waves that had swept over the jetty were now gone, and although there were pools of standing water still blocking her way, Naja navigated smoothly around them.

I wasn't sure what she could do—at this point a distraction would hardly matter, and Jackie had grown up with her in any case. It wasn't like Naja's sudden appearance would throw her off for more than a moment.

I stole a glance at Jessie, who was watching, expressionless, face like stone. Oh. Naja wasn't there to distract Jackie—she was there to stop her. And there's only one weapon that a snake possesses to stop someone.

I watched in grim fascination as Naja approached her. Jackie had her eyes closed now and had no idea anything was near. When Naja got within two feet or so, she reared up and spread her hood. Maybe she hissed, or perhaps a faint slithering sound penetrated Jackie's focus, or maybe that sixth sense of danger kicked in. She whirled around, just as Naja struck.

The cobra's strike caught her squarely in the throat, and

Naja hung on for a moment before releasing. Jackie grabbed at her with her hands, and when she held on, Naja struck again. Jackie staggered back, now clutching her throat. The venom must have been injected straight into a throat vein, because it was only a matter of seconds before Jackie fell to her knees.

This was a distraction with a vengeance and came at a crucial time, just when the spell that would open worlds had reached its culmination. The wall of force moving toward us stopped, wavered, and then started to break up, releasing massive amounts of energy in random directions. The waves that had been so docile surged up, again with the fury of a hurricane-driven storm.

Jackie somehow staggered back up to her feet and stretched out an arm toward the energy wall in a desperate last attempt to regain control. The storm wall started to stabilize just a bit until Naja, partially freed from Jackie's grip, struck a third time as Jackie tried feebly to ward her off. It was going to be a race between how fast the poison worked and how close Jackie was to completing the spell.

For a moment she stood motionless, as the wind howled around her. The waves lurched up even stronger than before. And then, suddenly, it was over. A giant breaker reared up, roaring and hissing, throwing up a huge wall of spray. It swept the end of the jetty clean, and after it passed over, Jackie and Naja were nowhere to be seen.

We all stood frozen in place, stunned. All but Victor. He grabbed my arm and punched Eli in the shoulder to get his attention.

"We need to get off this jetty," Victor screamed, loud enough to be heard over the roaring of the surf. "Now!"

Lou was already halfway back to the shore before he finished his words. Jessie stood there, immobile, staring at the empty space at the end of the pier.

Victor leaned over and shouted in her ear, "Jessie! Move! You can't do anything now."

He grabbed her by the arm and roughly pushed her toward the beach. Her eyes focused on him and for a moment I thought Victor was in real trouble—Jessie's not someone you can manhandle, no matter what the circumstances. But she just tore herself away, stared back for a moment at the place where Jackie and Naja had been, and then started running toward the relative safety of the beach with the rest of us.

One big wave hit Eli and knocked him off his feet, but Sherwood and I both grabbed him at the same time, keeping him from being swept into the water. Somehow we managed to all get back to shore without losing anyone, but it was close.

The wall of energy that had been advancing on the world was now in chaos. Huge streamers of energy shot out from it like eruptions from a volcano. Bursts of color exploded, shot through with lines of silver and patches of absolute blackness. It was like a Fourth of July fireworks barge had caught fire, and all the fireworks were exploding at once, whizzing off in random directions. And like a rogue fireworks barge, it was dangerous.

A giant crescent of energy shot straight up in the sky, then veered and headed right toward us. At the last moment it veered again, but came close enough so I felt the power of it pressing on my consciousness and vibrating like electricity running through my teeth. We crowded together instinctively like strangers caught in an unexpected blizzard. But that turned out not to be the best idea. Our huddled group made a small, compact target, and when another piece of the sky fell, it caught all of us as neatly as a teacup over a mouse.

Magical electricity coursed through my body. It sought out every nerve, every cell, every axon and dendrite. And went deeper still, until it coursed through my very DNA, squeezing and altering the very basics of who I was, what made me who I am. I tried to scream, but I had no throat, no lips, no tongue. I was pure energy, pure light, pure essence.

Then the light contracted until I was a concentrated globe, then a bright star, and finally a minute point of brilliant pulsing consciousness. Then even that contracted until everything went black.

TWENTY-FOUR

IT WAS A SURPRISE TO ME THAT I WOKE UP AT all. If I'd been able to formulate a thought at the time, I would have given odds against that. I lifted my head carefully, expecting any movement to set off waves of agony. But it didn't—in fact, I felt fine. Tired, of course, but without pain, and with none of that confusion and muzziness that is the inevitable result of being plunged into unconsciousness. I felt a surge of triumph. We'd done it. Against all hope, against all odds, we'd saved practitioner society and come through it in one piece to boot. Not exactly the way I'd envisioned, but that didn't matter, not in the slightest.

The rain had stopped and the sky had partially cleared. It was now early evening and there was even a bit of sunlight as the sun made a brief appearance, glinting off the water and dancing from wave to wave.

I stood up, still cautious, and looked around. Victor and Jessie were still lying on the beach, out cold, but Sherwood was stirring and Eli was already up and about, bending over first one, then the other. He glanced over at me.

"How do you feel?" he asked.

"All right, I guess." I looked around. "Where's Lou?"

"He's fine. He was sitting next to you, standing guard when I woke up."

Victor suddenly opened his eyes, lay quietly for a moment assessing the situation, and then sat up quickly. It looked like we all were going to come through this okay after all.

"How do you feel?" Eli asked him, in exactly the same tone he'd used with me.

A faint unease started nibbling around the edges of my consciousness. Victor stretched, flexed his hands, got to his feet, and took several deep breaths, considering.

"I feel . . . different," he said.

The minute he said that, I realized I felt different as well. I couldn't put my finger on what it was; I didn't feel bad, but there was a sense of something not quite right, something missing. Like Victor, I felt . . . different. Eli nodded gravely.

"I think I know what you mean," he said. He pointed his hand at a piece of driftwood washed up by the waves. "I tried to change that, but I'm not very good at that sort of thing anyway. Maybe you still can."

I didn't like the implications of what he was saying, and neither did Victor. He concentrated, gestured quickly, and the driftwood remained obstinately unchanged. The unease that had been nibbling around the edges of my mind became full-fledged anxiety. I reached out and used some talent to whip up a little sand funnel, a beach dirt devil. But when I reached, there was nothing there. The level sand stretched away, serene and untroubled.

I tried another trick, then another, then a simple illusion. Absolutely nothing. Victor was doing the same, but stopped at the same time I did.

"Anything?" he asked.

"Nothing."

The realization slowly dawned. We'd all lost our talent. The magical energy wave had been broken up and dispersed. Practitioner society was safe, unaffected—but we weren't. We'd been caught in the fallout when it broke up.

Jessie was now awake, too, and watching us. She made a quick gesture, with no result. She nodded her head and walked away from us down the beach without a word. Victor started after her, but Sherwood grabbed his arm and shook her head.

"Not the time," she said. "Leave her alone. How would you feel? In a single moment she lost everything—her talent, her Ifrit, and, worst of all, her own daughter."

"But she saved everyone else," Eli said. "All of us."

"True. But I imagine that will be a grim solace."

Sherwood was right. I felt bad for Jessie, but honestly I was more concerned with myself than I was with her.

"Do you think it's permanent?" I asked Eli. "Losing our talent, I mean."

"There's no way to know for sure," he said. "Time will tell. But given the nature of that awesome display of power, if I had to guess, I'd say it's quite possible. But I just don't know for sure."

I couldn't quite take it in. It was like unexpectedly hearing about the death of a loved one; for a while your mind is blank, unable to comprehend anything so huge and monstrous. Only later does it sink in and become all too real. And what about Lou? I remembered wondering what the Ifrits would do if their practitioners lost their talent. I looked around, but he was still nowhere in sight.

"You said you saw Lou?" I asked Eli again. He nodded.

"He was sitting right next to you."

Well, he wasn't next to me anymore. Maybe he'd been disoriented by the talent storm; even an Ifrit might have been affected by that awesome power. Maybe he was just around the rocky point, tending to some Ifrit business of his own.

I sat down on a rock, well away from the water's edge. I looked out over the water at the setting sun that turned the sky from blue to red and gold. The waves rushed in, gentle now and soothing, speaking of eternal tides and ancient shores. I knew Lou, as well as I know myself. He would never abandon me, no matter what. I calmly watched the sea and waited for him to return.

ABOUT THE AUTHOR

John Levitt grew up in New York City. After a stint at the University of Chicago, he traveled around the country and ended up running light shows for bands in San Francisco. Eventually, he moved to the Wasatch Mountains and worked at a ski lodge in Alta, Utah. After a number of years as a ski bum, he joined the Salt Lake City Police Department, where for eight years he worked as a patrol officer and later as an investigator. His experiences on the job formed the background for two mystery novels, *Carnivores* and *Ten of Swords*. For the last few years, he has split his time between Alta, where he manages the Alta Lodge, and San Francisco. When he's not working or writing, he plays guitar with the SF rock band The Procrastinistas and also plays the occasional jazz gig. He owns no dogs, although his girlfriend now has four.

You can visit him on the Web at www.jlevitt.com.

Also from *New York Times* bestselling author

SIMON R. GREEN

A HARD DAY'S KNIGHT

A Novel of the Nightside

John Taylor is a PI with a special talent for finding lost things in the dark and secret centre of London known as the Nightside. He's also the reluctant owner of a very special—and dangerous—weapon: Excalibur, the legendary sword. To find out why he was chosen to wield it, John must consult the last defenders of Camelot, a group of knights who dwell in a place that some find more frightening than the Nightside.

From the #1 *New York Times*
Bestselling Author
PATRICIA BRIGGS

RIVER MARKED

Car mechanic Mercy Thompson has always known there is something unique about her, and it's not just the way she can make a VW engine sit up and beg. Mercy is a different breed of shapeshifter, a characteristic she inherited from her long-gone father. She's never known any others of her kind. Until now.

An evil is stirring in the depths of the Columbia River—one that her father's people may know something about. And to have any hope of surviving, Mercy and her mate, the Alpha werewolf Adam, will need their help . . .

Available March 2011
from Ace Books